NEON EMPIRE

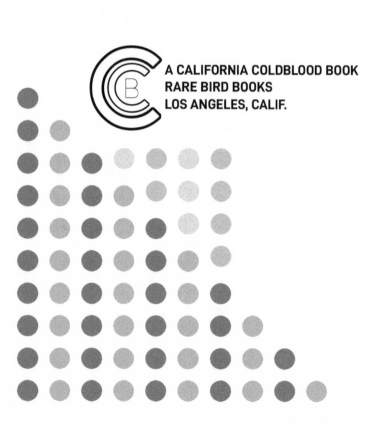

A CALIFORNIA COLDBLOOD BOOK
RARE BIRD BOOKS
LOS ANGELES, CALIF.

NEON EMPIRE

DREW MINH

Publisher's Cataloging-in-Publication data

Names: Minh, Drew, author.
Title: Neon Empire / Drew Minh.
Description: Los Angeles, CA: California Coldblood Books, an imprint of Rare Bird Books, 2019.
Identifiers: ISBN 978-1947856769
Subjects: LCSH Crime—Fiction. | Imaginary places—Fiction. | Dystopias. | Cyberpunk fiction. | Science fiction. | BISAC FICTION / Dystopian | FICTION / Thrillers / General
Classification: LCC PS3613 .I623 N46 2019 | DDC 813.6—dc23

NEON EMPIRE

Eutopia

THIS MEDIATIC METROPOLIS—THIS ALWAYS-ON torrent of sound and light—flickered before him. Massive digital billboards plunged into the raging streets below, stuck on selfie loops. Like alien hieroglyphics, pixelated noise flashed across the diodes, cycling between black nothingness, fuchsia, and vermillion.

In the plaza beneath the balcony, a battered drone tiger, freed from the Coliseum hours before, dragged itself past a group of rioters. Decapitated, its articulated neck exposing wires and sensors, it came within striking distance of a bat-wielding woman in a white bodysuit. Raising the bat above her head, she brought it smashing down on the tiger's back, then followed up with a swift lateral blow, knocking it over. Its legs, kicking at the air as its onboard circuitry tried to make adjustments, gave it the look of an overturned cockroach. It would keep at it until it either righted itself or, more likely, ran out of batteries. The tiger's momentum, like Eutopia's, was reaching an end. The man on the balcony—Cedric Travers—looked down on the chaotic tableau and for the first time since arriving realized he actually belonged in it.

Thirty minutes left, according to his watch. A thudding explosion rippled through the plaza below. A guy wearing a cape had hurled a Molotov cocktail toward the centerpiece of the plaza: a statue of Garry Kasparov leaping onto a chessboard. The flaming bottle smashed just opposite Kasparov, on a computer, and the bulky cathode monitor caught fire, flames licking across the chessboard and up Kasparov's leg as a young woman in a hooded cloak recorded the scene on her cell phone. As the polymer skin of the statue burned, the rioters scattered. A spotlight from a drone cut through the plaza and glanced off the sliding glass door behind him. The drone's motor screamed as it whirred off toward shots echoing in nearby urban canyons.

Cedric turned from the balcony and walked back into the apartment, which was in complete disarray—scattered boxes of designer drugs, piles of clothing, swag from nightclubs—the accoutrements of a professional with little appetite except for mood-enhancing pills and prepackaged food. He approached a shelf and pulled out a thick book on twentieth-century street art and lifted the cover to reveal a hollowed-out interior, filled with old letters, pictures, and a filigree engagement ring. He threw a memory stick in a backpack along with some old letters and pictures. Then he ran his fingers over the delicate, aged scrollwork on the ring and placed it in his breast pocket.

He headed out the door without bothering to close it and took eight flights down to street level. Holding an old shirt to his nose, he walked past a media crew shooting B-roll of the plaza. The pavement—littered with casino chips, spent canisters of tear gas, flyers for clubs, and bits of torn clothing—was bathed in the flickering light of the signage above.

He walked as fast as he could—without running, in order to avoid attracting the attention of surveillance algorithms—toward an unblocked street. As he walked toward Paris, a matte black Humvee passed him, the top of which was fitted with a sound cannon. The vehicle purred as it rolled toward the rioters. His pulse was quickening, but his gait remained steadfast and calm. Dressed in his dove-gray blazer and sneakers, he didn't fit the description of the troublemakers they were looking for. He was too old, wasn't dressed as extravagantly as the majority of the kids doing the looting, didn't run—for all they knew he was one of the many thousands of city workers trapped here.

After ten minutes of walking, he arrived at the corner of Paris, demarcated on the corner by a Chanel handbag store with shattered vitrines. In the pre-dawn light there was something eerily photogenic about the scene: displays ransacked, mannequins toppled over, arms ripped off as if a tribe of savages had invaded. Cedric stopped abruptly as a paddy wagon barreled past, sirens Doppler-shifting as it drove through an obstacle course of discarded gadgets and shredded clothing.

He walked on, passing gangs wielding makeshift clubs and carrying backpacks filled with loot, until he got within eyesight of the edge of the city. As he stopped in front of a bistro, a drone overhead hovered for a couple of seconds, its black optical dome glinting in the purple sky, before darting off after a crashing noise down the street. Somehow a chalkboard sign had managed to stay standing amid overturned café tables and woven-back chairs.

Entering the bistro through a wide-open door—into a dining room replete with zinc countertops and checkered marble floors—he called out.

"Hello?"

Satisfied when no one answered, he pulled out a beacon device and set it on the bar and activated it. Invisible signals began radiating out to a private mesh network, and Cedric, enjoying the relative silence in the bistro, grabbed a condensation-covered water bottle from a refrigerator and leaned back against the counter. Out there, Eutopia was burning, and it would be a few hours until reinforcements and evac helicopters flew in to start clearing out the city. The cool water soothed his throat as he took a slow sip of it. He pulled out a burner phone, also connected to a mesh network, and sent a message. Twenty seconds later he got a reply.

"*On my way. ETA 13 min.*"

Part 1

1.
Gamified

A JOLT TO THE CAR awoke Cedric Travers, and he sat up from his reclined seat, watching as the steering wheel turned left and right, adjusting to a pothole-filled section of highway. The car's autopilot had been engaged for a full hour, he noticed, while he'd been sleeping off a bender. He was so hammered he didn't remember much about the previous night besides trying to dance with a woman in a Oaxacan cantina and arousing her boyfriend's anger. The next thing he knew, he was coming to in the cold, concrete confines of a drunk tank.

News of his wife's disappearance two months earlier had sent Cedric into a downward spiral of depression and self-loathing. Not only had he squandered his chances to repair their broken marriage, his wife had been implicated in a terrorist attack. Internet message boards circulated the most outlandish theories he could possibly imagine—that she had planned it, that she was a corporate spy sent by a rival network, that she was among the dead that day—and the deeper down the rabbit hole he went, the more he started to doubt himself. It had to end. Unless he started something new, he could pretty much call it quits. Retrieving his great-grandmother's engagement ring, which he had given Mila many years ago, might indeed give him closure, but the nagging feeling that his and his wife's story wasn't complete was eating at his psyche. It was a crazy, lunatic thought, but he was certain Eutopia had corrupted her, just like Los Angeles had corrupted their marriage and his career five years earlier—as if the two cities were malevolent gods using and discarding humans like game pieces.

He pressed a lever, and his seat moved into a more comfortable driving position. The screen on the dashboard indicated he was still about fifteen miles outside of Eutopia. It was late afternoon, and he hadn't eaten anything since that morning. After asking the personal assistant for the nearest diner, the screen showed a few options in the outskirts. The best option would be to grab a bite before heading into the city, checking into his hotel, and exploring. He disengaged the autopilot and took the wheel.

A flat, desert landscape scrolled past his windows, distant rock formations sawing into the gray-blue horizon. Dirt roads wound off the highway here and there, leading to clusters of bobbing machinery slowly working in the distance—fracking wells. He drove on for another ten minutes until he saw low-rise buildings looming on the horizon. He passed a weather-beaten highway sign that read City of Parado, population 129. After taking the next exit, he drove down an old macadam road, past taverns, trailers, and a liquor store, until he got to a bend where an old steel-beamed bridge crossed some railroad tracks. Out-of-commission railroad cars stood on the old railway, covered with dust, weeds gathering at wheels. The nav system guided him to a main street lined with low wooden buildings—relics of a bygone era when Parado was a stop on the transcontinental railroad—and newer strip malls with mini-marts, fast-food restaurants, and massage parlors.

After two miles, he had already covered the main street

and was approaching the diner. Parked in front were dozens
of cars of all makes, models, and colors, but just opposite the
diner, separated by a chain-link fence topped with razor wire,
was a large hangar with Humvees parked in front. A few vehicles
circled the perimeter. Distinctly military in feel, but not. Cedric's
wife had told him Eutopia's administrators had hired former
military contractors to maintain order in the city. She had found
it off-putting at first—calling it the Green Zone in reference
to what happened in Baghdad during the 2003 war—but it
worked. Money was rolling in, distractions were plentiful, and
the unostentatious black matte of the contactors' uniforms and
vehicles blended right into the background.

After asking a waitress at the front of Suzie Q's for the
washroom, Cedric walked past rows of burly, wide-backed men
sitting at the counter. The diner was another relic revived by the
influx of money, its walls covered with old photographs of celebrities, a jukebox stationed by the entrance. Inside the bathroom,
he locked the door and looked at himself in the mirror, his palms
resting on the cool porcelain of the sink. His semi-bloodshot eyes,
four-day beard, and slept-in clothes gave him the appearance
of a tramp. He bought a razor kit from the vending machine,
then stood at the sink, splashed his face with warm tap water,
and proceeded to scrape away the stubble on his face. After his
five-minute makeover, he exited the bathroom, took a seat at the
end of the counter, and ordered an in-vitro burger, sweet potato
fries, and green tea.

BY THE TIME HE finished his meal, dusk was falling over the
desert. Beyond the sawtooth horizon, the alpenglow turned the
razor-wire fence surrounding the compound in front of the diner
into a jagged silhouette of tangled lines. As he summoned his
car and waited for its gullwing to open for him, a lone Humvee

ambled along the perimeter, sending up dust. He set the nav for Eutopia and drove the car back to the highway before engaging the autopilot again.

Up ahead, the Eiffel Tower thrust into the skyline, brightly lit against the night sky, fading from red to blue to a burst of white, which dissipated into thousands of points of sparkling lights. He was approaching the Parisian quarter, the gateway to Eutopia. From a giant billboard, two silver eyes appeared behind two slender hands forming a filmmaker's frame. The hands moved apart and the shot pulled out, revealing a shock of black hair around the eyes, jagged, anime-esque with its sharp lines. The shot pulled away again, revealing an alluring feminine face, then a white leather jacket over jeans that tightly hugged one leg and stopped halfway down the other, revealing a glowing prosthetic limb ending in a spike. *Welcome to Eutopia, the Place to Be Seen* flashed in neon letters over a stark black background. Cedric's mobile pinged with a message. *Turn on Location Services to Allow Eutopia to Pay You.* He clicked Cancel, then received another message: *Are You Sure You Don't Want to Monetize Your Stay?* He hesitated—knowing that doing so could be a trigger, sinking him back into the world he'd been avoiding—and clicked Yes.

After adjusting his seat to the full upright position, Cedric disengaged the autopilot and followed the nav directions to his hotel. The contrast to the surrounding desert, even the nearby strip malls of Parado, was jarring, almost like waking up after a long intercontinental flight, suddenly on solid ground in a foreign country. He steered past a small plaza filled with people on outdoor terraces carousing, snapping photos and filming themselves. The fronts of the cafés and shops looked weathered, deliberately painted with a patina otherwise achieved by years of rain, sun, and pollution. Plastic marigolds hung from wire baskets in small windows above the terraces, but just above that, in striking divergence from the microcosm of old Europe, a sheer wall of light shot up, projecting ads on a loop across

CGI renderings of a building façade—uncannily real-looking balconies and cornices, and, at the top of the building, an illuminated mansard-style rooftop the color of decades-old copper.

It was as bizarre, and jarring, as the old Hollywood studio lots—with their European streets next to typically American town halls and squares. He turned onto the Champs-Élysées, with its steady stream of cars, many wrapped with screens projecting advertising for drugs, clubs, and luxury wearables. A moving billboard, partially blocking his view, advertised an app called L-Uber, for P2P sex-on-demand, before the screen changed to an advertisement for Panadrine, a vape drug promising to cut the need for sleep, touted as the official drug of Eutopia. High-rises with surfaces of light lined the boulevard ahead of him, and, at street level, a who's who of luxury boutiques enticed the crowds with dazzling storefront displays. Just as he pressed the accelerator to keep up with traffic, four people flew over him, each whooping and screaming, arms outstretched. Attached to a zip line stretching the length of the boulevard, the foursome ended up on top of a replica of the Arc de Triomphe, draped, like the buildings all around it, in colorful cycles of ads.

Cedric, who had been in a self-imposed exile for the last four years after his career, his marriage, and his will to fight deteriorated, had, for at least that long, tried to avoid social networks and the bustle of big-city life. The energy around him now both repelled and attracted him. Mila had said to him that beyond the surface of the city, something revolutionary was happening inside the people inhabiting and visiting it. And if there was one person whose opinion he trusted, it was hers. Almost his age, she wasn't the demographic Eutopia was targeting, but she had a mind for trendspotting. As she saw it, Eutopia marked the beginning of a new kind of society. Those alerts he had received upon entering the city were probably part of it. Maybe all the ebullience around him had to do with the fact that everybody here was in some way getting paid for their stay. Getting paid to have fun.

He took a corner and drove past an anime-themed strip club and VR poker room. The street, sloping down into a tunnel, was a shortcut to the next zone of Eutopia. Sodium lights lined the concrete walls of the tunnel, the middle of which was divided by massive concrete pillars. When he came out of the tunnel, he was in Rome. To the right of him was the Coliseum, wrapped in flashy signage announcing a UFC fight taking place in a few days. He drove past Renaissance-style facades with opulent adornments, topped with projecting cornices that gave way to walls of digital screens, until he arrived at his destination: the Hotel Augustus.

A BRISK JUNE NIGHT—WITH wind blowing in from the surrounding desert—enveloped him as he walked past a mix of Asian and American tourists filming a street performer. At street level, the city was a fire hose of activity, gaggles of twenty-some-things amped on stimulants, filming each other, streaming in and out of casinos and sex clubs. There was a babble of Spanish, English, and the occasional passing conversation in French, German, and Mandarin. People were staring at billboards, some with their phones in front of them, interacting with screens that would occasionally project mirror images from their self-facing cameras, eliciting wild exclamations from crowds and sponta-neous dancing. He'd seen real-time audience interaction like this before, at Lakers games, another closed ecosystem of media and technology.

Some were broadcasting, he realized, while others were interacting with the giant screens looming above Rome's luxury stores, trattorias, and casinos. Cedric pulled out his phone, the interface glowing with the time. After entering the settings app, he enabled geo-tracking and disabled the ad blocker, a premium service he'd paid for years ago and had left on ever since. His screen was immediately covered with a glowing sky-blue interstitial ad for Panadrine—a sun glowing in the background cast a halo around the slogan, *Like a Boss.*

He closed the ad and continued walking, eager to explore the surroundings of his hotel. As he passed a group of young women—dressed in short skirts, sheer stockings, open-back boots—his mobile began to vibrate. On he screen he saw an ad for L-Uber, the sex-on-demand service he'd seen advertised earlier. It had pinpointed his exact location in Eutopia, and little male, female, and transgender icons appeared across the city. Double-tapping his screen, he could see the group of women that had just passed him were represented by pink female icons, slowly edging away. All around him were icons offering on-demand hookups, and if it weren't for the ad, he'd have assumed they were average visitors, like him. One tap, and he could summon any one of them in exchange for Eutopian cryptocurrency.

Walking back toward his hotel along a less trafficked side street, Cedric noticed the buildings around him begin to change color. The screens faded from Panadrine ads to pulsating hues of blood orange, and people around him began holding their phones up, filming their surroundings. A high-pitched whirring passed by overhead, and, looking up, he barely caught a glimpse of a drone. Just then, a black Mercedes careened onto the side street, nearly hitting a group of people who had been filming the changing building colors around them. After the sharp turn at the end of the street, the sedan sped in his direction, the ambient warning system from its powerful electric motor emanating an increasingly louder pitch. Three motorcycles turned the corner behind it onto the now cleared street, and, as the sedan raced past, followed a few seconds later by the motorcycles, the crowds who had been filming the pursuit on their phones turned back up to the screens. Instead of the alarming red hues they had been cycling through, the screens now showed what looked like real-time footage being broadcast from inside the sedan. Through a rear-window POV, there were three motorcycles inching closer and closer to the car, their headlights creating intermittent starbursts, saturating the screens around him with bright light. The footage intercut with aerial views from the drone, cutting back to inside the car, to street-level POVs from some of the onlookers, even occasionally to POV footage from the pursuers' helmet cams. An overlay slid across the lower portion of the screen: *Live Pursuit: #eutopia #paparazzi #arore* before sliding back out, followed by a relentless stream of live comments. As if they were predatory creatures—forces of nature ready to pounce at any moment—the motorcycle headlights hovered in the background, closing the gap with each hard brake, disappearing with each hard turn, and suddenly reappearing with renewed intensity.

Another overlay slid across—*A'rore -200, Paparazzi +200*—betting odds skewing in A'rore's favor. Cedric, with his phone in his pocket, was surrounded by people whose eyes darted from their phones to the digital signage, interacting frantically with their interfaces as the odds came and went. The screens cut back to aerial footage, showing the car make a sudden sharp turn, fishtailing, barely missing a taxi and coming to a stop. The nearest motorcycle in pursuit attempted to make the turn and failed, the rider rolling onto the street as the bike slammed into a Dolce & Gabbana storefront, the plate-glass window shattering. Helmet-cam footage from one of the other two motorcycles showed the immediate aftermath of the wreck as they zipped by. The screen cut to aerial footage of a mangled mannequin hanging out of the window, while the motorcycle, short-circuiting on the sidewalk in front of the store, sent off sparks. Scattered chunks of its shattered lithium battery burned bright, scarlet red, causing lens flares in the video feed.

Cheers went up in the crowd around him as the screen switched to a new live stream, this time from a front-facing camera on a phone. A woman with aquiline features and choppy, anime-style hair—perfect enough to be a CGI rendering—was exiting the car, the angle of the camera revealing the top of her torso, the car in the background, and, as she turned, the wreckage in front of the store. Her features were calm, relaxed, even in the midst of chaos. The video feed cut to the aerial view showing her full figure, as stylized as her hair: tall, slender, sporting a white leather jacket. Tight leggings tapered down to a motorcycle boot on one leg; her other leg was a glowing purple prosthetic ending in a spike. Next, a split screen showed the POV from police motorcycles in pursuit of the other two paparazzi who had just avoided wiping out in front of the store.

A'rore, as spectacular as she'd looked on the billboards, looked up at the drone cam, and the crowd around Cedric erupted in cheers again. "That's my girl! Just won me 2K!" said a bystander next to him. A tingling feeling came over Cedric as the strange tableau once again occupied the entirety of the screens—the smashed storefront, the downed paparazzo being attended to by first responders, A'rore exiting the scene, stepping back into the rear seat of her sedan. As the dopamine rush subsided, Cedric tried to place the last time he'd felt frisson on that level. Not since he'd screened his first movie at a festival and received a standing ovation.

2.
Pale Idol

"**O**H, FOR FUCK'S SAKE. This is the third time this month." A'rore pressed the phone to her ear with one hand and gripped the car seat with the other as Norton, her driver, took a tight turn, the sport-tuned suspension of the Mercedes rebalancing quickly. Opposite her, bracing against the back of the driver's seat with one hand, holding a camera to his eye with the other, a photographer documented her daily routine.

"The IT guys are trying to patch it now," a produced said on the other end, "but it looks like we'll be on air in time. I mean, I assume as much." They drove by another blacked-out billboard, then another flashing the message—*Your Ad Rev Belongs to Us*—in simple sans serif font. The billboard network had once again been hacked.

She hung up, placed her phone on the back seat, and watched out the window as they passed through Barcelona. Lately it had been attracting more and more of the lesser influencers and economy tourists taking advantage of budget airfares. There were more visitors than ever, and most were here to party. As they passed a sex club with a tall phallic neon sign exclaiming *Sexo! Dinero! Poder!* she swept back her hair so more of her profile was visible to the photographer, who promptly took a burst of photos.

Once again, hackers had interrupted her schedule, disrupted her revenue stream, but for what purpose? As Norton drove her to the Haussmann Hotel in Paris, where they were prepping for the interview, she tried to be mindful of the photographer. Nothing worse than looking upset—the gossipmongers would immediately seize on her mistake, and before she knew it, they'd be controlling the narrative. One bad angle, spread virally, could send her ratings tumbling.

She took a long pull on her Panadrine vape, lowered the window next to her, and exhaled a cloud into the late-afternoon sky. Just a few feet away from her was a group of drunk sombrero-wearing tourists, filming each other, unaware that the biggest influencer in the city—top ten in the world in terms of pure numbers—was being driven right past them.

It had been two days since she'd had any sleep. Last night's paparazzi chase had gone well—her numbers looked good, but not spectacular. She'd been plateauing for the last few months, and she was wary of losing momentum in the increasingly saturated influencer space. What confluence of events would it take to push her back to the forefront? As she hit the vape again, conscious of the photographer shooting another burst of photos, her phone rang. It was Sacha Villanova, the investigative journalist she'd been casually seducing.

"Hello, Sacha," she said in lively tone, belying her exhausting routine of stunts and appearances. "What's going on?"

"Hey there. I'm coming back to Eutopia in a few days. I wanted to catch up where we left off. Talk more about that thing."

"For sure. I can *definitely* make the time."

Sacha, writing for *VICE News*, had contacted A'rore earlier that year for a piece she wanted to do on Eutopia. Before meeting with Sacha, A'rore had vetted her credentials, realizing she'd been exposed to snippets of her work long before Sacha's initial email. As a reporter for the *Verge*, she became known for her under-cover work, exposing collusion between Silicon Beach entrepre-neurs and data-mining companies. However, instead of dwelling on the technical details, she psychologized the piece, exposing the reckless behavior of the companies' leaders. But Sacha wasn't without her baggage, either—according to her wiki, she'd been arrested when she was younger on drugs and stolen goods charges. These stories had resurfaced when her exposé on Silicon Beach came out, and, facing public pressure, the site retracted her story, citing her "sketchy" past. A few years had gone by, and now she was making a comeback.

It was during their first informal meeting that A'rore began articulating an escape plan from the city. After over two years as the city's main influencer, she was sensing fatigue. Not only had another rival city of influencers popped up in South Korea—parroting the same monetization tactics as Eutopia—but dozens of influencers were copying her style. She needed to pivot and make the conversation about her again.

—⁓—

SHE WAS MET AT the underground entrance to the Haussmann by a self-serious TMZ producer, who led her through the back entrance. The photographer, staying in the background, snapped a few shots of them walking. While they were waiting for the elevator, the producer—wearing thick-rimmed, tinted Dior glasses, her hair in a tight bun—looked disapprovingly at the photographer, then to A'rore, who said, "He's with me, for a story another site is working on." The producer forced a smile at the photographer just as the phone she was clutching pinged with a message. She lifted the phone, then said, "Looks like they're still having issues with the networks."

"This is literally the only time I have to do this," A'rore said. She was purposely injecting some false urgency into the situation, since it was—in the scheme of things—more beneficial to her to take the interview than for them to give it. Her career depended on these exclusives with gossip outlets, the bottom-feeders of the media world. A few years ago they'd helped launch her career when they'd leaked a surreptitiously recorded sex tape of her and a senator. Now she was doing maintenance work—which, along with her exhausting daily regimen, was part of her job. Stay top of mind, stay *relevant*.

When they got to the top floor, the producer led A'rore and the photographer past a maître d', who smiled and bowed his head while greeting them. They walked past crews of people prepping a bar and seating area for the night's crowds until they got to a VIP room where technicians were busy setting up lights and camera equipment.

"We'll sit over here," the producer said, leading A'rore to a Camden-style chair. While the photographer was busy shooting some establishing shots of the makeshift set—bright lights, a camera crew setting up a 360 camera—the producer continued. "I know you're under a lot of pressure, especially after that chase last night, but let's use this moment with the makeup artist to go over your talking points."

A'rore nodded as the makeup artist scooted next to her on a stool and began prepping her foundation.

"Keep it personal and keep it short. We're doing a full-length interview, but once it's released and dissected by the other channels, you know, whatever you say will be sliced into . . ."

"Six-second sound bites," A'rore said.

"You said last time you weren't able to get your point across. Just trying to help."

The photographer, panning his camera across the room, was busy getting a landscape shot, ending on A'rore looking up stonily at the producer while the makeup artist hovered over her, like an artisan applying finishing touches to a sculpture. A'rore's prosthesis—switched from yesterday's spike to a more comfortable ergonomic design—glowed blue.

A'rore, whose mind was foggy from sleep deprivation, barely registered the producer droning in her ear, listing the key points she needed to touch on. She raised her index finger, and the makeup artist stood back. A'rore rummaged through her handbag and pulled out a vape. Taking a long drag off of it, her eyelids fluttering as endorphins fired across her brain. She was present again, her eyes creased, her lips stretched into a warm smile.

"Sorry about that," she said.

"About what?" the producer said, oblivious.

"The interruption. I *totally* appreciate the download."

The makeup artist leaned back in with a sponge, and the producer continued.

"We'll intercut with footage of the paparazzi chase last night. Talk about your experience, not the paparazzi in general. Bring it home. They invaded your space."

The photographer, having finished some establishing shots, was making his way along the back wall, stepping over cables and flight cases strewn about the makeshift studio. Pausing, he lifted his camera and aimed at the trio.

"Perfect," A'rore said, "I know where to go with this." The sex tape of her and the senator, which resulted in his downfall, had been made by a journalist who had tricked his way into a room adjacent to theirs in a Manhattan hotel. He had placed contact mics on the wall, simultaneously filming them through an altered peephole on their door. "My life was almost ruined by unscrupulous gossipmongers."

"My suggestion: Keep it at 'Paparazzi ruined my life.' And have a physical reaction. Make it visible." The producer's phone pinged, and, after glancing at it, she said, "Good news! The networks are up again." She placed her hand on the makeup artist's shoulder. "There's shine on her forehead. Get rid of the shine." Then she turned to the technicians and said, "We're ready for the mics. Melody should be here in the next few minutes."

"Melody?" A'rore said. "Melody Noguera? You didn't tell me it was going to be her. I hate that cunt. You know that. This is off." A'rore shooed away the makeup artist and started to stand.

"Sit down, sit down," the producer said. "I can explain. Todd had to cancel at the last minute and we brought her in. Someone get her water." The producer turned to a PA. "Can you get her water? Don't just stand there." A'rore sat back in her seat, hearing her out. "This time we're strictly sticking to the script. No gotchas."

The last time she'd done an interview with Melody, two years ago, the journalist had hinted that A'rore was a political operative and that she had conspired to leak the sex tape.

"If she goes off script again, this interview is over," A'rore insisted. The PA, approaching A'rore with a bottle of water in one hand, was texting on her phone with the other. "Don't you dare tweet this."

A cameraman came over and leaned into the producer, saying something in hushed tones. Looking A'rore over, the producer nodded and sent the cameraman away. "We have to lose the white jacket," she said to her. "The white is contrasting too much."

"Yeah sure," A'rore said, easing out of her jacket and handing it to the makeup artist. "That bitch, does she even have followers? She's just drafting off me. Does this work?" She was wearing a faded black Stooges T-shirt, the sleeves cut off, showing her upper arms, which she had been focusing on with her personal trainer. After her arm lipo surgery two months ago, she was following a strict regimen to keep them firm, toned, and youthful-looking.

"That'll work. That's fine. Hey *sound*?" The producer beckoned the sound guy who was fiddling with cables on a mixing console. "What are you waiting for? Mic her up."

As the tech approached, a petite, peroxide-blond Latina wearing high heels and a navy-blue sheath dress walked in. She walked toward them, open-palmed with a wide smile revealing symmetrical white veneers.

"Hello, darlings!" she said, air-kissing the producer on both cheeks, careful not to muss her impeccable makeup. Extending her arm to A'rore, she knelt slightly.

A'rore, her face having transformed from a scowl to a radiant smile, took Melody's hand and said, "It's been *such* a long time. You look *amazing*, as usual."

"As do you," Melody said. The sound tech, who was standing by, held up a lav mic and A'rore nodded at him to proceed. "I'll let you finish. In a bit," she continued, putting her arm around the producer, steering her away from A'rore.

"*Tart*," A'rore mouthed before taking another long drag from her vape. Her lips pursed, she exhaled a jet of Panadrine vapor in their direction, the creases around her eyes flattening.

3.
Gray Eminence

C OFFEE IN ONE HAND, Cedric waved down a cab in the hotel's taxi stand. He'd spent the morning at the gym, sweating out the toxins he'd been accumulating over the last few weeks, and preferred a chauffeured ride to the police station over the hassle of driving himself. A cab pulled up, driven by a man with a dyed blond pompadour, and Cedric gave him the address.

"That's the police, no?" the cabbie said.

"It is," Cedric said, as he sunk into the back seat, the cabbie's eyes narrowing as they studied him in the rearview mirror. Despite the heat—already T-shirt weather at ten in the morning— the cabbie was wearing a polyester blazer. Together with his hair, he looked like a seventies-era record mogul.

"You a cop?"

"Far from it. Just gotta go there to pick something up."

"All right, boss," the man said, lowering his sunglasses and easing the car into traffic. He had his phone mounted to his dashboard, its front-facing camera engaged.

"That's not on, is it?" Cedric said.

"Just for me. Just for me," he said. "No worries, *amigo*."

Cedric nodded to the non-answer and leaned against the passenger's side window, well outside the camera's field of vision.

Walking home last night, past the international mix of would-be influencers and through the dazzling cornucopia of stimuli, he'd had the beginnings of a desire to understand the fabric of the city, what really went on when you lifted the veil. When he was younger, he'd backpacked through Southeast Asia, watched cock fights in Manila, and spent days smoking opium in the shadows of dilapidated temples in Laos. Like then, again he felt a compulsion to "slum it," as he called it—to give in to the temptations around him. The incessant siren call of sex, the mainlined injections of light and sound, and the promise of augmented pleasure through new analog drugs were all part of a world that was familiar to him—only here it was amplified. To a degree, every big city offered these things, but in Eutopia, everything had been driven to its logical extreme.

As the cab passed the last neoclassical storefronts of Rome—the brutalist communist-inspired architecture of Berlin in the distance—Cedric said, "Did you see that paparazzi chase last night?"

"That was a good one. I was working, but I could see some of it on the screens. They're *loco*, you know what I mean?"

"Did the cops arrest them?"

"I don't think so. They never do."

"Can't the city block their feeds or something?"

"You know the game where you hit the animal and it pops up somewhere else?"

"Whac-A-Mole?"

"*Si. Guacamole.* Yeah. It's like that."

"How long has this been going on?"

"Since I been here, for the last two years, at least. But things, they been getting worse since the Louvre."

"You seem pretty relaxed," Cedric said as the Fernsehturm, piercing the clear blue sky, passed over them.

"I have protection, just in case," he said, tapping his right breast pocket. He said it with firm conviction, leaving no doubt he was implying a gun, rather than a bulletproof vest. "Beside, money is good for now. More people are coming for the show."

"The show?"

"The life. The insanity. They like it. It feels like a movie."

"That attack at the Louvre. What do you think about that?" Cedric said. Maybe this cabbie-cum-down-on-his-luck-lounge-singer knew something the media didn't.

"Not surprising, man. I been here awhile, working this and that, and before that, things was getting worse all the time. Carjacking, burglary—every day in this town."

"Why do you think that is?" Cedric said. They passed Checkpoint Charlie Casino.

"People, they think it's easy to make money, and they frustrated. They want more."

"Should be pretty easy for the police to catch them. It's not like they're hardened criminals."

"Yeah man, it should," the cab driver said. "The city has their own private police. They all ex-military from Iraq and Syria. Badass motherfuckers. Maybe it's too much for them?"

That's right, Cedric recalled. Eutopia had been built on Native American land, which allowed them to skirt laws on sex and gaming, and police their own jurisdiction. As the traffic around them began to thin, the buildings got shorter. From the high concept of Eutopia, they entered into the strict twentieth-century American ethos of utilitarianism. Strip malls, like he'd seen on his way in, lined the roads, offering naked sushi bars, shooting ranges, and massage parlors. The cab driver took a right turn and drove past rows of tract housing and a detour leading to an airport, the landing strip covering a stretch of arid, hard-baked desert between them and mountains.

They neared a two-story building, painted the same adobe color as the strip malls in the area, with a concrete courtyard. Parked in front were matte black Humvees and sedans, each with livery adorning their doors—a white paw print encircled by crosshairs. *Eutopia PD* printed in all caps traced the top half of the circle. The vehicles—all black with tinted windows and comic book-style insignia—had a threatening yet stylish air about them, as if the designers had cribbed from a Third Reich aesthetics handbook. Two men wearing khaki cargo pants and tucked-in open-necked blue polo shirts looked down on them from a watchtower adjacent to the building. Holding automatic rifles, the mirrored lenses of their aviator sunglasses gave them an inscrutable, insect-like presence.

—ᨡ—

"I'M HERE TO PICK up Mila Webb's belongings."

Behind a bulletproof screen, the receptionist, who up until that point had barely lifted her gaze from the computer screen, looked up at him squarely, nodded, then typed something on her computer.

"Take a seat," she said, her voice slightly tinny through the speaker. As Cedric took a seat, she made a call, her mouth moving silently behind the thick protective screen.

The innocuous reception area—blue plastic seats, a water cooler with cone cups, a monitor showing Eutopia News Network—could have been a doctor's office, if it weren't for the security precautions and the two armed guards outside. Sitting there alone, Cedric wondered what his outfit said about him. Faded blue jeans, an old cotton T-shirt, sneakers—maybe he should have dressed like he was going for a job interview.

A few minutes later, a broad-shouldered man about his height walked out, hand extended.

"Inspector Monteiro," he said as Cedric stood up. While

Cedric tried to disengage from the handshake, Monteiro held on to it for a second longer, looking him in the eye.

"Hi. Cedric Travers."

With a buzz cut and a carefully shaved salt-and-pepper goatee, Monteiro looked like a retired linebacker, still formidable in his middle age. Wearing a pair of white chinos, a tucked-in blue shirt, and a loosened wide-cut red tie, if not for his Eutopia PD belt buckle and his Glock, he wouldn't have been out of place in a boardroom.

"Come on, follow me," he said, and led Cedric back through the door, which made a solid thump—the barely audible sound of servos auto-locking—as they moved down the corridor. Cool, sterile air engulfed them, in stark contrast to the heat outside and the tepid temperature of the closed-off waiting room. "My condolences about your wife, Mr. Travers. When I found out you were here, I wanted to meet you. I was the detective assigned to her case." They passed in front of a common area where some officers, dressed in all-black paramilitary attire, were lounging. "Do you want to grab a coffee or something before we go in the back?"

"Sure. I could use a water," Cedric said. "What do you mean 'condolences'? She's missing. She disappeared."

Monteiro ignored him as they headed to a vending machine, walking by two officers playing *Call of Duty* on a large, wall-mounted screen. Each wore a headset with electrodes on their temples. An on-screen avatar got sniped in the head, and one of the officers cried out and handed his controller and headset to a colleague, who was standing by. Monteiro purchased a bottle of water, handed it to Cedric, and led the way back out to the corridor.

"Travers, I'm going to be fully transparent with you. I think your wife was a decent person. No one had anything bad to say about her. She brought a lot of value to the city, from everyone I talked to. That's why it's all such a surprise—how she got mixed up in what she did."

"Inspector, I'll be up-front with you, too. I just came here to pick up her belongings. It hasn't been easy coming to terms with all this. I kind of just want it all behind me."

"From what I know, you seem convinced she's an innocent party."

"You mean what I said to the reporter? Yeah, of course, that's ridiculous. She wouldn't get involved with terrorists." Cedric had given an interview to a BBC reporter, only a brief snippet of which made it to a podcast. "Besides, Inspector, I would know if that were the case."

"Let's go in here," Monteiro said, opening the door to a small breakout room. Cedric walked in and sat down. "There's things about the case that aren't public. As I said, she was probably a good person who got mixed up in something." Taking a chair and spinning it around, he sat, bulging forearms resting on the seat back. Looking squarely at Cedric, eyes unwavering and unblinking, he said, "You still drinking?"

"What is this?" Cedric palmed the table and stood up, pushing his chair back. "All I want are the keys to her apartment."

Monteiro, still seated, kept a poker face. "You'll get them, Cedric. As long as you're on the level with me, you won't have any issue here."

"She was not an ideologue or a criminal. No way would she have been mixed up in what happened."

"How often did you speak with her?"

"We texted every once in a while."

"Regularly?"

"Well, maybe not in the last few months. We were both busy, I guess. I was trying to get a project off the ground. She was working all the time."

Monteiro nodded. "I see, that makes sense."

"What's going on? I *really* came here to pick up some things and leave."

"I want to believe you, Mr. Travers, and I almost do. But doesn't it bother you a little bit that she was involved in something like this?"

"There's a couple things. Groups like that, whatever they are, were never her style. Two, this whole thing, from the way it played out, could have been an accident."

In the days following his wife's disappearance, Cedric had scoured the Internet for information. Forums, social media, news outlets—there were dozens of competing theories. There was the heist narrative. Everybody had seen the witness footage, cobbled together from people who were in the Louvre at the time. Then there was surveillance footage of a woman wearing a hat, allegedly his wife, sitting in front of a large-scale cinema-graph, where, moments after she left, a smoke bomb detonated.

There were dozens of social media postings of the ensuing chaos, mostly shaky, vertically shot videos of people running, smoke rising from different locations in the museum, suggesting a coordinated attack. In one, a distinct explosion is heard. This was the bomb placed at the plinth of the robotic Venus de Milo. Another distraction, it was surmised, but also the origin of the terrorist narrative. When the bomb exploded, it short-circuited some wiring and started a fire, which spread and eventually destroyed the place.

Separate, leaked surveillance footage showed two other individuals calmly walking in the opposite direction of the panicked museumgoers, making their way to the museum's "augmented" Mona Lisa, lifting it from the wall, and heading for a service entrance. Here, an overzealous security guard tried to stop the two thieves, aiming a gun at them, only to be quickly disarmed and injured in the process. Conspiracy theorists said the thieves' technique was practiced, professional, suggesting military training.

"What makes you think it was an accident?" Monteiro said.

"It's just a hunch. It looked like a heist to me, where some things got out of control."

"The Louvre was destroyed. Innocent bystanders were killed . . ."

"By smoke inhalation."

"And your wife, who *was* there, is missing."

"Look, Inspector, I know the woman with the hat looks like my wife, but from what I understand, she was wearing different clothes in surveillance footage taken only half an hour before."

"You know what they say about lies? They travel halfway around the world before the truth has a chance to put its shoes on. There's *a lot* of fake news out there."

"You said there was stuff not known to the public?"

"We found her jacket and hat in the bathroom, matched her DNA to them. We also ran fingerprints from one of the thieves. ROFLEX. His group is behind the billboard hacking. Piece of work, this guy is. A disgruntled, wannabe social media star."

"You're saying she was working with this guy? ROFLEX?"

"It looks like it. I know it's hard to stomach, but I wanted you to hear it from me first. It was a terrorist attack. The robbery just funds their organization. Your wife, somehow, got involved with them."

"Inspector, I don't know if I should thank you for your candor or call a lawyer," Cedric said, standing up. "As I said, I just want this behind me. I came for her keys and to get her belongings."

"That's all good, Cedric. I'm glad you understand this is a matter best left to the experts." After casting a less than friendly smile, Monteiro got up and walked to the door, holding it open for Cedric. "You know what? I'm headed back to the city anyway, if you want a ride."

Cedric accepted Monteiro's offer, though he was puzzled. His trip to the police station was supposed to be quick—stop in, pick up his wife's keys, at the most deal with a couple of low-level employees. Why was Monteiro trying to tempt him into a mystery by threatening him to keep out?

"There's a lot of people that don't like the things we have. They don't like freedom or transparency," Monteiro said while they waited in his unmarked car at a stoplight. In front of them, crossing the street, was a newlywed couple and their entourage. The groom, with a long, lustrous beard, large sunglasses, and tailored white suit, walked hand in hand with his bride, who sported bright pink hair under a wedding bonnet, a miniskirt over tattooed legs, and four-inch-high stilettos.

"That kid you will be hearing about," Monteiro continued. "He tried to scrub his identity from the networks. But he couldn't."

They took the Continental Tunnel, which crossed under a canal that spanned a swath of the city. Doubling as the Seine in Paris and the Thames in London, it was like the rest of the city, scaled down with architectural details common to each capital. After the tunnel, Monteiro made a turn, easing into the denser city-center traffic. At the end of the boulevard stood the Arc de Triomphe, lit in waves of blue. A billboard atop the Haussmann Hotel replayed the car chase from the night before. "This is a nighttime city," Monteiro said. "She looks cheap in the daytime. Like a hooker."

Cedric only nodded as they drove. How many of the people around him were residents, how many were weekend visitors? How many were L-Uber users for kicks? How many, like Monteiro had implied, were on the precipice of committing crimes because they'd lost their social currency in Eutopia?

As if listening to his thoughts, Monteiro said, "There's marketing and advertising. Smoke and mirrors. Then there's real life. Look at that."

On the right-hand side of the car was a building with some boarded-up windows and evident damage near the top—gradations of charred black, a mix of paint and ash dripping down from where firefighters had drenched the flames.

"The Palais-Royal and Louvre. Or what remains of them."

"Aren't they rebuilding it?"

Monteiro looked askance at him and continued driving without a word. The Louvre was still in disrepair, which was odd considering the record speed with which they built this city, using best-in-class techniques from the architects that built Tianducheng and Dubai. Not one part of the building, from the faux masonry embellishments to the art it housed, wasn't saved on 3-D printable files. Monteiro drove to the edge of Paris, toward Rome, which housed executive apartments for the city's semipermanent residents, and dormitories and incubators for social media influencers.

"This place is in constant flux," Monteiro said, pulling to the curb. "Forty-percent churn rate in these residences after three months. It's the same way with everything in this city. Don't expect things to stay the same or go back to what they once were." Handing Cedric the fob to his wife's apartment, he continued, "I'd show you in, but I have a meeting."

They shook hands, and Monteiro again gripped and twisted Cedric's wrist in another overt attempt to demonstrate superiority. Everything felt calculated, threatening, and Cedric, in any other situation, would have brushed it off as the behavior of a random douchebag if it weren't for the connection they had through his wife. "I checked out your first movie," Monteiro said. "Pretty good. Some of the fight scenes could have been more realistic, but overall it was entertaining."

"Thanks."

"Good luck." The window slid up and the cop flipped a U-turn and drove off. Cedric thumbed the fob and turned toward the building, pausing, sensing a shift, like a change in atmosphere before a storm. It wouldn't be the last time he saw Monteiro. He was sure of that.

4.
Property Destruction

PULLING ASIDE POLICE TAPE, Sacha Villanova entered through the service entrance of the Louvre—the same one the thieves had used to escape. Wanting to make the most of her time in Eutopia, she had dropped off her belongings in her hotel room and headed straight for the burned-out building. She would be meeting with A'rore later that night, but first she wanted to explore the gutted structure herself. It was a great launching point for her investigative piece. Unlike many of her colleagues, whose stories relied on big data to analyze audiences and tailor their writing to fit, Sacha was old school. She preferred to go straight to the source. Get into the nitty-gritty, data be damned. The online chatter around the attack had spawned thousands of conspiracy theories. Whatever the real story was, she was sure that when the truth came out, it would define Eutopia.

In the Palais wing, she walked through a room covered with soot. Dust and debris covered gaming pods and slot machines, illuminated by a beam of midday desert sun cutting through a hole in the roof. She lifted her camera and shot a pic of the stark shadows on the now empty gaming floor, then another pic of the ragged hole in the roof. First observation—gut feeling—the place felt disposable, like tech, which is ironic because it looked on the surface like something built to withstand revolutions. A sign indicating this was Napoleon's salon pointed toward other wings, including the Louvre. Once stately gilt-bronze card tables and furniture littered the room. She walked toward the Louvre's galleries, past a bar and an artificially distressed étagère loaded with Parisian bric-a-brac. The ceiling above—what remained of it—was painted to craft the illusion of a luminous sky. Exotic birds traversed the expanse, the jagged line separating the ceiling from the sky beyond like a demarcation between real and imaginary worlds. She lifted her camera and took a picture with the flash on, to capture the contrast.

On her way to the Palais, Sacha had gotten word that finger-prints from one of the assailants had been recovered and matched to an obscure, would-be Swagly star whose accounts had since been deleted. Screenshots shared across news and social channels showed an unremarkable twenty-something's shares of hot content. His own posts, meanwhile, had received minimal—if any—social interaction. His activity had suddenly stopped a year ago, only to start again shortly before the Louvre. His last post, after a series of rants about the government, was the smoking gun, according to an off-the-record quote from the Eutopia PD: "#fucku #fake #bitches #getsum #riches #ROFLEX." With the post, he attached an image of the hijacked Rolex logo, adding the F in the middle, which had become the official insignia of a new anonymous hacking group. Could all this destruction really be attributed to him? Sacha wondered.

Sacha, walking past an overturned reproduction of Bernini's *Sleeping Hermaphroditus*—the wires and actuators that had brought it to life exposed—turned on a flashlight and swept it across the gallery. The walls, most of which had been covered by ultra-HD screens showing cinemagraphs, were now intermittently covered with blank black squares and rectangles. Now that Paris—the real Paris—was no longer safe to visit, this Louvre had drawn quite a crowd.

The curators had hired the best art reproduction experts in Xiamen, China, to take the most popular art objects from the museum and enhance them. Notably *La Gioconda*—often dismissed as overhyped and too diminutive to see behind the throngs of people crowded in front of it—was scaled up for the new Louvre. Larger and more vibrant, this painstakingly hand-painted version was itself one of a kind. *Nike of Samothrace*, the Greek winged statue of liberty, had been reimagined from the ruins, with its missing arms and head reattached. *Venus de Milo* got her arms back, too. Canova's famed *Psyche Revived by Cupid's Kiss* was given a fresh treatment—the two figures' animatronic skeletons covered by uncannily supple, ivory-white skin, embracing in fifteen-second loops on a slow-turning pedestal. Delacroix's *Liberty Leading the People* became sexier with a more voluptuous figure to suit modern tastes. Michelangelo's *Rebellious Slave* had rippling muscles that came to life with subtle subdermal enhancements.

Standing in front of the blank wall, where the Mona Lisa once hung, she recalled a scene in Godard's *Bande à part* in which a girl and her paramours view the entire Louvre in a record nine minutes and forty-three seconds. It was like the planners for Eutopia's Louvre decided to make an original reproduction that could be downloaded in a conveniently short visit. She snapped a picture and was about to turn around when the hairs on the back of her neck stood up. Someone was watching her from the shadows, she could sense it.

"Hello? Who's there?" she called out. "Hello?" Her words were met with silence, then a sudden flurry of footsteps as someone fled into the depths of the gallery. Her pulse racing, she gripped her flashlight and made a beeline back through the gallery wing, toward the service entrance, catching her breath as she lifted the police tape to step outside. She looked side to side, then leaned against the wall, halfway closing her eyes as she composed herself. It had been a while since she felt that rush, and she did not find it unpleasant.

Trespassing was only a minor offense, one she could get away with. She'd always been a risk-taker and thrill-seeker. Her first gig out of school, covering music for *Rolling Stone*, gave her that first taste for cocaine. At first, she only dabbled, but it got worse the more time she spent backstage on Gulfstreams and luxury yachts. Not only were drugs and partying endemic to the scene—she dove right in and immersed herself—she also dated a few musicians and her writing began to get noticed. Around this time she got involved with a minor DJ, who supplemented his income by selling drugs on the side. It wasn't long before she started supplementing her own income. With her connections, she became the perfect middleman for dealers looking to tap into the lucrative musicians' market. Soon she was supplying top acts, minor celebrities, the kids of celebrities. Things came crashing down when the DJ got busted and snitched on her. She was twenty-three.

Five years later she broke the biggest story of her career, an investigative piece on the shady world of data trading. But soon the hit pieces started coming in. She was stripped of her awards and the story went dark—the mere push of a button disappeared it from existence.

Walking away from the Louvre, Sacha wondered if the footsteps had been a figment of her imagination, a warning from her subconscious to tread carefully. The burned-out building, with its boarded-up entrances and blackened orifices, told her the story she was trying to track down was bigger than one social media celebrity. No matter how seductive she was, A'rore didn't care about stories; she cared about A'rore. She could be valuable or merely manipulative.

5.
Acronymious
(Six years earlier)

"**W**HICH ONE IS IT? I'm pressing the 'front' button, but nothing is happening."

"Have you tried the 'rear' button? Try that. Maybe it's miswired or something."

"*Damn* this thing."

"Where's Alexandra?

"It's new. It's probably just us not getting it."

"Did you try the 'rear' button yet?"

"I did. Nothing's happening. Damn it!"

"What time is it? Eight o'clock Hong Kong time. They'll be calling now. What about Neilay? He's handy. Can someone get him in here?"

"Didn't someone try this thing out beforehand? Jesus Christ."

"We're creatives. Not techies."

"Wrong. We're a digital agency. Aren't we supposed to be cutting edge?"

"Holy crap, this *piece of shit*. Fuck. It's frozen."

"Very helpful. Just curse at it. Curse at a slab of plastic."

"Have you tried turning it off and on?"

"Brilliant!"

"The screen is stuck. Look, I'm tapping the damn thing to death."

"They're logging into the webinar. I'll hold them off."

"Unplug it, genius. Try that and plug it back in."

On his knees, near the outlet, Curtis, junior coordinator under the chief creative technologist at Iverson & Beckenburg, pulled on the cord connecting to the touchscreen interface, waited for a few seconds, and plugged it back in. Just as he did, his boss, Alexandra, walked into the conference room, notebook and laptop under one arm, bottle of spring water in the other hand.

"What's going on?" she said, looking at her assembled team, who had straightened the moment she walked in. Two of them placed their cellphones on the table and leaned forward on their elbows. "While Curtis is trying to get this thing working, will one of you let Lab Networks and Wei & Hardy know we're dialing in?"

Lab Networks was embarking on a new venture they jokingly called the "adult Disneyland," appealing to post-millennials between school and parenthood, who had graduated to higher-paying jobs and had disposable income. Iverson & Beckenburg had been hired as a consult, providing the cultural insight—their marketing material boasted no one in the company was over thirty-five—as well as digital monetization expertise. Wei & Hardy, the joint French-Chinese architectural firm, had been hired to plan and design the new high-concept mini-city/theme park. Today was the "blue sky" meeting, where each group would present their big ideas to Lab Networks's key stakeholders.

"The light just came on. I think we're live," one of Alexandra's underlings said. Just then the large multi-paneled video screen on the wall in front of their conference table illuminated, showing the Iverson & Beckenburg team in the bottom right-hand side of the screen. To the left of them was the sharply dressed Wei & Hardy team. At the top was Lab Networks, calling in from their Venice Beach offices. Another caller dialed in, camera disabled, and popped up on the bottom left-hand side of the screen. In place of a video feed, a generic gray avatar appeared.

"Good morning and afternoon to all of you," one of Lab Networks's stakeholders said. "Glad to see we could all make it despite the technical difficulties."

A round of hellos rippled around the room and over the conference line. Everyone on the call made a short introduction, stating their name and function in their company. Each time someone spoke, the top image switched to them, and by the time they were finished, everybody was accounted for, except, conspicuously, the gray avatar on the bottom of the screen.

While a Wei & Hardy architect was talking, one of Alexandra's teammates slipped her a piece of paper: *Gray person in the corner must be Sokolov.* Alexandra nodded and smiled. Of course Dominika Sokolov would call in like this. Known for her ruthless business acumen, she was rumored to be living somewhere on her own private island, somewhere in the Indian Ocean. Alexandra's eyes kept drifting toward the gray avatar, the mystery of it like an unmarked package—intriguing, even though its contents could be dangerous.

"Three things," said the Lab Networks lead, a fit, SoCal-tanned, middle-aged man wearing an open-collared shirt. "There were three things we took away from the kickoff meeting. One: Turn fear on its head. Fear in Europe because of the migrant and terrorism crises. The right-wing populists have taken over and tourism is taking a hit. But people still want to visit. Europe is top of mind, in the news, which makes it perfect for our concept.

"Two: Surprise and delight. We have the best data scientists in the world pulling decades of records, collating raw numbers, determining which destinations and attractions engaged people most. People coming to our integrated city—let's call it that, and not a theme park—will get Europe's greatest hits without having to go there.

"Three: Massive ROI. This is a unique opportunity. Our digital experts at Iverson & Beckenburg know their audience and how to monetize them."

While the video feed was locked on the Lab Networks stakeholder, Alexandra noticed a few of her team members on their phones, texting. Or were they playing games? Muting their mic, she obscured her mouth and told them to put their phones away. Curtis, who had been appointed scribe, continued taking notes.

"Differentiating from Vegas and family-oriented theme parks is key," another Lab Networks stakeholder said. Dressed in a tank top, with designer glasses, she could have been a yoga teacher. "Which is why we want to go high concept. We're calling it Eutopia. This is where the super talented team at Wei & Hardy come in. Are you guys ready to share your screens?"

The wall of screens in front of Iverson & Beckenburg switched from the live camera feeds to a black screen, and an aerial CGI rendition of Eutopia appeared. Shown at night, it looked not unlike Vegas, like a little sea of lights in the middle of a black expanse of desert. The camera swooped in, like the establishing shot in a movie, and transitioned to specific monuments, including the Arc de Triomphe, the Coliseum, Buckingham Palace, the Fernsehturm. Then, panning shots at the ground level of the Ramblas, Dutch canals, and cafés with people milling about. After the ninety-second sizzle reel, the screen switched to a sketch of the Louvre, showing the Palais-Royal and the glass pyramid in front of it.

"We're really proud of what we've done here," one of the Wei & Hardy architects said with a heavy French accent. "This was a labor of love for me. Like a love letter to the continent. To the past." The screen cycled through more sketches of moments and details for Eutopia while he continued. "Because of the size we are limited to, on the Navajo Nation territory, we found it very beneficial to work with the data teams at Lab Networks to pinpoint which attractions we should prioritize, intermixing, as you can see, enough detail at ground level to make it an authentic-feeling experience. We don't want to repeat the same mistakes made in Tianducheng, where they went halfway with their copy of Paris. We are focusing on big picture and small."

After dozens more slides showing interiors and proof of concept examples that had already been built— Hollywood lots, Roman malls in Vegas—the Wei & Hardy lead stopped on a slide listing a consortium of architects from China, Europe, and the United States.

"Each is best in class at what they do. For top-notch, forced-perspective monuments, we have experts who worked on Universal Studio's Harry Potter World, already working with us to exploit our limited space and achieve maximum impact. We can emulate the old through the use of concrete, rebar, and polystyrene skin. It will look better than the real thing. For hyper-efficient building times, of course, this is where our colleagues in China are unmatched. For authenticity, we have the best consultants out of Hollywood, to apply the touches we need for believability. The end result is a city we all agree we would not just want to visit but also to live in. I truly believe, even if people had the chance to go visit these places in Europe, they would prefer to come here."

Alexandra jotted down a few ideas. The firm's presentation was so *literal*; she had been expecting more of a spin on the big ideas. The architects at Wei & Hardy, winners of an Aga Khan Award, had a reputation for cutting-edge design, and, it almost seemed, they'd been swept up by nostalgia, presenting their straight-ahead vision as a radical departure from the avant-garde of architecture. Yes, she *got it*, what they were trying to do, but it was only creative masturbation.

Alexandra thanked Wei & Hardy and, when given control of the screen by the conference leader, played her agency's own sizzle reel—a strategically short fifty-six-second showcase of who they were as a company. Conditioned by Instagram, her data showed the most engagement with videos that were less than fifteen seconds, with long-form videos showing diminishing viewership after the sixty-second mark. The sweet spot was somewhere in between. With a breezy indie folk-pop accompaniment, the video showed their Williamsburg office: a large, open space with a bike rack and young, busy-looking account managers walking around with tablets and laptops. Stats appeared on the screen, boasting over a hundred designers, creatives, technologists, researchers, strategists and digital project managers. Next, the thirty-plus *Fortune* 100 companies they worked for and twenty-plus industry awards. Finally, the fifty-eight miles per day they clocked biking, and the over three hundred cups of coffee they drank.

"We know your audience because we *are* your audience. We grew up in a world where Facebook had already been established as the backbone of the Internet, practically a utility."

The screen switched to a slide showing icons for dozens of social media platforms, with statistics for hours of usage per day, along with age and gender demos.

"But we're not here today, of course, to tell you about what you already know. Social is huge and we all know that." Pressing the clicker in her hand, she paused, waiting for a clip of Wayne Gretzky slapping in a goal, then a short reaction GIF of Michelle Obama giving a thumbs-up. "Anybody remember what Wayne Gretzky said? 'I skate to where the puck is going to be, not where it is.' Mila Webb, one of our top digital supervisors, currently working on the Ford account, will take you through the three biggest trends on the horizon and how we're going to harness them for maximum ROI."

Mila was the second-oldest person on her team and had been a huge asset since arriving. Inquisitive, bright, and thorough, she brought an element of maturity in a company whose employees tended to last, on average, six months to a year, until another agency offered them a new job with a better title. One of their top national account directors, she had been with the agency for just over a year. Also, Mila was married to the film director Cedric Travers and had produced his sci-fi fan-film, which had just gone viral on YouTube. Mila was ambitious, like Alexandra, and was definitely going places.

"Geofencing, leveraging GPS technology to target mobile ads to precise geographic locations," Mila said. "As you all know, this, along with demographic and psychographic targeting, is the foundation of programmatic ad delivery across the web. Companies like Snapchat are adding geofenced filters to their apps." Switching to onscreen examples from Snapchat, Instagram, and Twitter, Mila continued, "Filters that only work in certain locations. Think of the possibilities to incentivize the public to go to places. This technology is nascent—barely exploited to its full extent.

"You need to ask: Beyond the beautiful city the very talented specialists at Wei & Hardy created," Alexandra said, "what are your KPIs, and how can you guarantee strong ROI?" Nodding, the stakeholders at Lab Network stayed silent, like rapt pupils in a classroom.

Mila clicked out of the presentation to show them live video streams across Facebook and Twitter. "Live streams are just in their infancy. Technology is finally in a place where anybody with a hundred-dollar cell phone can broadcast live from almost anywhere on the planet." On screen, Kendall Kardashian was giving a tour of her Pacific Palisades mansion. "Right now, there are over three hundred thousand live feeds in the US alone." A heat map appeared on screen, showing clusters of activity on the East and West Coasts.

"We have one more big thing on the horizon, a game changer for event- and location-based digital marketing," Alexandra said.

"Then we'll tell you how they come together under one overarching theme."

"Beacon technology. Near-field interactivity with a second screen," Mila said, as the screen switched to a video of crowds in Times Square interacting with a digital billboard. Selfies from the crowd appeared on the giant billboard branded with the YouTube logo. "There is a huge opportunity with outdoor screens. We're just now opening up the programmatic out-of-home market, where digital billboards can be targeted to specific audiences. You have a dozen sports enthusiasts around the billboard, show them an ad for Adidas. You have an over-forty male audience around it, show them an ad for Cialis." Ripples of visualized laughter spread across the bottom of the conference screen.

"How does it all come together?" Alexandra said. "This." The now iconic image of Kim Kardashian West with champagne cascading onto her prodigious rear end appeared on screen, eliciting chuckles across the conference line. "Kim broke the Internet last year. She showed us the future. Her brand is herself, and like Kim, millennials and post-millennials will each be their own mini media companies. Given the unique opportunity to create a city for this audience, the pathway couldn't be more clear. Make Eutopia the place to be. Incentivize them to live-broadcast their lives. Geofence these streams with digital swag, like filters and custom emojis, and give each of them the chance to make money while having fun. We envision a city for the new transactional generation, where everybody has the chance to be a star. Lab Networks will charge premium CPMs, the kind the *Fortune* 100 brands we work with will be dying to pay for."

There was silence on the lines as the teams at Lab and Wei considered what Alexandra and Mila had just presented. The vision they had presented, of a microcosmic Europe, would require a fundamental rethinking to accommodate thousands of screens.

After a polite thank you from the lead stakeholder at Lab

Networks, Wei & Hardy were conspicuously silent. Alexandra had expected tension, as she usually did with creatives who didn't understand monetization and brand building. Par for the course. As the meeting wrapped, she thought about taking the rest of the day off so she could visit the new Thalassa spa in Midtown, where she'd be able to work on her laptop while getting a much-needed pedicure. "I'm actually kind of excited to see how this thing turns out," she told Mila as they filed out of the conference room.

6.
Social Cache

A GIANT DIGITAL SCREEN ACROSS the plaza from Mila's apartment showed a couple of girls in the street, dressed like the woman whose images had followed him around town since arriving. They had A'rore's hairstyle down, her post-punk outfit, and even a glowing shell covering the lower half of their left legs, imitating the prosthesis he'd seen her wearing the previous night when she'd stepped out of her car after the paparazzi chase. One of them looked up and started pointing, and soon both were jumping up and down, flashing their breasts, having seen themselves on the giant billboard.

After a few seconds, the signage cut to a map interface with male, female, and transsexual symbols across it. *Sex. On. Demand. L-Uber.* Next, a well-coiffed businessman surrounded by scantily clad secretaries pulled on a vape pen, exhaling a massive cloud. *Panadrine. Like a Boss.*

The screens were hypnotizing enough, but below in the plaza, where a statue of Kasparov battled Big Blue, there was a hive of activity, as visitors from around the world milled about hoping to be seen. A café just across the street, with Parisian-style glass-topped tables and mesh-weave chairs, was full of characters, notably groups of Korean high rollers with shopping bags around their tables. Gold-plated items glinted in the late-morning sun: watches, chain-link straps on handbags, designer sunglasses, phone cases.

A distant explosion, like a large firecracker, startled Cedric. The café-goers down below froze as well, shrugged, then continued whatever they were doing.

Mila's executive apartment looked onto a swath of a boulevard lined with casinos, luxury boutiques, bars, sex shops, game parlors, and specialty food shops. A simple but spacious one-bedroom on the top floor of the Hotel Pigalle, it was equipped with a kitchenette, a large bathroom, and two televisions. It wasn't the kind of place Cedric would ever have imagined her inhabiting. When he was "in" in Hollywood, they'd lived in Venice in a historic cottage, which they'd carefully renovated to preserve its character.

The place had been turned over by Monteiro's forensic crew, looking for clues to corroborate their suspicions about Mila. Turning from the balcony, Cedric approached some books scattered around a coffee table—thick, expensive, limited-edition art books she had been fond of collecting. A book of early twenty-first-century street art, an illustrated edition of Dalí's *Diary of a Madman*, a biography of Edward Bernays, a Duchamp monograph, and his own book, *The Pitch*, a barely fictionalized account of his quick rise and fall in the movie industry.

The book had been met with critical success but was a commercial flop. By then he had cemented his persona-non-grata status anyway. He was considered difficult to work with, and *The Pitch* was his attempt to set the record straight—a behind-the-scenes look at the entertainment industry. He thumbed the cover, flipping through the pages. Mila had warned him about publishing it, but he'd gambled with his ego and lost. Reeking of desperation, failure begetting failure, his career nosedived while hers took off. In one of their last attempts to salvage their marriage, they tried to conceive, only for Mila to suffer a late miscarriage.

He walked to an open closet near the door, where some of her clothes were scattered. Picking up a white cotton shirt, he held it to his nose—lavender and a faint hint of perspiration. He pictured her last days in Eutopia rife with stress. She'd always been an overachiever, working extra long hours at the agency. Who knew how many moving parts she'd had to manage as the experiential director in this city? The billboards, the bustle on the streets, the massive confluence of DIY media and 24/7 enter-tainment—if anything, he was sure she welcomed it as a challenge and a welcome distraction from her previous life with him. He folded her shirt and slipped it into a slot on a hanging linen shelf, then took a cursory look at the jumble of clothes and shoes.

Hanging on a half-wall, adjacent to a table in the corner that served as a desk, was a white board with green lines demarcating start and stop points—a rough outline of campaign flights—with dates written in her confident, precise handwriting. The date of the Louvre incident was marked by a point in the middle of an ongoing campaign that had started earlier that year. Monteiro and his team had surely used this to corroborate their theory about her involvement. On the bottom right-hand corner of the board was a round sticker with a stylized *A* on it, an emblem that looked familiar. In a tray on the desk, next to an LED candle, Post-it notes, and business cards, was an array of branded pens she'd probably accumulated from visiting account executives. One in particular stood out.

A disposable vape pen labeled Panadrine. Had she been taking it? These days, CEOs and business leaders almost always attributed their superhuman ability to work eighteen-plus hours a day to the drug. It was like a cult, and it just didn't seem like her to buy into the hype. The pen was probably a piece of swag from a vendor at a trade show. As Cedric twisted it in his fingers, the temptation to take a small drag off it slowly faded, like an ebbing tide. He placed it back in the tray, pushing the rest of the items around absentmindedly. Where could she be keeping the ring? Did she have it with her, wherever she was?

His eyes drifted back to the sticker, recognizing it as a logo he'd seen around town. "Search A'rore," he told his phone, and the engine took him to a wiki. Gazing back at him through silver eyes, accentuated by dark mascara, was Eutopia's top influencer, according to her bio. The image looked like a still from an interview, her hair a lustrous sheen, jet black, asymmetrically cut, undulating surfaces culminating in flame-like points. There was something familiar about her, but he couldn't quite place it, as if a recollection of someone or something like her but not quite her was hidden in the labyrinth of his memories.

He was about to click on a link to an archived video of one of her earlier appearances, pre-Eutopia, when a change in the room's ambient light distracted him. Hearing another distant explosion, he turned toward the balcony. The sky had darkened with rain clouds—odd, since the day up until then had been clear.

By the time he left the apartment a few minutes later, the rain outside had picked up. As Cedric paused under the awning of the Hotel Pigalle to wait out the downpour, a man joined him. Using the tips of his fingers to flick off the water from his thinning head of hair, he said, "You look surprised." People across the plaza and on the boulevard median were dashing into stores and under doorways.

"It didn't look like that kind of day," Cedric said. "Not with the drought and all, you know."

"I can tell you haven't been here long enough to learn about cloud seeding." Leaning out slightly, just enough so he could point to the sky, the man said, "They fire off a few silver iodide rockets, and a few minutes later—boom—rain."

"So that's what that noise was."

During the Beijing Olympics, the Chinese had pioneered technology to launch particles into the atmosphere to nucleate clouds, causing moisture to build up. Farther west, where Cedric came from, weather modification was becoming more and more prevalent due to the decade-long dry spell—but he hadn't experienced it directly, until now.

"It's supposedly to cool off the city, keep some stuff irrigated, but the joke around here is that they're seeding the clouds with amphetamine dust to keep us all awake."

"I wouldn't be surprised," Cedric said, chuckling.

"It's part of what makes this place tick. The energy, that always-high feeling."

All highs, no lows. The man had just articulated something Cedric had been thinking since arriving. It was almost as if everybody were in a trancelike state, monitoring their social channels, connecting to billboards, transacting with each other. And it didn't stop.

"Are you here for the poker tournament?" the man said, this time looking directly at Cedric. His wispy blond hair, damp from the rain, was combed straight back, showing gaps where it was thinning. About Cedric's height, with a slighter build, he had the unassuming air of an accountant. He didn't fit the hoodie-and-sunglasses stereotype, though, for poker tournament players. Perhaps that meant he was a formidable opponent, dressed down to seem less intimidating to his competitors.

"No, just here for a visit."

The rain had passed over their part of the city, and the sidewalks and streets reflected sunlight, like sleek bodies of water. Looking back toward Berlin, the man asked him if he was going that way, too. Cedric said yes, not because he had intended to do so, but because he had nothing else planned besides finding a spot to eat, and he was curious to find out more about the city. They passed some stumbling, drunk Chinese tourists live-broadcasting themselves, jabbering, waving, and laughing with their audiences as they filmed selfies in front of the Kasparov statue. A South American couple—preppy, dressed like Macy's mannequins—cursed loudly as they had to go out of their way to avoid the group.

"Are they all tourists in this town?" Cedric said.

"Pretty much, but a lot of them are trying to tap into influencer dollars, so you have long-term visitors. I guess I'm one of them, but I'm here for the poker."

"I feel pretty old here," Cedric said as three garrulous girls passed, dressed like members of the Avengers.

"Well, the older generation has Vegas now. Even the retirees that come to this place are millennials who struck it rich in the third Internet boom."

"The retirement community of the future."

As they walked past a group of Japanese tourists, filming each other, making *V* signs and interacting with a giant billboard, the stranger introduced himself as Fred Green. Just a semi-pro poker player grinding out a living as he went around the country.

A guy with a ragged beard and torn velour track suit was getting cuffed by an officer. Fred noticed Cedric watching the scene unfold.

"There's a growing homeless contingent here. A lot of them are guys who came here to mine social media dollars and fell on hard times."

"Jesus. Are they doing anything about it?" Cedric was looking for the lowdown on this place, not filtered through Monteiro—although he wasn't sure about Fred. Still, an insider's view, which Fred seemed to possess, might help him figure out what happened to his wife.

"Besides locking them up? Nah. Not that many tourists seem to notice. There's *always* a live chase or scandal or something going on. Never a dull moment between the ads."

"If it bleeds, it leads."

"You've heard of Dominika Sokolov?"

"She's the media mogul, right?" Cedric said. He'd been in the industry and followed the trades enough to know all about her and her empire, of which Eutopia was a small part, almost more of an experiment, according to Mila. She'd been named *Forbes*'s most influential person in media about a decade ago after the massive success of her multichannel network. She'd been credited with destroying the old-boy networks that dominated the twentieth century, but in recent years she'd become grist for the tabloids, with stories focusing more on her eccentricities than her business acumen. "Isn't she a recluse or something?"

"Oh, she's in charge, I think, no matter what anyone says."

"All they ever talk about is this wildly rich woman with extravagant outfits and too much makeup."

"This place would have been totally different if it weren't for her."

Cedric, knowing his wife's role in the initial planning phases of the city, didn't say anything. He was getting interesting information from this guy, but he couldn't be sure he didn't have an angle, or was somehow involved with Monteiro. "How exactly does she run this place?" he said, as they approached the spinning, neon-rimmed windmill sitting atop the Moulin Rouge Sex Club.

"Like any other business nowadays—remotely. She has her operations team on the ground running logistics. All the clubs, casinos, etcetera. She's probably more personally involved in the public relations side of things since she's pretty much *the* media queen. I mean, that's what she's famous for, and public perception is everything."

The bright red blades and structure of the windmill—an exact replica of the original—stood out against intermittent waves of cyanide blue on the surrounding screens, like a lurid beacon in the waters of a collective libido. Crossing the street, they encountered a crowd of people forming around something. The screens, which had been showing animated color gradients, transitioned to a sweeping, handheld shot of a crowd. It took a couple seconds for it to register with Cedric that this was the same crowd he was about to enter.

"Speaking of public perception. That's A'rore up there," Fred said. The surrounding screens now showed a selfie of the city's icon, and, about twenty people deep into the crowd, A'rore was standing on a raised platform, her glossy anime hair waving in front of her eyes. Live shots of her and fans streamed across the billboards, an aggregate audience number rapidly ticking upward while comments started appearing with the hashtags #moulin-rouge #arore. "She randomly appears like this, announcing where she'll be minutes before." A'rore was handing out cards, and fan-shot video feeds showed her chatting with people, mugging with the seductive cool of an old film star. Women and men were clamoring and jostling to be in her proximity, a kind of mass psychosis he'd only seen at major galas. Like David Atten-borough documenting a strange new species of primate, Cedric watched with bemused detachment.

"What is she doing?"

"No idea, but my guess is she's handing out VIP passes to a club somewhere. Some of these things are hard to get into because of the amount of social clout they attract. Just getting in and getting tagged by the level of people in them can raise your status. You're lucky to be here. You might get tagged in someone's photo with A'rore."

A'rore held up her phone, shooting another selfie with the crowd. Cedric, having worked in the entertainment industry, where so much hinged on youth and beauty, had been around too many charismatic individuals to count, whose supernova personalities had a captivating quality about them, drawing you in at a glance and sucking you into their orbit.

"The weird thing is that even though she's the star, it's almost more about the fans and their audience," Cedric said. People were pushing each other, vying for optimal sight lines where they could capture themselves and A'rore in the same shot.

"Getting a selfie with her is the most lucrative social trophy that exists. I don't have one, but I imagine they're making money off it or they wouldn't be so crazy about seeing her." The crowds jostled them, twice the amount of people now as there had been a mere three minutes ago. A'rore had disappeared from her perch, and on the billboards around them fan-perspective streams showed her in the back seat of a black sedan with sunglasses on, reminiscent of a rock star being pursued by groupies. As her driver started pushing forward, the digital signage around them switched to her POV, shot from her eyewear. "Look at that. They give people exactly what they want to get them here."

"Themselves," Cedric said, more to himself than for Fred to hear.

Like a troop of primates dispersing after their alpha, the crowd began to thin as soon as A'rore's vehicle drove away. The two of them continued walking, and, as they approached an intersection, Cedric's phone vibrated. He stopped and took it out of his pocket. From an anonymous sender, it was a random string of numbers—*4.5059252*—with a message reading, *"watch your step."*

"Who is this?" Cedric replied as people flowed around him.

He sent the message and stepped into the street, and a sixth sense seized him. A car, just about to crash into him, slammed on its brakes, stopping within a mere foot of him. Adrenaline coursed through him as he made eye contact with the driver, a young woman who looked just as startled as him. She drove off, and he could see his companion on the other side of the street, waiting for him.

—ɯ—

CEDRIC PARTED WAYS WITH Fred shortly after the A'rore sighting, agreeing to meet him later. He had warmed up to Fred and was eager to see if this unassuming poker player knew anything about his wife. Despite himself, he wanted to know more. It was like, with each passing moment, he was illuminating a cave with a lantern, revealing bits and pieces at a time. What was it that had drawn Mila to this place and kept her here?

Crepuscular light limned strands of clouds above the hard lines of the city horizon. The sun was about to set, and Eutopia's high wattage began to pop. As he passed gaming establishments—interspersed between clothing stores, sex clubs, and gadget boutiques—he thought of his wife. She had always been competitive. The first time he met her, at a Snapchat party in Santa Monica, he had been flirting with one of her colleagues, an intense, whip-smart blonde wearing bright red lipstick, almost the mirror image of Mila, who despite the auburn hair could have been her sister. He'd found himself in a faux debate with the blonde about advertising versus art—more of a cerebral mating ritual than a genuine conversation—as they drank Japanese whiskey at the bar. He was already an established commercial director, making a decent upper-middle-class living churning out advertisements for major brands—things like household items, packaged goods—and he was hard at work on a passion project, a sci-fi short he had been trying to get made for a couple years.

"Advertising, billboards, preroll—it's not inspired, it doesn't come from the inside," he said.

"But," the blonde said, "you just told me what you do for a living. Isn't that hypocritical?" For someone who made his living from Fortune 500 brands, of course it was, but he wasn't going to admit it.

"I'm just being real. There's a difference between being an artist and a technician. I work with so many people who refuse to see the difference."

"I have this friend in the Lower East Side in New York who designs eyewear for Prada, and she does amazing work. You can't

deny what she does isn't art, even if she makes it for a corpo-
ration."

"I wouldn't put the two together," Mila said, who had heard
the last snippet of their conversation. "If it takes a committee to
make, to decide on color and material and each contour, then
it's more of a product." She finished her barb with a smile and
completely took the heat out of their conversation. The blonde
exited shortly afterward, the tension between the two palpable.

"Thanks," he said. "That conversation was getting a little too
conceptual for me. I was just playing devil's advocate. She was
trying to convince me the Super Bowl ads this year were master-
pieces."

"I hate that tart," Mila said. "Of course, I was bullshitting.
Everything is collective nowadays, including art." Cedric couldn't
help but agree with her—even if he didn't want to—and marveled
at the way she had maneuvered herself into his space. She moved
up fast, wherever she worked, and as he walked through Eutopia
he could see how this hyper-gamified city would have a certain
appeal to her.

He passed café terraces, bars, and brightly lit luxury
boutiques filled with twentysomethings, all filming themselves
and each other. He'd been to Europe before the populist uprising
had ruined the tourist economy, but now, in his forties, he was
probably one of the few in the city of Eutopia who'd actually
been there. The people around him could only compare their
experience to digitized celluloid footage, glamorized depictions
in movies. This idealized version, without any of the strife of the
real thing, was just an elaborate backdrop for social media. Still,
if these recorded digital snippets ended up in a time capsule,
only to be discovered by our future selves, he thought, one would
be hard-pressed to distinguish Eutopia from its inspiration. Like
the fake blue-sky scrims in a studio back lot, without the wide
perspective, within the confines of a camera frame, you could
almost fool yourself.

Pausing in front of a hybrid gym-restaurant—where buzzed Eutopians could walk on a treadmill and sip Soylent meal replacement beverages while regulating their social media feeds—he pulled out his phone to access the map app. He had to swipe through a large interstitial ad for Club Rossebuurt—where A'rore would be making a guest appearance—before accessing the app's home screen. After accessing the map app and pinpointing the Haussmann, he walked over a breezeway, past dozens of street buskers, toward the bright, swirling signage of the Haussmann.

A few minutes after arriving, as he took in the buzzing atmosphere, Fred pinged him to meet near the VR arena. A giant screen depicting a live virtual environment showed a first-person perspective of a soldier at a checkpoint in what looked like the Middle East, armed with an AR-15, facing down a bomb-strapped jihadi insurgent. The player, wearing a VR headset and motion sensors, was standing in the middle of a platform, acting out the scenario. As he moved his arms, on screen a burst of gunfire erupted and the jihadi's head exploded, brilliant red chunks flying out from a cloud of blood vapor. The player knelt and took aim at another jihadi while his credit score racked up a few thousand points.

They continued toward the poker rooms, heading past slot machines and dance games, where people were dancing against each other and avatars, arms waving, popping and twerking in a frantic attempt to outscore one another.

A WHITE, GLOWING NIMBUS of e-cig vapor surrounded their table like a halo, broken up by passing waitresses, only to take shape again with the next round of exhalations. The secondhand vapor, whatever it was, perked him up, and the oxygenated air of the Haussmann had the effect of making him hyperalert. The stakes were much higher than just winning chips off of other players. Fred had given him the lowdown on how Eutopian-style poker worked when they arrived.

"Every table is connected to a global audience with a potential reach of eight hundred million viewers. Everything we say and do is simultaneously translated into five languages in real time. They're betting on our hands with a twenty-second delay in order to prevent unfair advantages for the live players."

"So it's like meta-betting."

"Pretty much. It's an extension of how the city itself works."

Cedric agreed to sit in on a few cash games, even though he wasn't anywhere near a pro poker player like Fred. "It's a bunch of tourists and drunk fish," he said. "Just sit in for a few hands and have some fun." Their table was indeed full of "fish," as Fred liked to call them—tourists here just to share on their social channels, shoving all-in with terrible hands. Then there were others, chatting amicably with each other, who seemed like locals—possibly employees of clubs and restaurants—who were making extra cash off the tourists.

A large screen overlooking their floor, flanked on either side by betting odds and live feeds of other sporting events, showed the action at each table, the players represented by their social media avatars. Cedric, who had deleted his accounts a couple years ago, was the only one represented by a gray avatar, and was all the more conspicuous because of it. Fred's was a picture of himself, unremarkable-looking next to dozens of carefully selected avatars taken from video games, comic books, anime, and action movies. Their game, consisting of players with moderate social reach, was peaking at around three thousand live viewers. As drunk tourists dropped in and out of the table, their chip stacks grew, and so did their global odds.

After a bad beat from a tourist who struck a flush on his pair of jacks, Cedric sat out and watched a short stream of abusive comments flutter up from their screen. Fred, who was faring better, ended up clearing chips from the tourist on the next hand, amassing a decent-size stack.

Forty-five minutes later, when he had cashed out, Fred met Cedric at the bar. Cedric was nursing a tequila sour and Fred was sipping a whiskey and soda when a tall, thin man walked by them with an entourage of thick-wristed men wearing suits. The thin man, with carefully sculpted facial stubble, cut through the tables, making his way toward the back of the room, his tapered beige blazer standing out against the wide black backs of his counterparts. Part of the entourage broke off and went around the bar to their right, out of their line of sight.

"That tall guy. That's Eddie Costello, one of the bigwigs here in Eutopia. Chief Entertainment Officer."

"Really?" Cedric said, his interest piqued.

"Yep." The tone of Fred's voice was a pitch lower than normal, and his posture had stiffened. As if reading Cedric's mind, he said, "The guy is kind of a celebrity, I mean, to those in the know. They say it was his idea to bring A'rore to the city."

"It looks like he made the right move." Cedric was eager to ask about his wife, but Fred had hastily downed his drink and set it on the monitor-laden bar counter behind them. Getting off his stool he said, "Let's get out of here."

Cedric followed him, noticing a member of Eddie's entourage had reappeared at the other end of the bar.

—◊—

AS THEY WALKED OUT of the Haussmann, passing through the bright curtain of lights near the entrance, Cedric wondered out loud about their sudden departure. "Are you in some kind of trouble?"

"With the guys I beat?" he said. "Nah. That was chump change for them. The regulars cleared me out before so it's payback. I just needed a change of atmosphere."

As they walked, the brisk night air tightening the skin on their faces, Cedric thought of confiding to Fred the reason he had come to Eutopia. Suddenly paranoid, he badly wanted a confidant and he chalked up his skepticism about Fred to years of hobnobbing in Hollywood, where opportunism was the name of the game. They made their way past a hookah and wine bar— where a woman wearing an embroidered bra, chemise, and full-length skirt beckoned them in. Cedric was about to politely decline when a woman started shrieking, "My purse! My purse!" A motorcycle's engine revved and accelerated. Everybody around them paused and looked up from their phones, trying to locate the source of the commotion. The taillights of the motorcycle disappeared between two cars as it split lanes and jumped a red light. A large screen over a Nike store switched from a club advertisement to aerial drone footage of the motorcycle zipping and weaving through traffic. People around them aimed their phones at the screen, typing emojis and acronyms that appeared in a real-time stream. Another drone darted past in the direction of the motorcycle. Cedric and Fred looked at each other and shrugged.

"Not as exciting as last night," Cedric said.

"You're already jaded," Fred said, a smile spreading across his face. "I know just where to go, come on."

7.
Bleeding Edge

S HE *WAS* SEDUCIBLE, A'RORE thought. Sacha was the kind of young woman she respected. Somehow, Sacha was impervious to the superficial allure A'rore knew she exuded. She wasn't among the millions who followed A'rore, who added to her coffers via thousands of dollars in daily income from her exclusive makeup line, or the ad revenue pouring in from her live feeds. But that didn't make A'rore resentful. It made her desirous.

"I think," A'rore said, sitting across from Sacha in their first-ever face-to-face meeting, "that the accident was the best thing to ever happen to me."

They were in A'rore's penthouse suite, with panoramic views of Eutopia from twenty-three stories up. The boulevards, like vital arteries, showed a constant, steady flow of movement. The monuments, like vital organs, their surfaces laden with LED lights synchronized to her heartbeat, mirroring the calm, steady mood she was in. A physician had just administered her bi-weekly vitamin IV drip, which she was taking to combat chronic fatigue syndrome. Filled with vitamins A and C, magnesium chloride, calcium gluconate, and nicotinamide—Sacha had taken notes from the physician with A'rore's permission—it was a cocktail that gave her a much-needed energy boost. A nice side effect was vasodilation, which gave her complexion a youthful glow.

When A'rore mentioned the accident, she brushed her hand against her prosthetic—stylized not to simulate a real leg but to accentuate its artificiality. Today she was fitted with a "cloaking" appendage designed by Sophie Oliveira Barata. Inspired by Cortana version one, her favorite character from the *Halo* franchise, the limb was laden with a dielectric metasurface, which made it invisible. Barata had programmed intermittent glitches that momentarily revealed amethyst-colored scan lines and circuitry.

"I'm surprised to hear you say that. Your accident must have been traumatic."

"It's something I don't talk about much."

"We don't have to."

"I want to. I want to. Is this being recorded?"

"Yes, but it's just for my notes. Anything can be off the record, and whatever I write I'll let you have first look."

"I'm fine with it, but you know, like everything else I'm showing you, I just want to open up and take you inside myself." A'rore paused contemplatively, carefully choosing her next words. She had planned on being "transparent"—but whatever she revealed still needed to be curated. Her heroes—mythologized by the entertainment industry—were at once vulnerable and godlike. "It's weird, because when I lost this part of me in the accident, when my leg was crushed, I thought it was over."

"In what way?"

"My modeling career. So much depended on perfection. I was on a runway one moment, and the next some drunk guy plows through a red light in Manhattan and T-bones the cab I'm in. I spent weeks in the hospital, months in painful rehabilitation, so I had lots of time to think. I'd already been through a lot at that point, after the story with Senator Erickson broke. I'd lost my contract with H&M, and I was this scared girl, because I had basically cultivated my life to do this, to look beautiful, and what else was I going to do? What else could I do?"

"And from that low point, how did you find something positive?"

"I knew I had to own who I was. When I was learning to walk again, I met with designers who really had amazing, amazing technology. I wanted to have a closet full of prosthetics, one for every day and every mood."

"You kind of became a poster girl for the posthumanist movement."

"They were doing things people thought were crazy just a couple decades ago, inserting subdermal magnets and RFID chips, enhancing their senses. But really, if you think about it, it was just the next step in body modification after tattoos and piercing. I mean, people were wearing glasses, then contacts, but if you can have a bionic eye and see better than twenty/twenty? That's what I'm talking about."

"Your prosthetic certainly became your signature. What do you think about your copycats?"

"I don't condone amputating your own limb just to get a cybernetic one, but look, this was going on before I came along, and really, who am I to judge?"

"Is there any other part of your body that's enhanced?"

A'rore's lips parted, but she paused. When she'd discovered Sacha was writing about Eutopia, she knew this might be her chance at coming clean. She felt, for some reason, burdened with guilt.

"You know how they say movies are as good as they are because of the suspension of disbelief? I really think everything is like that. Everything in real life. I am exactly what people think I am."

"An ideal of something. An archetype."

"An idol. An influencer. Whatever you want. There's nothing fake about me. There's nothing artificial. I'm augmented everywhere, of course. It's like color versus black and white, you know. I'm showing more of the spectrum."

Sacha, who'd spent the entire day with her, casually chatting with her as she went about her daily routine, had noticed from the moment she met A'rore that there was more to her than met the eye. A'rore was opening up—it was palpably cathartic for her—because Sacha wasn't, or didn't feel like, at least, the type of person to judge.

"You're like, to a lot of people, a kind of perfection. What is it like?"

"People have no idea what I go through. I was born with good genes. I won't deny that and I hope it doesn't sound condescending. But maintaining this," she said, lightly cupping her breasts, then gripping her quads, "is time consuming and costly. I already had full C cups by the time I was fourteen. I augmented them to Ds when I was eighteen. My nose, it's been refined—rhinoplasty to further chisel it, but nothing that would make me unrecognizable." A'rore's shoulders relaxed and she could feel tingling at her extremities, the same euphoria she felt when she took a hit of Panadrine, almost like a light orgasm. It felt good to talk about this, get it off her chest.

"Time chisels at you. Just last month, you know, I had blepharoplasty to tighten up my eyes. Also this part," she said, rubbing the crescents just under her eyes, "this part was also tweaked to eliminate dark circles. I need to have a constant glow. My entire brand depends on radiating sexuality and vitality. Look, Sacha—and I don't know how much I want you to put in your story—but there isn't much on my body I haven't stretched, lasered, or veneered," she said laughing, revealing a perfect ivory-white set of teeth.

Sacha studied A'rore with the objective, detached air of a psychoanalyst. She had perfect facial structure, it was true. Her jawline was angular, defined, but not too hard or masculine. Perfectly plump lips—were there dermal fillers in those as well? She'd seen the photos of A'rore before she was famous, when she was known as Elizabeth Bowe, and she had always looked good, but since her transformation into A'rore, she definitely had that ineffable quality about her, that *something* that gave her an elite aura. She was also, very obviously, seducing her, and Sacha had to admit that this more vulnerable side, together with her poise and confidence, was sexy.

They'd met earlier that day at the gym on the top floor of the Brandenburg Hotel in Berlin. A'rore was winding up a private boxing class with Floyd Mayweather Jr., who was in town promoting an upcoming mixed martial arts fight at the Coliseum.

"I'm going to give you an all-access pass," A'rore said, when she heard Sacha was going to be in town. "Like one of those 24/7 documentaries on HBO." On hand were some members of the local press, a Deadspin sports correspondent, and half a dozen members of Mayweather's entourage. Ducking, bobbing, weaving, a right cross followed by a left hook, followed by a hook to the body, A'rore finished her combo and stepped out of range as Mayweather swiped a focus mitt past her head. Obviously staged for the press, A'rore's agility and coordination impressed Sacha nevertheless. After the focus mitts and a jump rope session, which she was able to complete despite her prosthetic, A'rore grabbed a towel and dabbed her forehead with it before draping it around her neck. After a couple posed photo ops, Mayweather and his entourage left the gym followed by the correspondents.

"The reason I come here, to the Brandenburg, is because they have the best cryosauna in town," A'rore said as they walked through the gym. "Have you ever had a session?"

"No, I haven't."

"It's extremely therapeutic, the same principal behind ice baths, or the sauna and ice swimming in Finland." They entered the cryo antechamber where a technician greeted A'rore with the professional yet friendly demeanor of someone who'd done a lot of business with her. The machine itself was a brushed stainless-steel tube with nitrogen mist coming out of the top, like a time travel machine in an old sci-fi movie. Disrobing in front of Sacha and the technician, relaxed and chatting at the same time—the natural ease of an exhibitionist, comfortable with her own body—she continued, "Your body gets tricked and reacts as if it was going into hypothermia. What that means is blood goes from your extremities, your hands and feet and legs, to your core. There the blood picks up nutrients, oxygen, and enzymes, then gets circulated back around your body the moment you jump out of the cryosauna."

Sacha admired A'rore's body, athletic, extremely toned, youthful in its tautness and gait. Her rear—that could have been augmented, too—was firm and bulbous, her breasts like a CGI rendering of the perfect woman's figure.

The technician handed her a thick gray sock, which she put on her "organic foot"—as she called it—then sandals and thick woolen gloves. A'rore stepped into the cylinder, dispersing the nitrogen cloud already formed inside it as she closed the door behind her. The temperature read minus -109° Celsius. Sacha lifted her phone and took a picture of the back of A'rore's head, which looked like it was floating on a cloud. Three minutes later, when the temperate had dropped to -160°C, the technician disengaged the door to the cryosauna. Her skin was pale from the fleeing blood and tight from the cold nitrogen mist rolling off it as she slowly stepped out, trembling. As she took a thick white burnoose from the technician, wrapping herself in it, she said, "It's almost like meditating in there. For those three minutes you are focused entirely on your body."

Norton, A'rore's driver, took them to their next destination, a meal at Roy Choi's 24/7 breakfast bar in Piccadilly Circus in London. "He's an ex-stunt driver who worked on the *Transformers* movies," A'rore told Sacha as Norton drove them through

Eutopia, avoiding the congested main boulevards, taking sharp, yet controlled turns around corners that suggested a latent aggressiveness in him, waiting to be actuated. Norton's square-jawed face was scarred, leading Sacha to surmise an accident had ended his entertainment career. She made a mental note to research him for a sidebar to her piece.

At the breakfast bar, in a VIP booth atop the Regent Club—while eating smoked mackerel, berries, dark fair-trade chocolate, almond milk, and porridge—A'rore told her today was her "on" day, and that especially after the workout, she needed to "absorb" some nutrients.

"I've been intermittently fasting for the last few months, which is doing amazing things for my energy. My physician is monitoring my biomarkers, and since I've started my BMI has dropped two percent to the ideal range. Elite athlete level."

Sacha, who had spent a fair amount of time around type-A entrepreneurs back when she was reporting on Silicon Valley data vendors, recognized A'rore's compulsivity. She found that the less she said with A'rore, the more she talked, using Sacha as a sounding board for her ideas, equal parts confessional and philosophical.

"I'm kind of obsessed with immortality," A'rore said, laughing. "I guess you could say that. I don't know if I want you to put this in there, because they're going to think I'm crazy, but, off the record, I take thirty pills every morning, and seventy more throughout the day."

"Wow, and here I am with my daily multivitamin and coffee."

"It's all to promote sexual health, brain health, and longevity."

"You're in amazing shape. Why are you worried about something like longevity?"

"I guess, on so many levels, my job and my livelihood depend on eternal youth. I'm—off the record, of course—at the age when the biological clock starts ticking. I'm past my peak fertile years, and you know," she said, half-smiling at Sacha, "the competition is fierce from these bitches."

—∿—

BY THE TIME THE day wound down, Sacha felt drained. A'rore's routine—even if it was for show—was exhausting. A'rore was now preparing for her club appearance at Rossebuurt. As she dressed, Sacha helped herself to a glass of water in the kitchen and noticed glass vials of Genotropin sitting on the counter next to the faucet. She queried quickly on her phone. Human Growth Hormone. Jesus, this woman was a walking pharmacy.

"Let's jam," A'rore said, walking out of her bedroom, wearing a blond wig, dark mascara, and a long-sleeve mesh shirt with a studded choker around her neck. Black hot pants over sheer pantyhose descended down one leg to a leather biker boot. Her other leg was outfitted with a new prosthetic skinned with a live screen showing green digital rain on black. "Love this one, inspired by *The Matrix*," she said, when she saw Sacha examining it.

They took her VIP elevator down to a back entrance, where Norton was waiting, his heavyweight boxer's frame filling out his black suit. "It's still early," A'rore said, "but I'll need more time with the makeup girl since this is a nude shoot."

8.
Lines of Flight

WHEN THEY ARRIVED AT Club Rossebuurt, in Amsterdam's Red Light District, a line stretching around the block had already formed. Fred and Cedric queued up, the surrounding digital signage showing live footage of multiple police chases happening around town.

"It's lively tonight, even for Eutopia," Fred said.

The multitudes around them were animated, talking about the live chases and the upcoming photo shoot with A'rore. "This is only the second time she's done one of these for the public," said a wiry young man with a shaved head and chrome paint sprayed across the lower half of his face, like one of the war boys from *Mad Max: Fury Road*. "Last time I missed the cutoff by nothing, like three people in front of me."

Fred, who had been watching the live pursuits on the surrounding billboards, now fixed his attention on the club. "I don't think we're going to make it inside without an invite. Look at this line. I should have bought some VIP credits back at the Haussmann." Display windows wrapped around the Rossebuurt's entrance, each containing a scantily clad woman or two, posing against a strong red glow from within. The top half, up to the pitched gable facade, was wrapped with a screen showing GIFs made by club-goers, all hashtagged with #rossebuurt #eutopia. At the entrance there was heavy security presence, and a parked matte-black cruiser with the EPD livery Cedric had seen at the police headquarters earlier.

"Is everything all right?" Cedric said, noticing Fred's nervousness, suspecting it had something to do with the security in front of the club. Just an hour earlier, Fred had wanted to get out of the Haussmann, and now, at their new destination, he also seemed uneasy.

"We should go," Fred said, placing a hand on Cedric's shoulder.

They'd taken a Lyft ride to Amsterdam from the Haussmann and were on the Damrak, the area's main stretch consisting of coffee shops, fast-food stalls, and red-fringed window parlors where, for a few credits, anyone could go in and broadcast a live peepshow with exclusive photo filters.

Cedric kept up with Fred's quick pace—barely—as they passed under the glow of a neon-rimmed vape bar, through a sugary-smelling cloud wafting out from an artisanal pancake shop. "I have a feeling we didn't meet by coincidence," Cedric said.

"We don't really have time to talk, but I'll explain everything to you."

Cedric slowed his gait, signaling his intention to part ways. "Don't fuck around, man. You're giving me the creeps."

"You have to trust me, that's all I can say. We're in danger," Fred said, again picking up his pace, turning down a pedestrian side street after looking over his shoulder.

Cedric felt compelled to follow, his reasons unarticulated, his motions propelled by equal parts curiosity and dread. Just by association, he knew, whatever was going on with this guy implicated him as well.

As they breached the other end of the side street, arriving at a group of people waiting for their turn to cross another thoroughfare, Fred turned again, leading him toward a concrete, multilevel garage, to a set of stairs leading down into the structure.

"Let's cut through here, to the other side," he said. The galvanized steel door squeaked open on its hinges and thudded shut behind them as they walked through the well-lit ground floor, echoes of the street commotion seeping in.

"Look, whatever trouble you're in, I don't want any part of it."

"You *are* part of it," Fred said as he walked between rows of charging cars, almost jogging, the smell of synthetic rubber and oil invading their nostrils. "I wasn't on the level with you earlier, but you have to understand you're in danger. I know about you. I *know* who you are."

When they were two rows deep into the structure, the metal door they had come through slammed shut again. Two men, wearing motorcycle helmets with visors pulled up, were approaching.

Fred tugged on Cedric's arm and split through another row of cars, cursing under his breath. Had he expected this all along? Cedric's mind leapt for a second to the spate of crime across the city that night, the chases and robberies being relayed across the network and broadcast for all to see and follow.

Two motorcycles rolled into view, the intense purple-white beam of their xenon headlamps swiping across the cars and landing on Cedric and Fred. Shielding their eyes against the glare, and aware of the two men approaching them from behind, who had now removed their helmets, revealing balaclavas underneath, they bolted across the lane toward one of only two lines of flight. As they dashed through another row of parked cars, the men behind them began closing the distance, their boots pounding the ground.

As Cedric saw two more men appear in front of them, tires screeched as one motorcycle rider spun his bike around while the other accelerated to the opposite end of the row. They turned toward each other, each rider with visor pulled down, high beams still on, and bore down on Fred and Cedric.

Fred made a dash at an angle, between the motorcycle on the left and the assailants in front of them. Cedric, still assessing his best move, was overcome from behind. A thick, muscled arm reached around his neck, but Cedric lowered his chin, preventing it from getting a strong grip. He could feel the choke coming on as his assailant attempted to grasp his own bicep to tighten the vise. Cedric twisted and elbowed as hard as he could, hitting his attacker in the abdomen, a spleen shot that dropped him to the ground immediately.

One of the two men in front of them came rushing forward, his right hand sporting a black knuckle duster. Feinting a jab with his naked fist, his right hand came in over the top with a haymaker that would have coldcocked Cedric had he not rolled it just in time, using his attacker's forward momentum to crouch and shoot forward, head against chest, right leg hooking behind, tackling him to the ground.

As he gripped his attacker's arms, preventing him from swinging wildly, another man ran toward them. Just as the top of a boot connected with his head, Cedric heard a tremendous, deafening explosion. His entire body went rubbery, his impact with the concrete diminished as the assailant below him shrimped out, rolling Cedric's body as it fell on its side, limp.

First, voices, distant-sounding, as if his head were submerged underwater. It took immense effort to open his eyes, his concentration focused on every muscle in order to lift his eyelids. The overhead strips of lighting created a starburst effect before his eyes fluttered shut again. Hearing boots scuffing the ground nearby, and alarmed by the throbbing at the back of his head, he again strained to crack his eyes open, barely enough to see Fred about two car lengths away. Standing over his prostrate body was a thin man, wearing a black leather aviator jacket and white-striped motorcycle helmet with an upturned visor. He knelt down, resting on his haunches, jeans not touching the floor, and began going through Fred's pockets. Pulling out his wallet and flipping it open, he slipped out a memory card and some cash, pocketed it, and tossed the wallet to the ground next to Fred. He patted him down then stood up.

"That's all we need," he said, his voice sounding distant and muddled. Cedric, eyes still barely cracked open, shut them all the way when the thin man turned toward him.

"What about him?" another voice said, somewhere behind his line of sight.

"He's not a problem," the thin man said, "at the moment."

Footsteps, then kickstands snapping shut, followed by the smooth purr of electric motors as they drove off. After counting in his head, trying to give himself time before moving, lest the attackers come back to finish him off, Cedric finally opened his eyes. He rolled to his elbows and, using his forearms, dragging his legs, he crawled over to Fred, who was taking clipped, shallow breaths.

"Fred," he said. "Fred. Are you all right?"

No response. He laid his head back on the concrete, exhausted from the effort. More voices. People approaching.

When he came to again, he was on a stretcher, just outside the parking structure. A large screen on the side of the building showed aerial footage of something—it looked familiar. Here. And someone. Him.

9.
Boomtown

O NLY SIX MONTHS EARLIER, the story Sacha had proposed on Eutopia was about to get killed due to purported budget concerns. The original plan was for her to steward a long-form multimedia piece for VICE's news channel. They had already scouted the city and had their contacts lined up when, only a week before leaving, news came down from corporate that the P&Ls for the project weren't in line with the year's budgets, which had been slashed across the board. There were rumors around the office, however, that Sokolov herself had put in a call to VICE's chief stakeholders, threatening to leverage her considerable sway in the media industry to cut off VICE's content distribution channels. She knew about Sacha—everybody in tech did after her exposé—and didn't want anything negative to come out about Eutopia.

Then, four months later, Sacha's editors told her the story was on again, that there was "renewed" interest in it, and that the data scientists had discovered positive web traffic trends around the topic. But another rumor circulated, this time about an eccentric billionaire named Ethan Lewin who was funding the story because of a gripe he had with Sokolov over a clip that aired on one of her channels. A controversial figure himself—a venture capitalist who had ties to conservative groups—he was outed as gay in the clip. He'd been rumored to be behind various lawsuits dogging Sokolov's media empire, and people openly joked about him being behind the push to get Sacha's story out there. She felt conflicted. She could play the game, but the most important thing was to write the story with integrity. Ever since Eutopia first launched it had been mired in controversy. The breakneck construction helmed by Chinese firms had been blamed for the deaths of dozens of construction workers, there were aggressive monetization schemes, and, increasingly, violence was spreading in waves across the city and gripping its online followers.

Riding shotgun next to Norton, with a photographer sent by *Vanity Fair* snapping candid shots of A'rore in the back seat, Sacha had received the first news reports of what turned out to be an extraordinary—even by Eutopian standards—crime spree. Alerts urging her to follow live pursuits pinged her phone every few minutes, and screens kept popping up showing live feeds from police drones outside. Even A'rore made an offhand comment about it: "Wow, tonight feels unusually *electric*."

By the time they made it to the VIP level of the Rossebuurt, where only those with over thirty thousand followers were allowed entry, Sacha was making plans to escape the curated routine A'rore was subjecting her to and document firsthand what was happening outside. After all, calling this an "exclusive" photo shoot was a joke. *Vanity Fair*, who was sponsoring the photo shoot, and who would host it behind a paywall, was the second publication to pull this type of stunt. The first had been pulled off by Facebook a few months earlier, only that time she wasn't completely nude, posing in extremely revealing designer lingerie by Bordelle for top Facebook influencers. This fully nude live shoot with *Vanity Fair* was the next step. Sacha could easily extrapolate what the next logical step would be after this, imagining more explicit scenarios.

As the clubgoers around her mingled with each other, she overheard snippets of industry-centric conversation. There was talk of conversion ratios and rival geo-locked social media cities springing up in Asia and Latin America, and plenty of one-up-manship when it came to A'rore sightings. The sentiment, she gathered, was that A'rore's popularity had peaked about a year ago, and that, though she was still popular, her best days were behind her.

"This is *interesting*, kinda desperate," said a cap-wearing man next to her at the bar. After scanning her profile with his augmented glasses, he introduced himself as a fellow writer, for *Juxtapoz Magazine*. "But everybody knows she needs to capture the media's attention again, and these little events are just keeping her above water. They come off as stunty, you know? Eutopia, A'rore—problem is there are copies starting to spring up that are arguably just as good."

Without any formal announcement, A'rore, wearing a silk kimono, strode to the middle of the room, the *Vanity Fair* photographer staying in the background. Security guards were ushering the dozens of VIPs in attendance to the edges of a large semicircle. A professional photographer, hefting a Hasselblad, captured multiple angles of A'rore, whose instincts as a former runway model kicked in. With a large window behind her, showing the expanse of the city outside, she began posing demurely, her back turned to the audience and the photographer.

"She's still keeping her poise, but it's true, her traffic is plateauing," Sacha said, her eyes still fixed on A'rore, whose body's contours could be seen through the translucent kimono she was wearing. The window she was posing against was fitted with see-through LED screens, the colors of which constantly shifted, as if she were standing in front of stained glass come to life.

"Out of curiosity," the *Juxtapoz* writer said, "what are you in town for?"

"I'm working on a long-form piece about the city. A'rore of course figures heavily in it."

"Ooh, very cool. *Especially* if you're doing it," he said, in a flirty tone.

A'rore unclasped her kimono and shrugged it off her shoulders, letting it slide from her body as her hands came up and crossed over her breasts. Her legs still crossed, her prosthetic stiletto boot emitting intermittent nodes of digital rain, she turned her head so that her profile was visible. The photographer angled his camera for a portrait shot, got up, angled his camera again, and took another picture.

Meanwhile, some of the VIPs in attendance had their phones up and were filming, including the *Juxtapoz* writer standing next to Sacha. On his phone, with the exclusive hyper-targeted geofilter engaged, using hashtag #AroreExposed, he was shooting short bursts of video for his own network of followers. A'rore turned to the right, placed one hand on her head, and tilted it back, while her other arm still covered her breasts. She smiled, then turned her head back toward the window and spread both hands out, as if she were a demigod about to sprout wings and take flight. The sides of her breasts and hips limned by the light coming from the windows, she slowly reclined, a modern-day Venus, the cameras surrounding her like mirrors casting her image to mortals around the world.

After about fifteen minutes of posing, an assistant came in and draped A'rore once again in her kimono, while her VIP audience clapped and whistled. Music faded up, and A'rore was escorted to an employee exit. Sacha, using the distraction to break away from the prying writer next to her, made her way toward the elevator and took it down to the main floor and the main entrance of the Rosseburt.

It was as she was walking through the Red Light District,

past the virtual peep show arcades, that the hairs on the back of her neck and forearms stood up and her heart began beating faster, for no perceptible reason. She'd felt this sensation in the ruins of the Louvre, and years before when she was under investigation. She paused to look into the storefront display of a designer drug boutique. About three stores down, a man in his twenties, unremarkably dressed in jeans and a gray café racer jacket, had also paused, looking into another vitrine. As she resumed walking, her suspicions were confirmed when she looked back and noticed the man was following. Holding his phone and swiping his screen, he gave off the appearance that he was engrossed in his own social media feeds, but her gut feeling told her he was watching her. She could feel it, ever since she had left the Rossebuurt.

She hailed a passing taxi and hopped in, giving the driver directions to Barcelona, where there was a chase underway. As they drove past, the man made no effort to disguise his intentions, his gaze following her.

"Barcelona, huh? There's been a bunch of muggings and bag snatches out there. The chases are all over the networks," the cab driver said as they took a corner onto a main artery leading to another portion of the city. The back seat of the cab in front of her displayed rotating advertising for the city's clubs and casinos, below that a scrolling ticker with alerts on the real time chase taking place on the Ramblas.

"Yeah, it's been a crazy night, right?" Sacha said, perturbed at the thought she was being followed. Was it a random creeper? An agent of Sokolov? She had learned to respect her own instincts as a reporter, even if, at times, they seemed paranoiac on the surface. The hunch was almost always right for her.

"Par for the course in Eutopia," he said with evident mirth. "Every few days there's a upsurge in crime. It's like as soon as the criminals get some rest, they're back at it again, a few days later."

"It's gotta be scary for you. I mean, you're pretty vulnerable driving this cab."

"Ehh. Not all that much. They know I carry barely any cash; almost all the transactions are done in-app. A couple of my coworkers have been carjacked, though."

Outside they passed a building wrapped with a still of A'rore from the photo shoot, her back to the camera, legs crossed, arms spread out. The cab driver, eyeing Sacha through the rearview mirror, said, "And A'rore, too; Didn't she do something?"

"Back there in the Red Light District. A live nude photo shoot."

"Ah jeeesus," he said. "Why is she even a thing?"

"I know, right?" Sacha said, ingratiating herself to the cab driver. It was important to understand the sentiment on the streets, removed from the filter of social media. "I guess she brings a lot of attention to the city."

"It'll be her, then another A'rore to replace her. This place always has something going on."

They were approaching the Monumental Hotel in Barcelona, a large shopping structure built to look like a bullring. Wrapped in screens intermittently displaying the brownish-red byzantine facade of the continental original, it marked the beginning of Barcelona, which consisted of a main pedestrian thoroughfare called the Ramblas, tapas bars, gaming parlors, one-hour hotel rooms, and an artificial beach lined with *chiringuitos*.

"Is there any place in particular you want to go to?"

"Right here is fine," she said, getting out next to a group of Asian tourists clutching Louis Vuitton and Chanel shopping bags. She nudged her way through them to an opening. They were commenting on a screen above a bar showing yet another live chase. A motorcycle with a passenger clutching shopping bags was gunning down the side of the Ramblas, and though she couldn't understand the people around her, she gathered it was one of them who had been robbed. The drone footage showed the motorcycle splitting lanes, arriving at a roundabout and taking it back in the opposite direction, the Monumental Hotel in the background briefly before the drone swooped in for a tighter shot. Waves of whistles and jeers rippled up from the end of the Ramblas as the motorcycle raced back up toward her end of the street.

The crowd around her turned from the screen, anticipating the speeding motorcycle thieves, when two police cruisers blocked the road. The motorcycle approached, its bright blue headlamp darting nimbly through traffic, then started fishtailing as its rider squeezed the brakes. The passenger hopped off the bike, dropping the loot and losing his helmet before running off. After the driver came to a full stop, he dropped his bike and helmet, then ran off in the general direction of his accomplice. Two policemen pursued them on foot.

There were cheers from the crowd around her as a tween girl dressed as a K-pop idol ran and picked up the bag the thief had just dropped. Holding out her phone, she took a selfie, her arm holding the shopping bag thrust high, behind her face. Seconds later her selfie appeared on screens all around them, real-time comments and share icons streaming up from the lower third of the picture. Sacha, who had been filming the spectacle on her phone, pocketed it and moved away from the crowd toward the entrance to a casino. In there, hopefully, was a bar where she could sit and type out some notes in peace.

On a settee near the railing separating the bar from the casino floor, she began organizing her notes for the day. The sound of cheering from a lucky spin on one of the roulette tables cut through the ambient noise. A large screen wrapped around the circular bar showing highlights from the UFC fight earlier that night at the Coliseum. As a violent, rapid-fire edit of the main card's fights played out—with each successive bout leaving the ring mat more bloody—betting odds scrolled below.

There was something about the man who had followed her earlier. He wasn't the usual creeper. There was also the person watching her in the Louvre, who had run off into the depths of the ruins. Somehow, they seemed connected, but the connection wasn't clear enough to articulate in her notes. These thoughts were still at the periphery of her intuition, and as the waiter set down her Diet Coke, she scanned the people surrounding her at the bar—young professionals who had flown in for a few days, singles flirting, a dusky couple, probably from a gulf state. None stood out as suspicious.

The UFC fight highlights on the screens above the bar switched to live news coverage, showing vertically shot video from inside a parking structure. It appeared to be someone walking toward two men lying on the floor of the garage, both motionless. Closed captions on the screen said this was eyewitness cell phone footage of the aftermath of a mugging that resulted in one victim's death. After some talking-head commentary, live footage from outside the parking structure showed one of the victims getting wheeled to an ambulance past a loose throng of people surrounding the crime scene, many of them filming the sequence on their cell phones. The man's head was bandaged, but otherwise he seemed alert.

Looking through her social feeds, she didn't find any official news on the identities of the victims, but one person getting retweeted mentioned the similarity between the victim on the stretcher and Cedric Travers, the film director. Some people in the comment thread were already pointing out that he was the estranged husband of Mila Webb, the city's experiential director, the one who had been accused of being involved in the terrorist attack at the Louvre.

It wasn't the only crime that night—there had been various bag-snatchings, muggings, and carjackings—but this one had resulted in bodily harm to someone who, if the rumor mills were true, happened to have a direct connection to the incident at the Louvre. After finishing her drink, Sacha got up and walked through the casino to the exit, the wild speculations on the networks adding color to an incomplete picture in her head.

10.
Cognito Mode

H IS URINE STREAM CAME out dark brown, but the doctors told Cedric not to worry—it was normal after taking a hit to the liver. The battery of diagnostic tests the hospital ran on him showed no serious damage anywhere besides a mild concussion. His brain was foggy, however, and he wasn't sure if it was because of the trauma to his head or the oxymorphone the nurses had administered. Aided by online stories and television footage from the set mounted in the corner of his room, he was able to piece together some of the events from last night, still scattershot in his memory.

He'd already seen some of the drone footage of himself getting wheeled to the ambulance, but there was also CCTV and bystander video of other violent muggings throughout the city that night. Some of the footage—disturbingly—was shot POV from the helmets of the thieves as they tore through the city on their motorbikes causing acts of mayhem. The logic behind the attacks escaped him and seemed to be equally controversial on social media, but nobody argued about the larger story of a crime wave sweeping Eutopia.

Even the Eiffel Tower and the Fernsehturm were pulsing orange, indicating the city's urgent health situation, as its algorithms pulled sentiment analysis from comments across the city's networks. The wall-mounted television said "Crime Wave Pushes Eutopia Health to Critical," and the next image was a selfie A'rore had posted earlier that morning with the message "Stay safe, Eutopians."

Wall Street data analysts showed global traffic to the Eutopian network hit a monthly high during the crime spree, accompanied by rising share values for Eutopia's holding company, Lab Networks. If anything, the morbid curiosity of the online audience proved a boon to cynical investors' faith in the city's value.

He was—despite his best intentions—part of the fabric of the city already, a point not lost on Inspector Monteiro, who had paid him a visit earlier that day.

"You're becoming famous, Cedric," he said from a seat in the corner of the room, legs flung out, relaxed hands hanging over the front of the armrests, a wry smile spread across his face. He'd just finished informing Cedric that his companion had died of massive head trauma sustained in the assault, and how lucky he was to have escaped relatively unscathed.

"I'm one of dozens, apparently," Cedric said, turning his head from the inspector to the television screen, showing the news on mute. "So I guess I'm not the only one graced by fame."

"You don't have to feign ignorance. You know people are starting to make connections between you and Mila."

Cedric stayed silent for a beat, not sure if he wanted to get into a disagreement with Monteiro, then said, "Sure, I guess."

"It's part of the reason I'm so busy lately. It's a complex city, lots of moving parts, lots of whack jobs from all over the place trying to get rich overnight."

"Have you caught anybody yet?"

Monteiro paused, crossed his legs, and looked down at his fingers, drumming the edge of the armrest, as if he was contemplating a chess move. "Yes," he said, "we have a few suspects in custody." He then looked at Cedric and continued, "Tell me about your acquaintance. How did you know him?"

"Fred?" Monteiro's face remained expressionless as he waited for Cedric to talk. "Green, or something like that. I think that's what he said his last name was. I ran into him yesterday, up near Mila's apartment. Just coincidence, but he seemed to know a lot about the city." Cedric found himself locked again in a mental duel with Monteiro, not sure how much he should reveal, and not sure exactly what he wanted. Already, by saying his acquaintance had insight into the city, he'd tipped Monteiro off that he was starting his own private investigation into his wife.

"What did he tell you?"

"He's a professional gambler, or, was. Mostly told me about the best spots in the city for grub and card games and shows. He seemed to know his way around. I guess he'd been here a few weeks or months. I can't remember."

Monteiro's brow furrowed as he shifted into a more rigid posture in his seat, his gaze unwavering. "And that's it," he said. "He tells you where the best poker rooms and strip clubs are and nothing else?"

"Was he in some kind of trouble, Inspector?"

"No. But you may be if you keep mingling with the wrong elements."

"*We* were the ones attacked."

"No need to be defensive," Monteiro said, slowly standing, looking down on Cedric on his gurney. "I'm not saying you personally were responsible. I'm saying some people invite trouble, if you know what I mean."

After telling him he'd be in touch soon for an inquest, Monteiro left the room. As he used the button to sit up in the motorized reclining gurney, a throbbing pain shot through his core as his bruised abdomen contracted. He swung his legs off, pausing before easing himself to the ground, already dreading the moment he'd have to bend down to lace up his shoes. There were ambient sounds of technicians pushing equipment down the corridors and stray voices of nurses exchanging patient notes. Cedric watched a commercial for a luxury spa in Paris on the muted screen in the corner. His mind flashed to a recollection of the attack, when one of the men was standing over Fred after rifling through his pockets. His gut feeling that they weren't part of a run-of-the-mill mugging—one of the dozens across the city that night—but rather part of something larger, gripped him like the ominous refrain of an orchestral piece. The experts trotted out on the news segment, video-conferencing from satellite offices around the world, spoke about the whole thing so matter-of-factly, it was as if it were all a mere integer value on a data scientist's spreadsheet. He was already yesterday's news.

As he was exiting the elevator on the lower floor of the hospital, Cedric made eye contact with a woman who was about to enter. There seemed to be recognition on her part as she held his gaze, and he also thought he knew her from somewhere, but he couldn't quite place it—perhaps due to the concussion and the opioids dampening his cognitive powers. As he was about to pass her, she said, turning to him, "You were one of the victims last night. The mugging in the garage near the Red Light District."

"Maybe," he said with a forced grin, unconsciously rubbing the bruise on his head. Who was this brunette with dark, steady eyes? She had a no-nonsense aura about her. In fact, she reminded him of his wife.

"I'm Sacha Villanova. I'm a journalist for VICE, writing a story about Eutopia. The influencers, the gaming and social networks, the more sensational aspects of it. I'd like to talk to you about what happened."

As the elevator shut behind them, he started walking toward

the exit, Sacha keeping up with him. Before speaking, he made a quick assessment of her—denim jacket over jeans, Converse sneakers, petite frame, intense energy. Sacha Villanova. Where had he seen that byline before? "Sure," he said. "But how were you so sure I was one of them?" He'd left his bandage upstairs, and besides the bruise under his hair, the only other visible contusions were hidden beneath his shirt.

"The video and pics of you last night. Some of the speculation on Twitter and Reddit. Really, it's just a coincidence that I ran into you just now."

After leaving through a rotating door, they stepped underneath the cement ceiling of the entrance, the dry desert air outside contrasting sharply with the cool air of the lobby. The bright light of the midday sun reflected off of their surroundings. Cedric squinted, his eyes sensitive from the painkillers he had taken. They stopped next to a line of waiting taxis, and she continued.

"So you're Cedric Travers."

"That's me. I keep my profile on private, but I guess I didn't expect to make it into the twenty-four-hour news cycle."

"That's the Internet for you," she said, punctuating her sentence with a tight-lipped but not unpleasant smile—another quirk that reminded him of his wife, who was able to deliver blunt truths gently. "There are traces of you on the networks, even if you've been out of sight for the last few years."

"I'm ancient history in Internet years."

"I wouldn't go that far. People are speculating and linking to your movies."

"I guess it's unavoidable, right, when you step back into the spotlight like this."

"Eutopia is a place to be seen."

Cedric laughed, despite his desire to avoid this reporter. It was true, what she said, even if she meant it ironically. From the moment he drove into the city, the city had lived up to the marketing team's vision. His shoulders relaxed and his arms uncrossed as he looked down on the intense woman who had just threatened to further mediatize his life.

"You know why I'm here, don't you?" he said.

"I don't know what you're mixed up in, or why any of this happened to you and your friend last night, but I'm certain you came here because of your wife. That, among other things, is why I want to talk to you."

She pulled out a slim metal case, popped it open, and handed him her business card.

"Call me," she said, as she backed up toward the building entrance. "Think it over and call me. We can help each other out." She smiled again and gave a small wave as she walked away, probably—he guessed—to find more victims from last night for her story.

He put his sunglasses on and decided to walk back to the hotel. The map on his phone showed it was only a thirteen-minute walk, and, despite the raw bruises making him acutely aware of each step, he needed the meditative walk in the open air. He didn't know what to believe. His intention all along was to come to terms with the past—what was and could have been. He ignored the stories, sure of his wife's innocence, also deeply skeptical of the narratives that got promoted and debunked in ever-shorter cycles on the Internet. But what if Monteiro, despite his brusque, off-putting behavior, had a point? Was this reporter, like Fred Green, also going to lead him into trouble? The idea of this shadowy group corrupting his wife, the determined air of this woman to uncover the truth, even the suspicion that she herself was more than what she presented herself to be, added layer upon layer to the mystery he felt himself getting drawn into.

He pocketed her business card, having decided to contact her in the near future. As he stopped at the curb, just as a car sped past, he realized this wasn't the first time he'd crossed paths with Sacha. The Moulin Rouge, after he and Fred had witnessed A'rore's brief public appearance. He had no doubt it was Sacha at the wheel of the car that nearly hit him as he walked in a distracted daze.

—ɯ—

ON HIS WAY BACK to the hotel, he stopped at a trattoria where he read about Sacha over a light meal of salad and grilled lab-grown chicken strips. She'd written for several high-profile websites including *The Verge*, *Wired*, and *Buzzfeed News*, where her focus was on emerging technology and gaming. Extracts from her stories were familiar, having been quoted or sourced in news reports he'd seen from a few years back, although admittedly a lot of it was too abstract to really capture his attention. He knew it was important—like how she went undercover as an account executive at DataKai, uncovering unscrupulous data-mining techniques and the infantile culture of impunity in upper management—but like most people he didn't fully understand what it all meant. It didn't have the same visceral, easily understandable impact like the civil wars breaking out in Europe, or the daily bombings in tourist resorts across Asia. His wife, who was working in the industry, understood it, but at the time it was too far removed from his daily life for him to give it much thought.

Her writing was clear and concise, and she dove into the personalities at the center of her stories. A cursory scan of the published output posted on her social channels showed she was critical of the merging of gaming philosophy and mass culture. Was she a technophobe? She didn't seem like a back-to-nature Luddite, but the events of the last forty-eight hours, the tenuous connections Monteiro was trying to make between a subversive organization and Cedric's wife, raised a lot of questions about her motivations. And how exactly, if she was critical of the city, was she allowed free rein to work there?

At the bottom of a Wikipedia page about her, there were more links, including a brief profile of A'rore, "the anime-styled selfie star with supermodel looks whose omnipresent gaze dominates the city." Echoing what Fred told him yesterday, Sacha wrote about how A'rore was brought into the city as part of a strategy to attract young, transactional-generation visitors, how she was part of an ambitious scheme created by Dominika Sokolov: "While she's on her private island, Dominika's crack team of experiential managers, poached from leading New York and Los Angeles agencies, are in charge of keeping Eutopia at the top of trending topics across social media."

Earlier, while he was eating, distant explosions from silver iodide cannons echoed though the city, announcing imminent rainfall. As a slight drizzle began, he quickened his pace. The opioids the hospital had given him were wearing off, and the aches flaring up in his body were mnemonic triggers, reminding him of the danger behind the saccharine facade of the city. As he crossed the street to the hotel entrance, he began to feel a familiar sense of unease. Kitty-corner to the hotel was a black Mercedes with tinted windows, and though partially obscured by the rain, inside there appeared to be a driver and a passenger, both observing him. As if to punctuate his sense of dread, once he was in front of the hotel, about to enter, the car drove off swiftly, its tires hissing and crackling on the wet asphalt as it sped away.

11.
The A-Game

THE MOST VALUABLE LESSON he ever had wasn't how to fight. It was how to detect anomalies. What were mere hunches for some people—feelings they couldn't understand, if they even had them, feelings that were almost always ignored—for him were clear indicators of trouble. He'd sharpened his observational powers while deployed in Iraq, and while he feared every day away from the hellhole of Ramadi that he was losing his edge, he was still a formidable observer. Cedric Travers had been a person of interest to him ever since he was alerted of his arrival. Trying to get a read on him was impossible, but nothing in his body language seemed to indicate deceit. He'd been forthcoming about his intentions, but Monteiro knew all too well that circumstance and context can drive a lost man to extremes. Travers, Mila Webb's ex, had the *potential* to cause trouble.

He found out Cedric was attacked the same time everybody else did, as it was being livestreamed by Eutopia's channels. It couldn't be a coincidence. He'd already considered putting some of his assets on this case. In only two days this guy managed to get attacked and blow up for fifteen minutes on social media. His deceased companion, so far a John Doe, also raised red flags. Even so, Travers's story about how he met him, as convenient as it seemed, was delivered without deception. He'd watched this man—this has-been, failed artist—and saw clearly what he was. A person without purpose, but a person on the verge of something. Like the insurgents who dressed as farmers, trying to blend in, or terrorists in Europe hiding in plain sight by adopting Western clothing and mannerisms, something was off that only trained eyes like Monteiro's could see. He was so good at this that it pleased him when another person he had been tailing, Sacha Villanova, met with Cedric. Without a doubt, it wasn't a coincidence. Even though he had seniority and didn't necessarily need to do grunt work, he enjoyed working on the ground, doing surveillance himself, and when he took the next shift tailing Villanova, he was unsurprised when she appeared to be heading back in the direction of the hospital when she left her hotel. Of course, all the victims of the last night's crime spree were there, including his boy Travers, and what better way to embellish her hit piece?

She had been flagged by an officer as soon as she was seen in A'rore's entourage. When she checked in to her hotel, one of his assets there sent him a one-sheet on her: her bio, links to her work, as well as her current projects for VICE. His experience in the Middle East had given him a deeply distrustful view of the media. When they sensationalized collateral damage and inter-rogation techniques, it was always with the intention of making his men look bad to conform to a kneejerk pacifist narrative. The liberal PC bias was toxic and painfully, glaringly obvious to anyone brave enough to be objective. They never showed nuance, never explained the context of the war, and they paid the price when the jihadis started massacring people across Europe.

As he watched her conversing with Travers in front of the hospital, he took another sip of his energy drink and placed it back in its pouch, hanging from the dashboard. She was one of dozens of persons of interest in the Code Yellow category, meaning she merited elevated interest and light surveillance. This meeting with Travers raised the stakes to Code Red—a designation he reserved for suspected sleeper cells. On a second screen he reviewed the report from the previous night where she showed clearly suspicious behavior as she exited the club where she had been with A'rore. Checking her six, an obvious indicator she was up to something and knew she was being tailed, she eventually evaded surveillance, only to reappear again in Barcelona.

With her disreputable past—busted for drug-dealing—and her penchant for sensationalist reporting, she was likely a disruptive agent, and if there was one thing he was good at, it was understanding threats to the baseline, which it was his duty to maintain. His father, who had also served, used to play this game with him when he was a kid—the A-Game. Sometimes, when they were on their way home from a restaurant, he'd surprise Montiero with a pop quiz. "How many workers were there? Was it a man or a woman sitting at your three o'clock? What color was the car parked near the entrance?" His father wasn't a kind man, but he taught him to have an almost animal awareness of his surroundings.

One of the biggest leaps he'd made—which he'd applied while training SEALs after his second tour in Iraq—was learning to step out of his head, detach himself. In his first SEAL platoon, field training on an abandoned oil rig, as his formation moved across platform levels, past rusting machinery, traversing see-though metal grating—a jarring, complex environment for his team—suddenly everybody froze, except him. He pointed his gun in the air, took a step back, and saw the whole situation. On an unconscious level he knew what to do next and issued the command that unfroze his formation: "Hold left, move right." Detaching oneself was critical, and when he trained his soldiers—SEALs, or his security detail now in Eutopia—it was the single most important lesson he gave to them.

Going to the private sector was more lucrative, but he missed combat. He couldn't believe he was a middle-aged man now. When he was in his early thirties, in combat, he was certain he was going to die, and he welcomed it, the warrior's death on the battlefield. Goddamn this place, Eutopia. This fakery and pageant, these kids immersed in their gadgets, removed from the real world. Rolling along Route Michigan—the constant threat of IEDs ripping through your body, the adrenaline of knowing your life was on the line, your fellow soldiers' lives on the line—there was nothing else like it. The purpose, the meaning, the camara-derie. What was *this* theater he was participating in?

For the past two years, Eutopia's baseline was a few days of relative calm, followed by a crime wave, which came in bursts, as if mugging, purse-snatching, vandalism, and homicide were a virus, peaking before going dormant again. Two to three times a month, enough to keep his men sharp, on edge, ready for possible urban warfare. This controlled chaos, in a way, helped contain the city of anywhere between three and four hundred thousand visitors and residents, whose noses were stuck in their cell phones, or whose peripheral vision was blinded by their focus on their augmented reality environments, chasing down top-tier social media influencers, watching the fluctuating odds on the dozens of events happening around the city at any given time. These self-involved people, with no real common purpose—unlike his brothers and sisters in the hell of Ramadi— were, in fact, the enemy, each like potential insurgents disguised as commoners.

He took his energy drink back out of his old grenade pouch and took another swig. Villanova had just handed Travers her business card and was walking into the hospital, where he knew she was going to try and interview other victims. After placing the near-empty can back in the pouch, he made a mental note to put his men on Travers's tail as well. Whatever Villanova was trying to stir up, he knew it was going to affect the baseline.

His phone on the passenger's seat vibrated with an incoming call from central command. He picked it up.

"About the inquest tomorrow with Cedric Travers, we need to debrief you."

12.
Unreliable Witness

J OLTED AWAKE BY HIS phone ringing, Cedric picked it up, absentmindedly thumbing the screen, activating the speaker. A coordinator for the police informed him he was due at the inquest in two hours and gave him directions to the location. He had completely forgotten about Monteiro's request the previous day when he came to visit Cedric in the hospital. After arriving back at his hotel—exhausted from the last forty-eight hours, but equally affected by the painkillers the hospital had administered—he had fallen into a deep sleep for eight and a half hours. His sleep tracker showed regular peaks and valleys, indicating healthy circadian rhythms and an 89-percent sleep quality, a minor consolation as he lay in bed scanning headlines on his phone. The global markets were down, performing lower than analysts' predictions; civil strife in southern France was threatening to cross the Pyrenees into Spain, where a North African refugee crisis was overwhelming the country; young Prince George in the UK was embroiled in a sexting scandal involving a purported picture of his genitalia. *Buckingham Palace Has No Comment on Crown Jewels.*

After transferring payment to the cab driver, he walked between two patrol cars toward a nondescript building off Eutopia's main strip. Adjacent to the city's jail, and about a quarter of a mile away from the police headquarters, it was strictly utilitarian in design, unadorned, and built in a way that suggested strip mall inspiration. Inside he approached the reception station, where a broad-shouldered woman—her swollen trapezoids stretching her polo shirt, attire reminding him of the contractors he'd seen at the police HQ the other day—took his name and told him to take a seat. Behind the receptionist, on a faux-wood-paneled wall, "Eutopia Hall of Justice" was spelled out in brushed steel letters above a Libra scale emblem.

A few minutes later, a uniformed officer led him down some corridors to the inquest chambers. Somewhat surprisingly, it was a small-scale television studio, with a grid of lighting rigs overhead, a control room separated by a window in the back, and two video cameras on raised pedestals being adjusted by operators. At a dais in front of the cameras was a pale-faced man, gaunt, with a loose-fitting navy-blue Eutopian PD jacket. He turned and pushed chrome-framed spectacles back into place on his large nose, briefly making eye contact with Travers.

"That's Gregory Nyland, deputy coroner," Montiero said, joining Cedric.

Nodding, Cedric said, "I thought this was an inquest, not a talk show."

"It's an inquest, but we have to provide a live feed to the jurors. Some of them are here, dialing in from around the city, but some are elsewhere around the country. It's a representative sample, the most efficient way we've found of carrying out the process."

Was this another extrajudicial perk of being on Native American territory? Cedric stood rigid, with a slight, knowing smirk, as the deputy droned on for the virtual audience of jurors.

"The inquest process is pure because it allows for the objective presentation of facts, leaving the ultimate decision to the public," he said in a nasally voice, his eyes looking directly at the camera after glancing at a tablet. "That's you, the jury." He paused, picked up his tablet, and, after a swipe, continued. "It's important to understand that this is not a trial. Rather it's a means to determine the cause of death. Before I proceed, are there any objections from those present? You may do so by raising your hand in the chat room and enabling your microphones."

A screen behind the camera operators, near the director's seat, showed a live chat with a dozen participants. Travers shrugged off his jacket and dabbed his forehead with his shirt sleeve. The overhead lights, like an array of suns heating up the strange inquest chamber, were stronger than the AC being piped in to offset them.

Nyland held up his tablet and swiped to the next screen, which also appeared in the chat room—a bullet-pointed list titled, "Known facts."

"The victim was dead on arrival at the hospital," he said. "Referred to in our documentation as John Doe, he was found with false profiles on his devices, but it is not within the scope of this inquiry to determine his identity, rather the cause of his death. After repeated attempts at revival by the EMTs at the scene, and in transit to the hospital, the blunt-force trauma suffered by John Doe proved to be beyond their capacity to treat. Multiple contusions to the body and wounds to the hands indicate a struggle took place. Considerable trauma to the head indicates a fall and collision with a hard surface, consistent with the location the victim was found in."

As the deputy spoke in detail about the man's fractured skull and brain swelling, Cedric leaned in to Monteiro. "Fred Green. I told you that's what he said his name was."

Monteiro shook his head, not taking his eyes off the deputy, and held a hand up, palm facing Cedric, before mouthing the words "Wait here." He approached the dais, introduced himself, and gave a rundown of facts from his own investigation. There were no surveillance cameras in the building because it was new and they hadn't yet been installed. "However, Deputy Coroner Nyland's description is consistent with the forensic evidence on the scene. We also have leaked cell phone footage shot by the first witness on the scene to corroborate this." A clip played in the chat room and on the mirroring monitor near the director, showing the same shaky, vertically shot footage that had spread across social media, featuring Cedric and his now nameless companion on the garage floor. "As to a motive for this crime, we had none that night and for the next few hours, but the next day we appre- hended a suspect." Stills from surveillance footage appeared in the chat room before he continued. "Cameras outside the garage showed a suspicious person leaving the garage at a time consistent with the attack." A still of a man wearing a balaclava appeared on screen, then another of the same individual removing it, then another of him stuffing it in his pocket. "By reviewing surveil- lance footage in the surrounding radius and matching the physical description of the suspect leaving the garage, we were able to trace his steps and later ID him after he entered a gentle- men's club in the Red Light District."

While Monteiro went through some technical details involving the capture of the suspect, a director's assistant told him to approach the dais and take a seat. Monteiro presented Cedric to the jury, explaining how, according to his own statement, he had been attacked by a group of men, some on motorcycles, all wearing balaclavas, and how he attempted to defend himself before succumbing to their blows. Two officers brought in a wiry man of medium height, with the weather-worn skin of someone who'd been sleeping in the elements, not unlike the men Cedric had seen panhandling at freeway entrances and intersections in Hollywood. With a fat lower lip, bandaged nose, and swollen-shut left eye, he appeared dejected and passive, his chin drooping. "This is the individual we captured yesterday. His wounds are consistent with a struggle," he said, then ordered one of the guards to place a balaclava on his head. "Mr. Travers, we know this may be difficult for you, considering the trauma you suffered, and your concussion, but do the clothes and build of this individual match one of your assailants?"

As Monteiro fixed his gaze on him, Cedric's eyes widened. He pressed his lips together. After a pause and a short exhalation, he said, "I can't say. He's wearing, I think, the same clothes, but he looks too small." The man, forced to spin slowly by his handlers, also had his image cast to the chat room, where the jurors viewed a split screen of him and the dais with Monteiro and Cedric.

"Your memory, like I mentioned, may be jarred by the blow you received last night."

"As I said, it looks like he's wearing the same clothes, but I do remember being attacked by someone who looked taller. And stronger."

"It wasn't well illuminated in there, and you were hit hard, but Mr. Travers, are you sure it's not just macho pride at being hurt by a smaller man?" Cedric didn't respond, and Monteiro continued. "We know there were multiple attackers, and he could have been one of them. You've corroborated that, and forensic evidence suggests this." He ordered the officers to remove the balaclava, and as they did so, the man's stringy hair was pulled up with it, flopping back down to cover part of his forehead. "Remember, ladies and gentlemen of the jury, this is the same individual we caught on camera leaving the garage. This is the same individual we arrested after IDing him in the gentlemen's club, with some of the murder victim's belongings and the balaclava. All the evidence points to this man's involvement in the murder of your acquaintance, John Doe."

"I'm sorry," Cedric said. "I know it looks like that, but I can't go on record saying I'm sure he was one of them."

After deliberating privately with the deputy coroner,

Montiero cleared his throat and ordered the guard to remove the suspect. With a hard-set jaw and narrowed eyes, he waited for the coroner to formally close the proceedings.

After being dismissed by Monteiro, Cedric was escorted out of the station, where he waited in the shade after summoning a taxi. The intense southwestern sun was at its apex, the air outside dry and hot, and the natural foliage of the hills just beyond the Hall of Justice was like the backdrop to a Western. Beyond them, the rock formations, offshoots of the continental divide, almost seemed like a giant screen on a Hollywood backlot, next to the hyper-modern stylings of Eutopia, part of a modular set of time periods and settings marking the iconography of pop culture.

On his way back to the city, the more he mulled over it, the more disturbed and disgusted Cedric was by the farcical inquest he'd just been a part of. He was, after fewer than a hundred hours in this city, thrust into an elaborate stage play put on by Monteiro and his privatized police force. The underlying motive to it all remained a mystery. Why pick such an obvious patsy when at least five real attackers were still on the loose? Who stood to gain from all this? Somewhere there was a connection, a thread he needed to grasp to lead him out of this labyrinth.

Later that afternoon, after a nap and a shower, he headed out for a bite to eat in a café. He was beginning to feel like the cipher in his own movie, getting sucked into a black hole despite his better intentions. As he sat, contemplating his next move, a man stood in the middle of the plaza facing the café, while a woman recorded him with a camera. Sporting a brash velvet blazer and a teased-out Afro, he was talking, gesticulating at the surrounding architecture, giving his social audience a tour of the Italian quarters—another would-be influencer vying for pole position next to the city's main star, A'rore. Cedric was jaded, having been through the mill of the entertainment industry in LA, having seen the end of the old entertainment empire and the rise of the new, when YouTubers converged on the city to network and push their channel subscribers and reach many more eyeballs than the stale old studios could ever dream of. These kids, each with their own carefully crafted brand, drove a stake through the heart of the old model, a sirocco blowing in, wiping out the last vestiges of art for art's sake.

After the inquest with Monteiro, he was more curious than ever about the subterranean machinations of the city, and the attempt to corrupt him made it personal. He began typing out a message to Sacha Villanova, proposing a meeting time and place. However, just at that moment, a tall, broad-shouldered man walked past, between Cedric and the influencer in the velvet blazer, holding a black motorcycle helmet with a white stripe. Leaving his message to the reporter unfinished, his eyes locked on the man as he walked away. He'd seen him before, a couple nights ago. Fred had pointed him out in the casino. He was one of the men who walked past them after they finished their poker game, who had so unsettled Fred that he wanted to leave as soon as possible. And that helmet, it looked a lot like the one worn by the guy standing over Fred as he took his last breath.

As the man disappeared into one of the side streets branching out from the plaza, Cedric got up and hurried after him.

13.
Barefoot and Broadband

"THAT'S IT, YES, RIGHT there," she said, as his hands kneaded her lumbar region, fingers sliding under the sand-washed silk sheet draped over her rear, causing her fingers and toes to involuntarily curl. Dominika Sokolov had had a particularly frustrating day—month, in fact—and massages from Frederico were part of a daily ritual to balance out the inconveniences of island life. Kiko, her pet name for her cabana boy, was a decent masseur, not the best she'd had, but she could sense he was distracted, his movements rote and dispassionate—not the sensuous bliss-making he'd promised on his profile page. Perhaps it was the pretty new servant girl from Martinique, staying in one of the bungalows on the eastern end of the atoll. Only a month and a half into her stay on Celine Island, her hideaway in the Seychelles, this was discouraging. Flying out a new cabana boy would mean an interruption of at least two to three days, which wasn't ideal, and certainly wouldn't cover her needs, and the locals she'd spied, both here and in the capital—a helicopter ride away—didn't meet her strict criteria of masculine beauty and dedication to craft. And besides, the whole point of her hideaway and her bevy of boy toys was so she could free herself from the burden of excessive distractions.

The electrical grids had been acting up since she arrived in late May, and she'd flown out two different crews of experts to inspect the solar panels and wind turbines powering her twenty-five-acre island. With two dozen servants housed in a dozen bungalows, the main villa where she stayed, and two guest villas, the island's inhabitants needed a steady supply of the creature comforts found in the capital, let alone any modern and connected city.

When she bought the island from a French heiress—who sold the already tastefully appointed retreat for a cold $90 million due to legal problems she was having with the French government—the whole idea was to create space between herself and the rest of her life. However, by nature she couldn't remove herself completely from the top-level operations of Lab Networks and Soko Media, and that meant she needed to communicate fluidly with her executive officers and stakeholders. An Internet connection was a basic utility, but her limited access to it reminded her of her days earning her computer science degree, in the nineties, using a dial-up modem before broadband came along.

Blowing in from the three open walls of her terrace, the cool, refreshing ocean breeze gently tickled her exposed skin as Kiko lifted the sheet and placed it, loosely folded, on a nearby ottoman. The trills of passerine songbirds drifted in just as the first drops of warmed essential oil pattered down the nape of her back, followed by the pressure of Kiko's palms and fingers rubbing it in, down the sides of her abdomen, her legs and inner thighs. She'd let him know from the first day of training that she expected a "complete" companion, as she called it, and that he was allowed and encouraged to make advances. She paid him handsomely, more than he could make at some midrange resort in the Bahamas.

Although she'd had her boy toys back when she split her time between Los Angeles and New York, they weren't hers exclusively, and even if she wanted that level of attention then, she wouldn't have been able to appreciate it. Running Soko Media and Lab Networks, raising her teenage daughter—largely without the help of her husband, whose work as an entertainment lawyer had him shuttling back and forth between Los Angeles and Beijing, where he had his mistresses—took utmost discipline.

Her typical sixteen-hour workday began at four a.m. with emails, then a workout, followed by phone calls and meetings and lunches. Once or twice a week she'd get her release with a boy or two, but this relentless rhythm—which she'd maintained since her undergraduate days—was beginning to take a toll she wasn't aware of, like cracks slowly creeping through the foundation of a house. One day her secretary found her in a pool of blood after she'd fainted at her desk, fallen to the floor, and broken her cheekbone. After MRIs and extensive examinations by her physicians, a tumor was ruled out. She'd suffered from nothing other than exhaustion.

Maintaining her empire and balancing her duties as a mother with the tiny bit of "me" time she had to have in order to stay sane had been sustainable for twenty years, but her biological clock had caught up with her. Her physician prescribed her regular low-dose injections of HGH to help her maintain her pace, and although it reinvigorated her already high sex drive, something still felt off. After hiring a lifestyle guru, who convinced her that in order to be happy she need to relinquish control, she began searching for a retreat. The guru had regaled her with anecdotes of his clients, type-A personalities all of them, who, after years of high achieving, had burned out and suffered aneurisms and premature cardiac arrests. She decided to nip the problem in the bud. After visiting spots in Belize, Guadalupe, the Exuma Cays—

which had become too saturated with nouveau riche—she finally opted for the Seychelles, about as remote as she could get.

"Miss Dominika, was good?" Kiko said, his hands resting on her lower back. "You like more the same?"

"It was fine, just fine," she said, phosphenes and patterns painting the backs of her shut eyes. The sound of his Uruguayan-accented voice had interrupted her daydream, and she was eager to fall back into it. "Carry on."

As Kiko moved on to stage two of her massage—using a feather tickler to build up her state of arousal—the muffled sounds of her villa's swamp cooler motors drifted in as they suddenly kicked on. It looked like the handyman, who had been working since early that morning, had finally been able to get the power back on. It had been over twelve hours since her last update, and she was anxious to view her performance dashboards. The level of detail she could get there outweighed the top-level feedback she could get over the phone, which, in times like this when the power was out, was the only way she could connect to the world.

After ordering Kiko to help her get into her burnoose and slippers, she walked back inside her villa to her office, where she had her laptop connected to three large monitors, two of them showing stock market fluctuations, the other reserved for chat logs and daily executive updates.

Scanning the updates, which had arrived a few hours earlier, she noticed nothing remarkable. Her team of data scientists, working in distributed offices around the world, were tasked with feeding her network executives daily insight into the hundreds of media operations she had running simultaneously. Hired from top Wall Street, NASDAQ, and Shanghai Stock Exchange firms, they had worked with her technologists to integrate data fed through APIs into a master control center, where she could get a holistic view of her entire empire, benchmarked against the global stock markets and competitors. It gave her a succinct advantage over anyone else in her field. Instead of disparate sources of information, to be mulled over and compiled by humans, supreme machine efficiency could collate and organize the gigabits of data in milliseconds.

"Winthorpe," she said, "show me performance results for Lab Networks for the last thirty days benchmarked against the same time last year."

"Hold on," her AI assistant said. "I'll pull that up for you." Another tech acquisition she had made four years ago, Winthorpe had been built using the same sophisticated machine learning algorithms used to beat the world's best human Go player in 2016. Beyond menial tasks, like pulling reports for her, he was always on, and, when given permission, he could regulate some of the more mundane optimization tasks that she had to oversee—minor optimizations to her trading desk, even strategic decisions when extreme reactivity called for it. After four years of working together, Winthorpe had learned Sokolov's decision-making process and even improved upon it. He wasn't susceptible to fainting spells, and since he lived on distributed cloud servers, she never had to fear downtime. Even when she was disconnected on her island, she knew she could rely on Winthorpe to make real-time optimizations.

Winthorpe refreshed her main monitor with a chart showing two craggy lines representing the performance of her flagship multichannel networks. "Winthorpe, expand out to show me the same year-to-year benchmark for the last ninety days," she said, and the craggy lines compressed to accommodate the longer timeline. Sokolov's brows furrowed as she scrutinized the data points on the screen. There was a noticeable delta forming in the last sixty or so days, which her analysts hadn't told her about. Perhaps she was relying too much on her data scientists and should cede more decision making to Winthorpe? This oversight—however subtle the changes might be—was exactly the kind of misstep she feared when she started relinquishing some of the day-to-day control of her companies.

Something outside her window caught her eye. Through the palm fronds gently swaying in the afternoon breeze, she caught a glimpse of Kiko as he walked away from the villa, his muscular, bare back russet-colored from the outdoor work she had him do around the villa. No doubt he was heading for a tryst with that little hussy from Martinique. Sokolov, who had always been fairly liberal—she was still technically married, and she and her husband had been polyamorous since the beginning—didn't mind that Kiko had his little flings. It was his performance with her that was suffering, and that's what was beginning to annoy her. His dispassion during the massage, which had followed a lackluster performance in bed the previous night, plus her intuition that something was going on with the servant girl, were the beginnings of problems, like a bad apple threatening to spoil the bunch unless she took quick action. Before she sent Kiko back to the capital, she had to make sure her next cabana boy was already on his way in. Perhaps she should hire two and play them off each other, have them vie for her approval. Masculine nature was simple—she'd learned to manipulate it early on as a young girl of fifteen, when she started getting looks from older men, friends of the family—and she was surprised she hadn't thought of this simple solution earlier. She'd have them compete with each other, perhaps even have them both smother her with attention at the same time. Of course she'd also have to get rid of the cute servant girl in order to set a precedent with the rest of the help on the island. They could do as they pleased, as long as her needs were catered to first. Her dominant role must never be questioned, and any infraction—she'd learned this over the course of her highly successful career—needed to be dealt with swiftly. Decisive, prescient, and ruthless—those were the three words *Forbes* used to describe her in their 2019 profile, when she was named the most influential person in media.

She lightly touched her hard-set face, tense from the disapproving looks she'd cast at Kiko as he departed toward the bungalows. After her last public appearance, at the private investors' gala she threw for the opening of her latest multi-channel city, she had been horrified by the snarky online chatter that followed, describing her appearance as eccentric, with "extravagant headwear only someone idiotically rich would wear" and "caked-on makeup." It was so damn hard to keep up your looks as a woman, and you weren't allowed to age grace-fully. And while she knew she could buy all the young studs she wanted, she wanted them to genuinely desire her, as they would a younger woman in her so-called sexual prime. Those age lines around her mouth were creeping back, as were shallow furrows in her forehead. She'd have to schedule a visit with her surgeon in Beverly Hills when she got back. In the meantime, her movement trainer—whom she'd flown out from São Paulo—could help her work on her butt and abdomen.

Glancing back at the screen displaying the ninety-day perfor-mance comparison, she said, "Winthorpe, show me the perfor-mance charts broken out by property." The screen refreshed showing dozens of lines, more or less following the same patterns across the timespan. One seemed to be ticking lower than average—her first multichannel city venture, Eutopia. Just four years ago it had been the hottest new concept in advertising and business. Now it looked like its performance was plateauing. Since its launch, other cities had retrofitted in order to compete with her innovative ad tech approach, allowing integrated gaming and ad revenue across multiple touch points. New multichannel cities in China had appeared, offering more competition—including one that was a barefaced rip-off of her concept, called Europia. After asking Winthorpe to pull up competitive charts, and to project one year into the future—factoring in global trends across the markets—she saw Eutopia might be headed for a disappointing fourth quarter.

"Winthorpe, flag Eutopia for me, and send me daily perfor-mance reports on network traffic," she said, and got up and walked to the adjacent room, which had 360-degree views of the eastern end of the atoll. She took a seat on her bamboo settee and contemplated the view, like a painter from the romantic period, appreciating the sublime immensity of the vast ocean beyond. Her guests in the Italian villa—the ones visiting from Shanghai—what would they be dining on tonight? She called her servant and requested the night's menu, as well as the outdoor movie theater schedule.

14.
Influencers and Outliers

EDRIC, ON HIS WAY to meet Sacha in Berlin, was sitting in the back of an autonomous cab when a news flash appeared on the touch screen monitor in front of him. A man had been found dead earlier that day in the influencer incubator zone—the area near where his wife had lived, which offered low-cost housing in hostel-style, multi-bunk-bed units rented to newly arrived aspiring celebrities who wanted to network and learn the ropes of social media influencing. The packages they were sold usually included seminars taught by social media experts and stars, and he had seen advertising around town and online offering heavily discounted prices. According to the news report, the man, who was found dead of apparent asphyxiation in an apartment, was named Eddie Costello, described as an "employee of the city." Cedric's eyes widened. Was this the guy Fred had pointed out to him in the casino the night he himself was murdered? The same guy he had followed? Engaging his cell phone, he swiped through the latest social updates for more news about the death, but only rehashed versions of the headline came through. There was some speculation that it had something to do with a honeypot scam gone wrong—that he'd been lured to a tryst with a L-Uber user and killed during a robbery. Nothing in particular about Costello—who, as the city's entertainment officer, was more of a behind-the-scenes guy. He felt hyperalert, as if he'd just inhaled pure oxygen. Everything he'd seen that afternoon a week ago was even stranger in retrospect.

As planned, Sacha was in the back corner of the Marx Bar, near an unfinished concrete wall decorated with bold, Soviet-era agitprop posters. She was reading her tablet, which she put down as soon as she saw him, the screen on a story about Costello's murder.

"I'm glad we finally have a chance to talk," he said.

"Thanks for reaching out to me," she said. "I wish it could have been earlier, but I was busy. I just got back in town."

He took a seat in the chair adjacent to hers, still facing the entrance of the bar. "I hope you don't mind. I just want, you know," he said, nodding in the direction to the entrance, "to keep an eye out. Things are starting to get weird here." Although it was early evening, the bar was already at about 50-percent capacity. People at the bar, a stylized slab of concrete in front of a colorful reproduction of the Berlin Wall, were chatting among themselves over Kalashnikovs, advertised on the wall as the bar's specialty shot, comprised of ground coffee beans chased by Stolichnaya. "I've had this feeling every since arriving, and even more so now, that I'm being followed."

"Well, you are, technically. Surveillance drones and CCTV are constantly compiling data."

He shrugged and said, "I don't mean that."

"I know, I was being glib," she said. "We could go somewhere else, if you want."

"No worries," he said, while glancing at her tablet. "So, you saw the news on Costello, the city's guy."

"Just now. It's pretty shocking, coming a couple months after the Louvre thing with your wife."

Cedric nodded, tight-lipped, contemplative for a moment as if he had just correlated the two events. The murder would probably get buried in the twenty-four-hour news cycle, under the weight of dozens of trending hashtags. After waving over a waiter and ordering an organic matcha tea, he continued. "A week ago, the day I pinged you, I saw this guy in public that I recognized from the night I was attacked with Fred, or whatever his name was. This guy, he was wearing the same jacket, carrying the same motorcycle helmet I saw in the garage that night."

As the waiter set down his tea, Cedric told her how he had seen Costello and his entourage in the casino shortly before they were attacked in the garage, how his companion had pointed him out and seemed nervous. "I followed him through some side streets and breezeways, more and more convinced he was one of the guys that attacked us. It was a gut feeling, maybe something about his gait, in addition to the motorcycle helmet, but it just matched in my mind." Sacha's dark, cocoa-brown eyes stayed fixed on him as he recounted the incident, his own eyes drifting upward as he recollected the day, then back down as he told her about it. "After about five to ten minutes of this, he gets to the back door of a larger building, like the service entrance of a restaurant, something nondescript. So he enters after waving a fob over a reader, goes in, and before it closes, I grab the handle. I wait there a few seconds, going over the pros and cons of illegally trespassing, considering my already shaky relationship with the law here. But I was too intrigued to let it go. This was the guy. So I open the door and slowly step in, and see that it leads to a corridor, and at the end of it there's some stairs, and along the side there's a couple of doors, also with fob sensors to unlock them. I could hear the guy's footsteps fading away, but at this point my nerves got the better of me, and, not wanting to get caught and get in any more trouble with the police . . ."

"Wait, wait, I want you to continue, but what's the trouble with police you're talking about?"

"They've been harassing me since I came here, and I didn't cooperate with them at the inquest for the guy who was killed with me. I'll tell you about it later. So I stepped back outside and decided to stake out the place from a bar at the corner. I took a window seat and just waited to see if the guy would come back out of the door."

He was about to continue when a guy—conspicuously nondescript for the bar, rather like Cedric—took a seat at a table near them. Cedric paused and tilted his head toward him, and Sacha nodded. "Do you want to get out of here? We can walk and talk."

After she gathered her tablet and dropped it in her handbag, they walked out of the Marx Bar and headed past Checkpoint Charlie and a recreation of the Berlin Wall. On the other side, Paris began, with a series of covered arcades, housing luxury shoe and clothing shops. "I'm sitting there watching the door," Cedric said, "and after about fifteen minutes I see none other than Eddie Costello and A'rore leave the building, and they're arguing; it was pretty obvious. Just behind them, a couple of bodyguard-looking dudes. I left the bar and followed them from a ways back, until I see them reach the main street where a couple of cars and drivers are waiting for them. They got in separate cars and drove off. But when I got to the street I realized that the door I'd been watching was to the back of the De Wallen Casino, right next to where we were attacked."

Instead of glass-topped arcades like continental Paris, these were fitted with massive curved LED screens, splashing psychedelic fractals synchronized with electronic dance music, piped in at low levels throughout the structure. Intermittently, an advertisement appeared, promoting a club or drug—a new advert he hadn't seen before promoted Narcolese, to counteract sleepless binges brought on by Panadrine. They cut through a small crowd of people filming a heavily tattooed young woman posing for an artist sketching her on a large, touch-responsive electronic canvas.

"That's not in itself unusual, seeing A'rore and Costello, since they work together," Sacha said.

"True, and I thought the same thing myself, except it was the helmet guy I saw who walked in the same door. He was one of the guys who attacked us, I'm sure of it. And then the news today about Costello's suspicious death."

"Yeah, I see where you're going."

"It can't all be a coincidence, especially after the argument I saw him in with A'rore. I've been here ten days now, and too many unusual things have happened for me to believe it was a random murder."

They passed Panadrine hookah bars, cafés selling bottled oxygen, bistros offering fois gras sourced from lab-grown goose liver, a souvenir shop selling kitschy 1970s-style postcards and Eiffel Tower replicas, even galleries selling hand-painted Chinese replicas of works by masters, once hung in the Louvre. It was beginning to feel like they were in a theatrical version of Paris that itself was pantomiming a version of Paris for tourists. The situation Cedric found himself in, despite his intentions to stay aloof, resembled a storyline he would have written for one of his movies.

Suddenly, fractals overhead began glitching, and the hashtags #AdRev #Pwned appeared, followed by "ROFLEX." After a couple of seconds, an ad for Panadrine appeared on the screen, followed by the fractal patterns. Cedric looked, with an inquisitive expression, from the LED screen to Sacha.

"ROFLEX again," she said, "the group that's been hacking the ad networks. They can infiltrate for seconds at a time before the real-time algorithms detect anomalies and start serving ads again."

"And isn't it the same group they're saying is behind the Louvre?"

"Oh, it looks like everybody and their mother has an opinion on that, if you're looking at the social chatter."

"The inspector on my wife's case seems to think so." Cedric continued a few paces without saying anything, lost in thought. Why did he get that feeling there was a link between Sacha, his wife, and the group behind the sabotage? Were these just suggestive thoughts given to him by Monteiro? "The more I'm here, the more I start to give credence to some of the rumors. The whole case, the way it's officially being presented, is so pat, so unnuanced. The woman I knew wasn't some crazed idealist, and I could honestly see her scoffing at things like ROFLEX," he said, pointing back at the section of the arcade they had just passed through, where the screens had been hijacked. "She'd say it was useless slacktivism."

"Didn't they find evidence—allegedly, of course—that some of the thieves were tied to ROFLEX?"

"All I hear is wild speculation."

"Cedric," Sacha said, gently gripping his arm and looking straight into his eyes, "that's why I'm here. There's a big story here, unfolding, and somehow your wife was involved. My hunch is she knew something big was going to happen that day and—don't take this the wrong way—that she might have been complicit."

"It's impossible. I mean, I didn't have a lot of contact with her over the last couple years—she was busy with her career—but I know her. She never would have been involved in a heist or, for that matter, a bombing."

They exited the covered arcades and entered a plaza, at the center of which was a fountain. A giant screen on a nearby hotel showed A'rore in a tight white bodysuit, jumping backward off of one of the city's high-rises, falling into a graceful dive, her purple-tinged hair flowing as she made one full 360-degree rotation before landing on the street below, fist pointed down in a superhero pose, cracks in the pavement webbing out from the force of impact.

"What I wanted to tell you the other day," Sacha said, "was that I had been chatting anonymously with someone in the city, supposedly high up, who wanted to whistleblow. We were only just beginning, and I was trying to gain their trust, but the communications suddenly stopped around the time of the Louvre and Mila's disappearance. My source gave me details only someone directly involved with the city could have known; in particular, they accurately predicted some recent events, including the Louvre. I think, Cedric, they were coming from her."

On his way back to his hotel, passing under giant screens showing euro-facades, he felt, despite his intentions to get out, an intensity pulling him toward the city, like a fish to a shiny lure. His wife, Sacha said after they had stepped into a hookah bar, might have come to the city as an employee, but maybe it became more than that. "If there's anything I've noticed in interviews with people," she said, "it's that there's a seductive promise here." Cedric, admittedly, knew what that was about, even if at this stage in his life he felt too jaded to fall into that mindset. The inward, navel-gazing self-obsession he'd witnessed in Hollywood was also present here. The hope and delusion you too could be famous. "The major difference," Sacha said, "is that here you can see tangible proof of fame, immediately. You gain followers, you earn advertising revenue, and the closer you get to the heart of it, the more social currency you earn. Sokolov is a genius."

Hyperalert from the secondhand narcotic clouds in the vapor bar, he was energized, even surprised somewhat at his budding desire to join the media-fueled circus around him. Perhaps, he reasoned, it was the only way to find out what happened to his wife. He'd just passed through the Red Light District and was about to take the last stretch to his hotel when two motorcycles raced past. Expecting another live chase, he glanced at a nearby digital wrapper showing an advertisement for the Arc Club—a quick-cut series of celebrity selfies taken with A'rore—before fading back to the neo-Renaissance facade of the Rome district.

He was suddenly reminded of one of his friends who dabbled in the kind of New Age things Southern California was infamous for. A big proponent of psychedelics, he had suggested them as a way for Cedric to break through his career malaise. Paraphrasing Aldous Huxley, he said the brain acts as a filtering mechanism in order to help us cope with the world, blocking out extraneous information so we can focus on the essential. What happens under the influence of psychedelics, he said, is that the filter is turned off, opening the tap, releasing a flood of information on the brain. It's like seeing the world through a child's eyes. Could he drop the filter he'd imposed on himself and break through this strange moment in his life? At the corner, two tourists wearing augmented eyewear were engaging with the signage. Others sitting in front of a nondairy gelateria were interacting with objects invisible to his eye, and an influencer in front of a Prada store was filming himself for his global audience. Short of becoming a guinea pig for some of the new cortical modems coming out—neural implants showing augmented reality overlays in your field of vision—the only thing he could do was purchase some AR eyewear.

In less than five minutes, he was walking out of a nearby Apple store, syncing his new eyewear to his phone, disabling the ad blocker he had reengaged after the night he was attacked. He'd kept it off for the most part since arriving, simply because he couldn't deal with the inundation of ads, alerts, and networking requests that kept coming in. It wasn't a full surrender, but his conversation with Sacha had triggered something, making him realize he was in too deep to turn back, and now blocking off half the world around him seemed arbitrarily intransigent.

Invisible objects in front of the trattoria appeared—rotating Eutopean coins some of the tourists were trying to catch, redeemable at stores and clubs around town. L-Uber users appeared like a swarm on his phone interface, advancing in clusters all around him. Even after refining the results to show only the elite L-Ubers, he was surprised to see some, at that moment just a few feet away, looking no older than eighteen, dolled up with bright red lipstick. In the lower third of his vision, a golden tiger slinked in, crawling on its sturdy haunches from right to left, followed by a glinting gold-rimmed logo for Tiger Max All Night pills. As he started walking, the logo slid off the screen, and more of his field of vision opened up, thankfully, allowing clearer navigation of the streets, yet multicolor flourishes still burnished everything around him—Eutopean coins in front of select stores, halos over influencers announcing social status, translucent auras around others indicating mood. A building's facade faded to the advertisement for the Arc Club—this time a fresh rotation of selfies with new celebrities and body parts, not too subtle promises of social boosting and sex— and he noticed that by focusing on a compass icon floating in the corner, a translucent arrow appeared, blinking, indicating "Arc Club, 7 min" with a pedestrian icon. Aural enhancers connected to the ends of his eyewear, transmitting via bone conduction to his inner ear, synced to his pulse, and an urgent, driving beat accompanied his walk as he followed the arrow.

Situated in the top portion of the Arc de Triomphe, the Arc Club was an interplay of shadows and accent lights, mint and cherry scents from vape clouds hovering over pinpoints of nuclear green and cyanide blue. Though many of the patrons inside had eyewear on, he took his off and hung it under his chin. Although he wasn't a newbie to the technology, which had been out for years, he'd never tried it more than a few times, even after it became fashionably mainstream. The benefits of using it came with the price of constant exposure to advertising—the irony of course being that both he and his wife worked in the industry, and they both used blocking technology. His short walk to the

Arc was the most time he'd spent in an AR environment, and he already felt overstimulated.

He'd never seen anything on this scale, in terms of real-life social networking, even during the peak of his career. Even without his AR glasses, he could see who had more social value just by the way others gravitated toward them. In fact, the centers of attention usually wore no AR gear at all because their social auras appeared to everyone else wearing the gear, and because they got tagged in the numerous videos and selfies being shot with them, they didn't have to do any work to promote themselves. Screens above the bar showed live footage from around Eutopia with comment streams, and everyone seemed to move in unison, whether it was a contingent moving toward the bar, the VIP rooms, the bathrooms, or the exit, as if they were a bee colony in a hive, working together toward a shared objective.

An hour in, after passively flirting with an account executive from Swagstar, a hot new Y Combinator start-up, whose curiosity was piqued when she noticed his profile and aura were dark—"you *must* be someone . . . only the highest status don't even bother"—Cedric was playing in a Street Fighter competition being held in one of the lounges, having downed two energy drinks mixed with vodka. Tonight he felt the strong urge to indulge—copious alcohol, even a puff on a cocaine vape a Snapchat ambassador had offered him. After a jab, cross, spin-kick combo, he KO'd his opponent with a massive Hadoken, and an onscreen message awarded him a trip to the VIP zone on the roof.

Spanning the top of the arch, with a pool and bar, the vantage point was the most privileged he'd seen—traffic radiated out from the monument—and the brisk night air was accentuated by unobstructed airflow. Low-end beats and synth hits wormed their way out from the lower levels, and a cross-section of the city's elite gathered around the bar, in reclining pods, on chaise lounges and ottomans situated beneath directional heat lamps. As he walked past the bar and the illuminated pool—hued lights synced with the music below, the rippling reflections like an ocean on an alien planet—he savored the open air and the lack of signage beckoning to him. He knew, in a way, he was like one of those jokey archetypes of old men telling youngsters to get off their lawn, but he couldn't see how the generations that came after him could acclimate to such intense and incessant stimulation. Maybe it came down to hormones and youth, maybe he was too old for all this. Maybe his wife, who was three years younger than him, had more youthful vigor. Then he remembered some of the pharmacological aids he saw in her apartment. There was that, too, which always helped.

Leaning on the building's edge, beyond the bubble of light and sound, he took in a lungful of the cool air. To his left and right, key monuments were pulsing with gradients of blue, boasting the city's good health that night. It was almost as if he were looking at a living tourist map, a dynamic topography ideally suited for this new world.

A feminine voice, low in register, interrupted his reverie.

"I can't decide if it's a caricature or the real thing. Or if it even matters."

Turning to his side, he was confronted with a dark silhouette, facial features briefly illuminated by the mood shifts in the pool lights. Glossy black hair, cut at a sharp angle, partially obscured her face, momentarily illuminated by the chrysanthemum glow of an engaged e-cigarette. Heavily rouged lips—the style of the L-Uber girls around town—exhaled a vapor cloud that quickly dissipated in the open air. Shoulders draped with a loose shawl, drooping down to just above a pair of legs clad in skintight material, she looked liked like a dungeon mistress who had stepped out for a cigarette break between clients. Her head turned toward the horizon still, she didn't bother to make eye contact.

"I'm inclined to think it doesn't even matter," he said.

"Then," she said, stepping closer while extending her hand, "what does, Mr. Travers?"

He extended his hand and gripped hers lightly, holding it longer than expected, as neither seemed in a hurry to unclasp. As he let go, he said, "I know you. I've seen you around." He could see more of her features now, her silver eyes glinting for a split second in the mood lights. Unmistakably, the same ubiquitous face he'd seen all over town. Tall for a woman, she had at least an inch on Cedric with her heels on. "But how do you know me?"

Several feet behind her, just visible in the shadows, was a broad-shouldered man, leaning on the ledge with his hands clasped in front of him. Although he was facing the pool, Cedric could sense he was paying close attention to the two of them.

"Don't mind him," she said. "He's my driver." The lower half of her right leg, he noticed, looked liked it had an extra layer of protection wrapped around it, like a form-fitted shell. "You don't have to worry, Cedric, if I can call you that."

"Whatever you prefer."

"You're wondering, of course, how I know so much about you."

Again, the palpable yet difficult to define feeling of dread he'd felt since arriving. "It's been you and him the entire time, watching me."

"I wasn't sure at first. You know, you're one of the few in this town that keeps his profile dark, but that only makes you more conspicuous. After you started getting in trouble, I was finally able to verify who you were." Her leg started emanating a low-intensity turquoise light, in sync with some of the monuments and buildings in the cityscape behind her. "I'm not surprised you don't remember me; it was such a minor thing. We met over a decade and a half ago. You gave me my first role."

She had triggered something in his mind when he had first seen her images around town, but still, he couldn't quite place her. "I had a feeling I recognized you from somewhere, but I wasn't exactly sure."

"It was an ad you were directing for BMW. As I said, really

minor. But it opened the door for me. You were instrumental in giving me that role, I know that."

"I do remember vaguely, but you were a lot different then," he said, his eye dropping from her flamed-out spikes of anime hair to her gently glowing prosthesis.

"A lot has changed since then."

"Tell me about it. But here we are," he said, and they both shared a complicit smile.

"Hey, why don't we go for a ride?"

The rugged figure behind her had approached the pool, and his square-jawed face was illuminated from below. His face half-turned toward them, showing rough stubble and a latticework of shallow scars, he nodded.

"Sure, why not?"

—◆—

THEY FOLLOWED HER DRIVER's lead to a private exit and elevator from the roof.

"So, this whole time I had a connection to your wife I didn't know about," she said. "She was good. She got it." As they sat in the back of her S-Class Mercedes, driven by Norton, her intimidating chauffeur, he felt himself being drawn into her world, like he'd passed a kind of threshold the moment he stepped into her car. There was a confluence of events, culminating in his desire to taste the fully enhanced version of Eutopia by turning off his blockers, but the barrier between the image and the real had been broken. Despite his cynical recusal from the theater of pop culture, he desired to be in her presence, to follow her to the end of the night, just to see what was at the heart of her allure, and, by extension, the city's.

As they drove through the city, anonymous, behind the tinted windows of her sedan, she mentioned casually that it was armored and bulletproof, a necessary precaution.

"I can see why," he said. "This place is a like a pocket of violence rising out of the desert."

"You experienced it firsthand, I know. We saw it. The thing is, Cedric—and you'll come to see this if you stay here long enough—people crave the violence."

"Believe me, I know that from working in the industry. But people want that in games and movies."

"What do you think is happening here?" she said. "I can start broadcasting myself right now, sitting with you, to millions of people around the world. Mila understood that."

Hearing her name gave him pause, and a sudden rush of longing came over him, a montage of good times, hope and loss. A'rore's profile was a blend of sharp and soft features, in dark relief against the colorful blur of lights passing by her window. Norton's face was also intermittently illuminated by the signage outside, and as he gripped the wheel of the powerful sedan, steering it into a new lane, the lights hit his face at an angle that once again accentuated the shallow scar tissue across his cheek.

"You must know by now I'm here for her. I just wanted to pick up her things, but this place is sucking me in."

"From what I know, or can guess, you became a person of interest when you started asking questions. That's how the EPD is. They like their storyline to be the only storyline."

"What about the attack? A guy died because of that. A guy I just met, but he seemed friendly."

"Unfortunate, but that happens all the time here in Eutopia. It's part of the fabric of the city. You and he were one of dozens of attacks that night."

"My wife, was she . . ." He thought better of a quip about her being "unfortunate." A'rore was revealing more and more, and he didn't want to spur any antagonism.

"We're not sure what happened to her," she said, head turning toward him, eyes steady, fixed on his. "It looks like, from the evidence, she was involved in a one of the groups trying to sabotage the city."

"ROFLEX?"

A'rore nodded. "I really know as much as you do. The rumors and theories are all over the place, but the most shared and upvoted ones . . ." Her voice trailed off as she looked ahead, then told Norton to park where he could, near what Cedric recognized as the burned-out remains of the Louvre.

"This is still my favorite spot in the city," she said, as they walked into an adjacent building with Greek columns and a triangular frieze. As Norton went ahead of them, the beam of his flashlight bouncing with his stride, A'rore continued. "This place used to be the Samsung Theater." Just then, the lights flipped on, revealing a sleek acrylic and concrete interior, white on white. "Even though it wasn't damaged," she said, "they closed this whole zone after the fire. It is, despite the name, an homage to the old city in Europe. The city's architects modeled it after the Orangerie where they displayed Monet's Nymphéas."

As she led him into a chamber, she said, "Eutopia doesn't, and never has, tried to be like the real thing. That's precisely the appeal. You'll see."

He followed her as she walked into the middle of an oval-shaped room with a concave ceiling, illuminated around the bottom rim with soft accent lights. The walls were smooth, seamless black glass, except for the entrance. Norton stayed outside as they both took a seat on a circular settee in the middle of the room. Was A'rore's interest in him genuine, or was it part of a ruse? As if she were reading his mind, she said, "I'm glad you came, Cedric. I don't forget people who've helped me out."

Close up now, her complexion was impeccable, skin taut, lips on the narrow side—yet perfectly pouty and plump—her hair thick, glossy, and radically angled across her face. Although she was the very image of radiant health, she seemed of indeterminate age. From their history he guessed she was around his age, yet with enhancements and cocktails of stabilizing hormones she could easily pass for someone in their mid- to late-twenties. A strange sex appeal radiated from her, not purely based on her physical attributes, but almost as if he'd been subjected to a megadose of pheromones. His inhibitions were lowering, and his natural skepticism was rapidly receding. He found himself surrendering to the seduction game he knew she was luring him into.

She took out a small chromium atomizer bullet and activated it under her nostrils, sniffing in a cloud composed of delicate white filaments, her eyelids fluttering, drawing his attention to her long eyelashes. After a slow, meditative inhalation, she handed the device to Cedric and said, "Try it. It's a new MDMA analog."

As he took the atomizer from her and activated it, the ambient light in the room dimmed to complete darkness except for a reddish glow coming from the device, illuminating a trail of vapor filaments rising to his nostrils. A rush of endorphins rippled through his body, euphoric waves lapping against the outer reaches of his perception. The darkness felt like a timeless dimension, unconstrained by the limits of his vision, as if he were on the threshold of an orgasm, yet he was alert and in full control of his faculties, as if he'd had the strongest and cleanest non-jittery cup of coffee ever. The room came to life, a living impressionist swirl of ultramarine, violet, viridian, pink, and red—shapes at once discernible and hazy. He was immersed, his entire field of vision flooded with the twinkling reflections of a mauve-and-orange sunset, flowers at once radiant and lost in the interplay of light and darkness. Everything seemed to undulate and stay still at once, and after some time, A'rore spoke.

"Monet flirted with abstraction," she said, her voice riding the crest of a wave of perception. "He took reality, reinterpreted it, and presented it in an unfamiliar way."

"He had cataracts, didn't he?" Cedric's voice felt disembodied, yet it flowed from his thoughts, which came naturally. "He saw colors differently than you and I."

"It's what he chose to show us. It's like we don't have a frame of reference, just this incredible play of colors and no horizon. He curated his reality and transformed his personal experience into art."

"What's been done here," he said, feeling a tingling sensation along the top of his head, as if he'd just heard a refrain from an especially moving song, "is the same thing as what's been done to the city, just on a smaller scale."

"That's it," she said. "The hyperreal. It's a city and lifestyle whose time has come. We're not imposing anything. People asked for it. Data maps pointed to it." As she said this, she moved closer to him. He could feel warmth radiating from her, and he leaned in closer, gazing at her semi-turned profile, the enhanced Monet painting a living, breathing backdrop.

Her hand rested on his thigh, gripping gently, drawing his attention once more to her. "Think of it like a gun firing in a movie. That's a language you understand. Without the hyperreal sound effects, it just falls flat. Menace, Cedric, isn't conveyed by realistic gun handling." As she said this, he could sense Norton's lurking presence at the far end of the room. "You can tell much more about a character's state of mind if they tremble while they hold it, if they exaggerate the weight of it."

He groped her waistline, firm from assiduous exercise, and they pressed into each other, his hands roaming her enhanced figure—wasp-thin waist, round rear, and augmented breasts just beneath her skintight outfit. Briefly, before falling back into her clutches, he had an intuition that she had also seduced his wife. Everything was calculated: her poise, her speech cadence, her careful choice of words, her scent—voluptuous notes of jasmine and myrrh filled his nostrils—and it seemed so effortless.

"It's all part of the spectrum," she said, "that enlivens this place." Mauve and violet hues from the screen surrounding them pulsed and glowed brighter as they drew into each other.

15.
Corrective Measures

Twenty-eight murders since January, in a city that gets over twenty million visitors a year, with a fluctuating population of around three hundred thousand people. According to the national crime index, violence in his city was soaring, but he had never been reprimanded for it even though he'd been commissioned as the city's chief inspector for the last three years. It was as if they expected it, almost encouraged it—and, in a way, it was also the narrative that justified some of the more controversial measures he had to take around town. In a potential battlefield, which this place was, threats had to be localized in order to isolate and weed out the insurgents. But every once in a while his department's predictive algorithms missed something. Like the terrorist attack a few months ago—that wasn't expected—now this, one of the city's bigwigs found dead of probable homicide. They had an algorithm for Code Yellow threats in the city—potentialities for trouble—and neither of these scenarios had been generated. Yet in each case he had the feeling that something wasn't right leading up to it. For the last couple weeks, since the arrival of Mila Webb's ex, Cedric Travers, Monteiro had felt a shift, a misalignment, like a rifle scope that needed zeroing. When he was in the NCIS two decades earlier, before predictive algorithms had begun to dominate investigations, a lot of his work combating transnational terrorism relied on instinct, which he still found to be sharper than the machines. Somehow Eddie Costello's death, he strongly felt it, was linked to Travers.

"India 101 to dispatch, send the 10-20 of that pending homicide," he said as he drove toward the main strips. The sky, dark purple, offset the familiar billion-watt cityscape of Eutopia. After a short pause, his GPS pinged and lit up with the address where Costello's body had been found. It had been a long day, and he had just finished his last reports when the call came in from the first responders. Discreet as usual, they didn't reveal the full nature of the crime scene, and at first Monteiro chalked it up to a routine homicide, probably some lowlife hopped up on meth who'd gotten into an altercation. However, one of the responders called him up personally when he discovered Costello's name on the ID found on the body. "You're gonna want to come down here," she said. "We've got a couple witnesses, and they apparently know Costello. They had seen him before."

The address the dispatcher gave him, the Snap Hotel, was familiar. It was in one of the more downtrodden parts of town, near the influencer incubators and hostels. He remembered paying a visit to a unit in the building over a year ago when he was investigating a network of motorcycle jackers. These pockets of criminality were the same the world over—there was always that physical nexus, in any city, where crime converged. It was like a necessary evil, preventing the miscreant behavior from metastasizing across the rest of the city, where it would be so dispersed—like Mogadishu at the turn of the century—that reigning it in would be impossible.

After taking the tunnel and navigating the less trafficked side streets, he found himself in the incubator zone near Paris, most identifiable by the down-market boutiques and preponderance of liquor stores and vape shops. Although there wasn't an official boundary line, most of the upscale visitors and more successful influencers never came here because of the lack of notable attractions and social lures. However, for those looking for the door to the score, or to get off on whatever sexual kink was their flavor, this was known as the area to do it.

He parked his unmarked Charger curbside in front of the Snap Hotel, near a twenty-four-hour walk-up pharmacy. A couple, having just made a transaction, walked past with a paper bag marked with a green cross, as he got out of his car and walked to the yellow-painted hotel. An officer at the entrance, controlling ingress and egress, let him in and directed him to the fourth floor. Three years ago, the Snap Hotel was a new, hip, acrylic-furnished, affordable place popular with young would-be influencers and short-term visitors looking to party. Naturally it attracted a rowdier element, and the wear and disrepair on the units and building had not been kept up with. Once bright canary-yellow walls were scuffed, furniture looked out of date already, and the floor of the elevator, a patterned carpet, was worn through in parts.

When he exited the elevator, he walked toward a sentry at the end of the hall. Upon entering a larger unit, fitted to be a mid- to long-term residence, he was greeted by the first responder who had called him.

"He's in the bedroom. Follow me."

Monteiro noticed the same archetypal patterns wherever he went, and this was no different. The scene of this crime, like the wannabe jihadi dens he'd raided, the thieves' and child-trafficking pimps' hideouts he'd busted, had that familiar fly-by-night feeling. Squalid, not really lived in or cared for. Stickers from clubs around town were randomly stuck on the walls of the hallway they were walking down. As they passed the kitchen, a full sink of dirty dishes and a poster of a male bodybuilder on a refrigerator were visible behind a half-drawn curtain.

"We found this place had been rented out using a stolen credit card and identity and, according to two witnesses, was being used as a hookup spot, where L-Uber users would bring back their tricks. The witnesses say they saw Eddie enter the hotel with a L-Uber user who went by the name SexxxyMew. We've pulled his social media accounts, and there are a bunch of selfie videos with barely any hits. It looks like he was slumming it here in Eutopia, making ends meet by prostituting himself."

Upon entering the room, a CSI tech slipped past Monteiro after giving him the nod. Gloved, he had a camera around his neck and was holding a tablet with notes. On the bed, facedown, was the half-nude body of a tall, mid-thirties, dark-complexioned male, matching the description of Costello. His arms, spread wide, had cuffs around the wrists, which were attached to the bed's posts.

"Give me a few," Monteiro said, dispatching the first responder. He needed to turn on his observation powers and let his first reactions come in unaffected by commentary. As the first responder left to deal with her technicians, who were still canvassing the apartment, he stepped carefully to the side of the bed. There were some signs of struggle, judging by a superficial wound on the corpse's wrists, where the metal edges of the cuffs had chafed his skin. The flat sheets had been pulled back, exposing a corner of the mattress. A nightstand nearby, with a small, red-shaded table lamp, had a bowl of condoms, a box of tissue, and a plastic bottle of baby oil, which had been knocked over, leaving a small puddle of oil dripping from the nightstand to the carpet. White powder, divided into uneven, dispersed lines, and a rolled-up flyer from a club were next to the overturned bottle of oil.

The corpse's face, turned toward the lamp, had wide-open eyes that were sunken and flat. Shining a light on them revealed dilated oval pupils and tiny burst vessels in the whites, behind a haze due to the onset of rigor mortis. A tie lay below the corpse's neck, which showed bruising consistent with ligature and pinpoint purple dots from ruptured capillaries. Shutting off his flashlight, he walked around to the other side of the bed, toward a sofa and coffee table. Pants, shirt, and jacket belonging to the victim were there, somewhat neatly draped over the sofa's armrest, with shoes nearby. On the coffee table was a small tripod, without camera. Everything indicated the body hadn't been moved, and that the victim had been lured into what he thought was a transactional sexual encounter. Immobilized by handcuffs, which appeared to have been voluntarily applied, he was asphyxiated by a necktie used by the perpetrator. The room, besides the nightstand, sofa, and coffee table, had no other furniture. As his first responder had mentioned, witnesses claimed this was a hookup pad.

Leaving the corpse behind, he joined the first responder in the adjacent room. A clothes rack with a variety of colorful jackets and shirts, some halfway off their hangers, was pushed into a corner. Hats, sunglasses, and T-shirts were strewn about, and pictures, stuck to the wall, all showed the same individual posing shirtless for selfies. Monteiro walked up to the haphazardly placed photos and scrutinized them, and a flash of recognition came over him. Although individuals like the one he saw posing in the photos were familiar to him, as if made of the same mold, something about this one stood out. Dyed green hair, fashionably unkempt, the drawn, over-taut skin of a stimulant user—a discarded wrapper for an ice vape on the ground and the powdery remnants in the other room confirmed this—intense, light blue eyes, which he was keen to show off in his photos, a lean, sinewy body. In better days, given his narcissism, he probably could have been a model. His face, however, had different scrawlings on it in each photo. In one it had "SexxxyMew" written across the forehead. In another it had "Sexxxy" on one cheek and "Mew" on the other. Another had "@SexxxyMew" written across his forehead and other nonsensical scribblings written on his cheeks and chest. The lunatic, capricious stylings were one thing, but Montiero knew he'd dealt with this individual before because of his eyes. It had been two years, but the man was one of his department's confidential informants, back before his turn as the SexxxyMew, when he was an influencer with a different handle, Thorgasm. He'd fallen off the radar, and Monteiro assumed he had left the city.

"Where are the witnesses?" Monteiro said.

"Back at the station already, giving statements," the first responder said. "One of them found Costello's body when he was returning to the apartment. Apparently L-Uber users used the apartment for their hookups, but for the last week or so the individual in the photo had been crashing here. The other, a receptionist, saw SexxxyMew and Costello enter the hotel together. Apparently, Costello frequented the Snap Hotel, and it wasn't unusual to see him there."

After another survey of the apartment, Monteiro left as the CSI unit began taking out all its tagged evidence. It had been a couple of hours, added onto an already late night, and he had to go back to the station now to talk to the witnesses. The crime was so commonplace that he normally wouldn't have involved himself, instead putting a junior officer on the case, but as it involved a city official, and as he sensed the death was tied to something bigger, he knew he had to take the lead.

As he took the elevator down, he made a mental note to look into SexxxyMew's channel—also noting the tripod on the coffee table, which may have filmed the deed—and look up Thorgasm in the database to see if he cross-referenced with any other infractions. The bar adjacent to the hotel's lobby was a mix of budget-traveling youth, many in-character, filming each other for their channels, and older, more haggard-looking individuals with an air of desperation, also dressed extravagantly, trying to reboot their relevancy with the younger set.

He had just passed the hotel's revolving door and was a few paces away from the building when the first jolt hit, rippling violently through the underground of the city. His knees buckled as he splayed out his arms to regain balance, and the pavement below him appeared to undulate. Alarms went off, echoing through the city canyons, off the smooth, flat surfaces. On the corner opposite his car, a geyser of water shot two stories high, flooding the street in the twenty-odd seconds it took him to steady himself before another rolling subterranean shock upset his balance again, as if he were on a yacht traversing choppy waters. Screens all around him glitched and went black, before coming on intermittently, showing snippets of A'rore. Screams joined the dispersed chorus of car and motorcycle alarms going off, and the cascade from the broken main kept coming down, the spreading flood lapping against his boots.

Part 2

1.
Rumor Economy

NORTON APPLIED THE BRAKES firmly as they breached the end of the tunnel, then accelerated again, expertly steering them through a turn and onto one of the main thoroughfares. Travers, sitting in the back with A'rore, was livestreaming their escape from a crew of motorcycle paparazzi that had followed them since they left a club in Piccadilly Circus. The S-Class's low-profile tires gripped the asphalt as Norton made precise adjustments to the car's trajectory, and Travers held on to the back passenger door handle with one hand and filmed A'rore with the other.

It had been a last-minute request, as her usual photographer had called in sick, and the night's experiential maneuver had already been locked in. Travers himself had coordinated it with account executives from Perez Hilton, *Hello!*, and TMZ, giving them a scoop that she'd be secretly meeting at an exclusive club with Ray Lee, a UFC welterweight champion. Earlier that night, Lee had dominated the main card of UFC 400, KOing his opponent in front of the Coliseum's boisterous spectators.

After photos leaked of A'rore and Lee conversing backstage, social media was buzzing with rumors of an affair—made all the more scandalous as his pregnant wife was in attendance at the fight. Chatter was peaking at the prospect of a new scandal involving the fighter and A'rore, who had a reputation as a serial home-wrecker.

It wasn't the first time Cedric had gone out in the field for a live campaign since beginning his new role as Eutopia's experiential director, but it was his first working on one of A'rore's popular paparazzi chases. Through the tinted rear window, he could see the single headlight of a paparazzi's motorcycle bearing down on them. A'rore, also livestreaming from a front-facing camera on her phone, was giving live commentary, while Cedric's POV would serve as B-roll for the live curators, intercutting the streams being displayed on the city's signs and on social networks across the world. He rolled down his window and held his phone out, capturing the chase in visceral fashion—his hand, trying to hold the phone steady, was buffeted by the wind and jostled by Norton's aggressive driving. Knowing the shaky footage he was grabbing would nicely complement A'rore's selfies, he held the phone there for another half minute, until another motorcycle appeared. As they continued their circuit around town, Travers glanced at the digital clock on the car's dashboard—approximately six more minutes until one of the paparazzi, a stuntman who had once worked with Norton, would veer off the road and jump his motorcycle into the canal in spectacular fashion. To reassure Cedric about Norton's driving skills before he agreed to join them on the chase, A'rore told him about Norton's past as a stunt driver on movies like *The Fast and the Furious*: "He's making a lot more money now than he ever did in Hollywood. And he still gets to do the thing he loves." Indeed, there was the faint trace of a smile on his face as he steered past cars and pedestrians, always inches away from impact, as calm and without regard for consequences as if he were playing a video game.

The night of their encounter, and her seduction in the Orangerie viewing room, she offered to make him the city's experiential director. "I don't ever forget," she said. "Especially people who've been there for me along the way." Their other encounter, fifteen years earlier, when she was an aspiring model and actress, and he was a young commercial director, hadn't seemed remarkable at the time, but it turned out to be an auspicious one for them both. She also missed Mila, his wife, she later confided, and hadn't been happy with Eddie, Mila's replacement. "It's unfortunate, really, what happened to him. I wouldn't wish it on my worst enemy. But Eddie was shady, what can I say. He got what was coming to him."

Her pillow talk amounted to a confessional, with sly implications about what went on in the city. Seeing her and Costello argue, only for him to turn up dead a week later, gave Cedric pause, but—and perhaps it was the MDMA affecting his judgment, as well as her charm—he found, despite himself, a desire for her approval after their first night together. Even the minor earthquake the night they met for the second time was barely felt from the heights of her penthouse, as they rolled in their psychedelic consummation, the signage around the city washing over in vermillion hues as her pulse raced with excitement. In the following days, as she used her influence to maneuver him into the director position left vacant by Costello, he tried to rationalize the move with his underlying need to find out what happened to his wife. Taking her old job, working from the inside, might be exactly what he needed to do. He'd come here with the intention of leaving with his wife's belongings and putting this entire episode behind him—their failed marriage, his flagging career—and moving on to something entirely different. He'd fantasized about the great American road trip, vast expanses across the I-10, hours upon hours of the dynamic American horizon, endless like the red rocks and cloudy skies of New Mexico. He'd come here a cynic, but A'rore, in her devious way, had enticed him into the inner realm. He was certain Mila, also part of that sanctum, had shared A'rore's bed, too. He'd no longer be a tourist. He'd be both a spy and a creator, if he played this correctly.

"With your director experience, you'll be perfect," she said. "You'll bring a much-needed, entertainment-driven perspective to the role." After getting approval, she herself extended the job offer, already anticipating he would take it. He couldn't resist— the craft of perception manipulation that extended outside of the digital realm, while spying from the inside. It was like the script to a movie he had always wanted to make.

She'd only hinted at the core mission of their experiences, in typically A'rorean fashion, enticing him with clues, perhaps to see how he would react. But it wasn't until he signed a sweeping NDA with the umbrella company—covering all material, conversations, and conduct, with a noncompliance penalty in the millions—that she started peeling back the onion layers.

"It's not about what people want," she said. "They lie to themselves all the time. Like the screensavers they have at work, depicting calm landscapes, tranquil beaches, idyllic meadows. That's what they say they want to their coworkers. That's their public face, their Facebook wall. The reality is, and the data shows it, they want excitement and danger. We're monkey voyeurs who'll pay good money to flirt with danger. No one sits for two hours, even in the best VR, just staring at a beach. They want SEAL team raids, porn, and car chases. Even if people did choose to watch the beach, they'd be expecting something to happen. Girls in thongs, boys in Speedos. A pervert or two leering in the background, tackled by a muscle-bound lifeguard. A few caipir-inhas to go along with it."

In his debriefing, he met with his core team members—young project managers and creatives who hailed from agencies on both coasts—as well as stuntmen who had worked with Norton. Most of them had worked with his wife, but none of them knew exactly what happened on the day of the Louvre. He looked at milestones documents for the weeks around her disappearance. In fact, everything listed on the commonly shared documents were more mainstream experiential events, like sponsored stunts by Ralph Lauren, livestreamed backstage access at concerts—nothing really remarkable, and everything he had assumed his wife was doing for the city. Then he was introduced to covert ops. This was the black book stuff he had to sign the NDA for.

"Not all of them, mind you, but some of the more publicized crime sprees around town, those are really controlled experiences," said one of his producers in a round-table discussion as they brainstormed new ideas. A man twenty years his junior, with old-school Americana tattoos on his neck, he'd been there for six months, and, like the rest of the small ops team, he was clearly excited about what they were doing—and being paid very well for it. "Tactically, it's a win-win for everyone. The Eutopian police give us latitude to carry these out, as long as they're given notice."

"Statistically we've seen lower crime rates correlated with regular, small doses of controlled crime," said the team's data scientist, a young woman, fresh out of grad school. "The people get their fix. Then there's copycats, but the police tolerate it because they're pulled out of the woodwork. Potential problem people are highlighted, tracked, and stopped before they can surprise us."

"The added value," the producer with neck tattoos said, "is that these experiences are genuinely exciting. They feel more real than your standard brand experiences. The increased web traffic is proof. Every time everybody profits."

—⚏—

HE STARTED OFF BURGLARIZING hotel rooms. Cedric had come up with the idea after learning how difficult it was to pull off a bag snatch. Even though a bag snatch made for good organic media—spontaneously shot footage from bystanders—logistically it was challenging due to countless variables when operating in the field, live on the streets. Cars, pedestrians, and good Samaritans could all foil an otherwise smooth operation.

After settling on an idea—they always planned a few weeks ahead of time—they identified the top influencers available based on the demographic they were prioritizing. In this case, they were going after women, eighteen to thirty-four, with high household incomes and an interest in luxury items—so they could tie the operation in with a Prada handbag promotion. His ad ops team plugged the targeting details into their social media dashboard—a master control center from which they could monitor all the major platforms and influencers in real time—along with the date range they were interested in. A list of influencers showed, in hierarchical order, the most to least influential based on total audience reach. Post interaction was another determining factor; if the influencers made posts that really engaged their followers, then the potential reach could be massive. They quickly identified three young women, ages twenty-five, twenty-seven, and twenty-eight, who matched their target demographic perfectly. Soon they'd be staying in the same hotel, the Soho Grand in London, making the logistics easier to pull off.

As a film director, he'd always been hands-on. Self-taught and from a rough neighborhood, he had made short movies with characters fictionalized from his real life. He'd always had to pull himself up by his bootstraps, and he'd applied the same mentality to his filmmaking. He learned the ins and outs of everything from screenwriting to gaffing, because he'd always assumed he'd have to do it all himself one day.

The burglary, code named Operation Night Crawler, took place exactly two weeks after they first ideated the campaign. After tracking the women on social media, following time stamps and locations on their posts, and corroborating with an insider on the hotel's security staff, two assistants and Cedric took the elevators of the Soho Grand to the twenty-second floor after the women had left their suite. Each donning baseball caps to hide their identity, one stayed behind near the elevators to act as a lookout, while Cedric and his other assistant went to the door, used a universal room card to access it, and slipped in the room, as furtively and smoothly as pros.

Steel and acrylic with wood paneling gave off a stately, modern, and English vibe, and the room, only inhabited for a day so far, had already been commandeered by the strewn-out contents of the women's large valises. They had just enough time to examine the layout when their assistant alerted them that their security contact had spotted the women reentering the hotel. They'd just left for the night—so perhaps they had forgotten something. Cedric's assistant, despite more time in covert ops, looked to Cedric for guidance since he was senior. Spotting a tablet computer on the desk near the media center, he told his assistant to snatch it. Meanwhile, Cedric rifled through the open valises, extracting lingerie. It was important to make the burglary intimate, with sexual overtones—that would resonate well over social media. After stuffing a negligee, several panties, and a bra into his hoodie's front pocket, he walked out of the room with his assistant, back toward the elevators where his other assistant was pacing back and forth, nervously looking at the screen of his smartphone. They summoned an elevator and got in, all three still wearing their baseball caps to obscure their faces from the overhead camera in the corner of the elevator.

"Good thing you came back when you did," he said. "Security told me they were just about to board the elevator. We're probably passing them on our way down."

Back at the war room—where they had a giant screen they used to monitor all network traffic—Cedric sat with his team of analysts and content curators. As expected, the women's posts about the break-in began getting traction within the hour. Pictures of their open valises with intimate garments—or what was left of them—hanging over the side, hashtagged #perv #eutopia #sohogrand, and live video feeds gave their audiences a chance to see the aftermath in a walk-through tour of the suite. The women started receiving thousands of comments and shares a minute. On the war room screen, they could see bursts of social activity, connections branching out from thousands of points. At the center of the screen were the three women's avatars.

"Demographic target is on point," his analyst said. "We're hitting over three million women right now in the US, between twenty-five and fifty-four." While intently monitoring the real-time chatter, they initiated phase two of the operation.

Coordinating with the Soho Grand management—who were in the dark about the covert ops his team had carried out— they managed to deliver the burglary victims three new luxury handbags Prada was trying to push, each outfitted with smart fabric technology. Synced to social media accounts, and using sentiment analysis, they changed colors based on whatever their users were posting. This, in addition to a generous apology from the hotel—their entire stay comped, an upgrade to a presidential suite, plus a voucher for a Gaultier lingerie boutique—was enough to send the women into another social media frenzy.

As he oversaw the media curation for the next twelve hours, marveling at the narrative he had envisioned coming to life, whose denouement felt fresh even though it had already been predicted, he recalled his conversation with A'rore in the Monet room.

Enhanced reality is what people had come to expect because, growing up, their cultural references had been Hollywood block-busters, where a realistic *pop* from a gun didn't have the same visceral impact as a *boom* augmented by sound engineers on Pro Tools. Like the advent of sound, then color, then CGI and AR, what he was doing now felt like the next logical step in the evolution of storytelling. By breaking the fourth wall, actually stepping into people's lives, making them participants in the story they were creating, they were pioneering the cinema of the twenty-first century. From the war room he conducted a symphony of messages and photos, broadcasting them via the city's signage, watching the feedback loop of commiserating followers edge ever closer to critical mass.

And then, a mere thirteen hours after the burglary story first went viral, the chatter sharply declined as the hive mind of the Internet shifted to the latest gossip involving Justin Bieber and an underage Sminx star. The city's billboards began cycling the latest A'rore selfies and designer drug ads again—a kind of electronic limbo until the next shot of mediatic adrenaline. They planned their campaigns strategically around traffic patterns and tentpole events, like holidays and big fights. In order to sustain traffic and ad revenue, they also had to be nimble and creative, ready to draft off of unforeseen trending topics.

"THEY'RE HAPPY WITH YOU," A'rore told him as they sipped a nootropic cocktail, micro-dosed with 1P-LSD, her silver eyes shining in the twilight as they looked over the city from a Red Light District rooftop. "I knew you'd be good, like your wife was."

He hadn't seen Monteiro since joining the team, but Cedric thought of him the day he moved into Mila's old apartment, and every time he ideated an experience for covert ops. With the success of the Soho burglary, he had begun to put his stamp on subsequent experiences. Vandalization, arson, A'rore's weekly paparazzi pursuits, all skirted the gray area between real and unreal, lawful and unlawful, and all seemed to have the desired effect of maintaining the status quo for the city. Whenever they had to coordinate with the police, especially the chases, which inevitably involved drones and patrol cars, he was the one that notified them an operation was underway. Those nights, when the denizens were stimulated, were always good for revenue, but they had catalytic effects on the more volatile elements of the population. Influencers on the verge of obscurity, desperate to make ripples on social media, might livestream their own robbery attempts, steal cars, or attack each other. Luring people with illicit temptations, the experiences they instigated brought the fringe elements out, allowing the police to purge the city of undesirables.

As he gazed upon the city from his wife's old apartment, feeling her presence more than ever since assuming her role and sharing a bed with her former lover, he thought through the operation he had planned for the next morning. A smash-and-grab burglary, it required precise timing and steady nerves, so he had run through the operation dozens of times with his team. In his head, he had gone over it many more times, anticipating all possible hurdles and how to overcome them. His wife had no doubt done the same thing when she was plotting experiences with A'rore and her collaborators.

This was the kind of real-world, hands-on creative work he never realized he wanted. Creating content for passive consumption behind a mobile screen or, with luck, via limited release in cinemas, felt so outdated, out of touch with the world he was living in. "Let's start the chatter" was a common refrain in their brainstorming sessions as they conceptualized experiences. The more people engaging, talking about the city, whether positively or negatively, the more people tuned into their geofenced revenue share streams.

He hit an L-theanine vape, feeling the calming effects wash over his body and neural networks. His colleagues, all very well paid and sworn to secrecy by the NDA, were motivated, he imagined, by the vanity of working for a cutting-edge company. Eutopia offered young, tech-worshipping transactionals a place to think as big as they wanted. Cedric, a decade older than them, sensed they all shared an idealistic streak—one he never knew he had. They thought they were part of a movement waking people up from a modern malaise.

He replayed the operation in his head again: *The dashboard interface shows them converging on the Apple store, right on time. He slides his balaclava down, lifts his phone, and gives the order to start operations.*

2.
Overnight

IKE A GLOWING ORB protruding from the black desert,
Eutopia appeared through Sacha's window. It seemed strange
at first—having woken up suddenly after only a couple
hours of sleep, the cabin still dark, the dropping feeling as the
plane descended—as if she were a space explorer, approaching
an alien life form composed of pure energy. The idea of Eutopia
never ceased to amaze her—the sheer audacity and ingenuity it
took to transform a tiny strip of Native American land into the
hyperconcentrated, bustling city it had become—and this was
her first descent into the city at night. The neon friezes, colossal
LED signage, billion-candlepower beams slicing through the
night sky, a galaxy of lights that consumed an estimated six
hundred megawatts of power per day—nearly half of Las Vegas,
and triple that of Disneyland.

Before boarding the red-eye flight to Eutopia, Sacha had
received a text message from Cedric Travers, with whom she had
been maintaining contact.

"I'll ping you tomorrow. We can meet wherever."

It had been a few weeks since she last saw him. She'd left Eutopia shortly after the minor earthquake rippled through the city, setting off car alarms and rupturing a few water mains. A magnitude 4.9, it wasn't the first that had hit the city. A year and a half earlier, similar seismic activity shook the city, and conspiracy theorists across social media blamed it on fracking at Eutopia's outskirts. In her notes, organized around central subjects, it had become one of many plotlines in her story on Eutopia. What had started out as a technology-driven story, with a focus on controversial construction methods, architecture, and ad-tech, had veered into something much more expansive, but she wasn't sure how it all came together. Her working method, for the moment, was to go by her intuition—to take it all in, without judgment, and make notes of the salient observations in her investigation. Whatever struck her as interesting or odd was filed away in her notes in the cloud.

Cedric had been one of those plotlines, but now he was becoming one of her central characters. They had exchanged messages since he'd become the city's experiential director, and he'd started teasing her with details from the inside.

"I'm not sure where it's taking me, but I'm getting closer to some kind of truth."

Similarly worded texts, hinting at extralegal activities and a personal mission—no doubt finding out what really happened to his wife—pinged her phone at all hours of the day.

"We need to talk. When are you back?"

"I think what I have is huge for your story."

Banking to the right, nosing forward toward the city, the plane passed through some low clouds and turbulence. The cabin lights went up, and the steward's voice came through the intercom, scratchy and monotone, a rote announcement he'd done hundreds of times before, perhaps even one or two times a day. "Ladies and gentlemen, we're beginning our descent. Please fasten your seatbelts and put your seats in the upright position."

Sacha's phone pinged again. An email this time, from her informants at Avion, one of the major shareholders in Eutopia. Praying for a steady Wi-Fi connection, she launched her mail app and, when trying to open the email, was greeted with a spinning wheel. After a couple more attempts, she rested the phone in her lap and closed her eyes, her mind drifting back to Cedric. She had the uncanny feeling he'd infiltrated some kind of cult, the same cult his wife had joined. The secrecy, the advocacy and enthusiasm, the shared sense of purpose—it was unmistakable.

Checking her phone again, Sacha was relieved to find the email from Avion had finished loading. Communicating over a secure, encrypted email service, the informant had reached out to her after seeing some of her columns and her byline, in which she mentioned she was working on a story on Eutopia. A system administrator, apparently, the informant didn't have access to the highest echelons of his company, but they had heard rumors around the water cooler regarding Eutopia. There appeared to be negative sentiment around the city's long-term profitability, which in itself wouldn't have been much of a news story for Sacha, but what interested her was the next thing the informant had to say. Upper management had apparently hired a corporate investigation firm to look into Eutopia. What exactly they were looking into, the informant wasn't sure. However, they had uncovered work orders showing a private investigator had come to Eutopia a few months ago, an operative by the name of Caspar Strand, whose undercover name was Fred Green. This happened to be the same Fred Green who was killed in the robbery in which Cedric Travers was involved.

All she got through the informant were work orders and a definite link between Avion and the private investigator, though no concrete evidence as to what exactly he was investigating. It was entirely possible they'd sent him in the wake of the firebombing at the Louvre, and the ensuing controversy, to see if their investment was at risk. But this email proved interesting. In it was a document, sent by Caspar Strand, aka Fred Green, to his firm, just days before he was killed. It contained a list of addresses in Eutopia, which appeared to be different small businesses she'd never heard of. She immediately thought of the dozens of the shell companies she knew had addresses in the city, using it as a tax haven—it was another one of her notecards, another storyline, another strata of the layer cake. She'd had fodder for plenty of shorter articles, but as things started coming together, she had to stave off the impulse to break the latest bits of news in the interest of the larger story.

The plane was descending now toward the runway, the strip of lights rapidly approaching, the Eiffel Tower, Fernsehturm, and the rest of the European mash-up boldly shining against the dark skies. She braced herself as the tires hit the pavement and the plane shuddered, the reverse thrust kicking in, bringing the aircraft to a rapid halt.

After gathering her belongings, consisting entirely of a carry-on with three to four days worth of clothes, a couple of SLR cameras, a tablet, and a laptop, Sacha wheeled herself to the taxi stand alongside the rest of the red-eye arrivals. Flying in from the East Coast, she was accompanied by fellow well-heeled Manhattanites heading to Eutopia for a few days of debauchery, as well as travelers from continental Europe and Russia—the ultrawealthy playboys who still had property there, whose own countries had now become no-go zones for tourists, whose service economies had nosedived, driving their countries into sectarian dissent. Another note for her story—the ironic image of Europeans coming from the old world to visit a replica of the old in the new. Concurrently, via Los Angeles, Koreans, Chinese, and Japanese were flying in to partake in their own mini-European vacation now that their governments had all issued travel warnings for Europe the fifth straight year in a row. It was ingenious of Sokolov to see the value of the European brand years before anyone else had, before the futility of a European tour—so popular with the jet-setting masses in the twentieth century—made only the idealized and augmented version a possibility.

When she stepped in her taxi and started the ride toward Eutopia, the first light of dawn, a dark violet gradient fading into magenta, began to appear. While the screen in front of her cycled through the usual advertisements for clubs and casinos, she swiped through the social media feeds on her phone. Suddenly the loop of advertisements stopped, interrupted by breaking news. CCTV footage showed a white delivery van ramming into a storefront, peeling back the protective metal fence. Drone footage showed what appeared to be an Apple store, with the tail end of the van sticking out of the entrance. Hooded individuals ran into the store while another, wearing a balaclava and speaking into a two-way radio, got out of the passenger's side of the van. The scrolling updates on the bottom of the screen read, "Live: Smash & Grab Break-ins Hit 3 Stores. #EutopiaSmash." She already knew she wasn't going to get any more sleep that day.

3.
Psychographic

NONE OF THE OLD television executives ever came right out and said, "We hope there's violence so that it drives the ratings." Much too on the nose, even for corporate America, given the inevitable negative publicity such a statement would have garnered. But Cedric knew they—like the board members, traffic directors, and data scientists he was working for—were after results. Their ambivalence to the methods was the same and equally obfuscated by language. He'd heard countless variations of the violence-equals-high-ratings argument in his virtual conferences.

"We know something is going to come along, and we know that it's going to drive traffic, and we have to act accordingly."

As he exhaled a Panadrine vape cloud—his brain felt like it had just been kicked into overdrive—he pressed a button on his phone and ordered the second phase of their smash-and-grab operation to commence. He'd just received an update from the traffic manager that everything was running smoothly—live feeds around the city had already been diverted to crime scene feeds, and they were pumping money into promoted streams across global social media networks, amassing a million-plus viewers in under ten minutes.

Via their closed mesh communication app, only accessible by his crew, he next ordered their largest vehicle to take the lead. The attention, having been diverted to the other smash-and-grabs that day, was focused elsewhere while the streets were clear around the Apple store. With the security forces distracted—and unaware for the most part that this was another covert op by his experiential crew—his team now had a small window of time to pull this off. Good direction, in his experience, never showed its hand. If for some reason the operation's authenticity were doubted, it would fizzle and die on the social networks. However, if pulled off correctly, and this looked like a job done by brazen criminals who had evaded Eutopia's forces, then it was a thing of beauty. Like a flawlessly delivered soliloquy, without a stutter, it suspended disbelief because the artifice was invisible.

From a getaway car, he delivered the next order. The delivery van, which they had stolen from a restaurant supply service on the outskirts of Eutopia, was lined up with its back facing the Apple store.

"Go!" he said, launching the next phase.

The delivery van driver smashed down the accelerator, and the van lurched backward with maximum torque for about three car lengths before ramming the front of the store. Large plate-glass windows gave way, shattering on impact, and the metal shutters inside caved in. Driving forward again, the van dragged debris out on the sidewalk, before stopping and spinning its tires until they gripped the pavement and sent the van careening once again into the store. This time it breached the shutters, which folded upward, allowing the van to squeeze in. He stayed seated in the getaway car while his crew rushed into the store, balaclavas pulled down, black hoodies on, hammers and crowbars in hand. His assistant held point by the opening, gripping his phone, watching for undercover cops or Good Samaritans stumbling into the scene. Cedric, meanwhile, watched the streets and kept a close eye on the elapsed time.

Their contacts inside the police department had let them know they'd have about three minutes tops to pull this off before the responders started arriving. During that time they'd have to loot whatever portable, high-value items they could find while the first drones arrived to start filming. Already, people were recording them from a safe distance at the end of the block. The city's health meters, triggered by store alarms and 911 calls, had already changed from blue to red on the surrounding building signage. Billboards, showing drone and bystander footage from the other smash-and-grabs—a pharmacy and a Rolex store— began scrolling news reports of the latest break-in at the Apple store.

They had one and a half minutes before they had to be out of the store and in their escape vehicles. Cedric's assistant, still planted outside, knelt down near the busted entrance and peered in, yelling out the remaining time to his crew. Past him, the occasional beam and starburst from a flashlight cut through the dark interior, as their crowbar- and hammer-wielding partners bashed in and emptied displays. His assistant looked back at him and gave a thumbs-up. With twenty seconds to go, and the signs just above the store starting to show drone footage of the break-in—a weird digital mirror in direct juxtaposition to the real thing—his assistant barked orders into the store. The people gathered at the street corner filming them knew it would be a matter of minutes before some of their own POVs would be picked up by the media curators and propagated across the networks, potentially netting them an easy few thousand dollars in ad revenue.

After Cedric ordered the assistant and the looters to commence the getaway, two piled in the back of the car while Cedric and the driver—one of the stuntmen Norton had brought in from Hollywood—stayed up front. His assistant and two other looters jumped on motorcycles and sped off down the semi-deserted early-morning streets, Cedric's getaway car following behind. While they raced through the canyons of screens, Cedric took another pull on his Panadrine vape to keep his neural synapses firing at their maximum potential. After he passed the vape to the backseat occupants, he flipped through the dashboard console screen until he got to the music interface. Linking it with his heart rate and sentiment monitor, the music player's algorithm chose a matching soundtrack—"Jesus Built My Hotrod" by Ministry—as intense as the vibrant vermillion signage they were speeding past. Under footage of the smash-and-grabs was a steady stream of comments and emojis.

After decompressing back at the war room, watching his latest event spread and morph across social media on the giant visual interface, he left the media curation in the hands of one of his managers. From his experience, the social media half-life of an event—even a novel one like this—was about eight to ten hours tops. After that, the hive mind focus shifted to the next celebrity scandal or violent spectacle elsewhere in the world. For the next few hours it was only a matter of pushing the posts that had resonated the most during the smash-and-grab.

Sacha had texted him earlier with the name of the hotel she was staying at, the Gaudi in Barcelona. Despite his need for sleep—it had been almost forty-eight hours with only two power naps and a half dozen hits of Panadrine—he hopped on his motorcycle and headed to meet her. He'd been exchanging messages with her for the last few weeks while she was out of town, hinting at the nature of the covert experiences he was directing. Pulled in three directions—passionate about the work he was doing, getting closer to the truth about his wife's disappearance, and wanting to reveal it all to Sacha for her story—he realized he could do everything at once if he was careful enough. He couldn't deny that knowing he was part of a bigger story, now that she was working on it, fed his ego. At his age—ancient by twenty-first-century standards with twenty-year-old billionaire CEOs and influencers commanding the world's attention—what else was he going to do? Nothing beat the excitement of realizing an idea and bringing a creation to life, and he'd never experienced anything as visceral as being a writer and filmmaker.

After parking his motorcycle, he sent Sacha a message while walking into the hotel's lobby. When no answer came, he took a seat against a far wall and took out his phone to see the latest traffic stats. Even though it had been a mere thirty minutes since he'd last checked them in the war room, a competing trending topic from halfway around the world could easily outrank the break-in by now. The comScore stats still showed tune-in to Eutopia at a healthy two million unique concurrent viewers globally. Swiping through the audience metrics showed traffic driving to Eutopia's main channel as well as repeats of live broadcasts from tourists from all over—China, Brazil, Norway, and the UAE. Behavioral and demographic data showed they were reaching their intended target of post-millennials with medium to high household incomes and affinities toward luxury goods, clubbing, and gaming. Conversion rates appeared to be strong as well, showing the strongest performance in the pharmaceutical vector, where Panadrine was the top seller.

Sacha still hadn't answered his message, and he scanned the lobby to see if she had decided to come down to meet him instead. Two lines had formed in front of the reception area, one for checking in, another for checking out, the former comprised of guests eager with anticipation, the latter comprised of haggard guests who'd spent all their social currency. In the sitting area of the lobby itself people were, like him, immersed in their tech, either on their phones, tablets, or watches. One girl was recording a POV video from her Snap spectacles, scanning the lobby of the Gaudi, with its kitsch modernista flourishes, wavy reception counters, organic motifs adorning columns, colorful swirls of broken tiles forming a floral mosaic on the floor. With no sign of Sacha, he pulled up his remote interface again to review the content generated from his smash-and-grab experience.

While the data scientists were in love with the peaks, valleys, and correlation factors of the data points rolling in, Cedric was still a slave to aesthetics. Swiping to a gallery of videos from the smash-and-grabs, he played some of the top-engaging clips. Invariably, it was the user-generated content that performed the best—handheld, imperfectly shot, intimate, first-person, and spontaneous. In terms of experiences, that's exactly what he was aiming to generate. When all was said and done, the story this would become had to feel like an authentic experience that millions of other users could relate to. The spectacle of the violent break-ins and the brand-name recognition they were able to draft off of made his operation synergistically perfect.

They rooted their social craft in the user habits of their target audience—post-millennials, aka transactionals. Using curated content, hashtags, and top influencers, they were able to generate what he called "concentric circles of buzz."

"It's about cutting through the clutter," one of his media strategists said during the kickoff call for the campaign. The curated component—compiling top posts and ordering them into a narrative—were posted during high-traffic times, in the morning, at lunch, and late at night, when people were most active, stalking people they were interested in across social media. Then they'd include a mix of thirty to forty hashtags related to Eutopia, brand names, and a slew of trending topics related to drugs, fashion, and clubbing.

It was a win-win for art and commerce.

He'd been timing the experiences, whether a carjacking stunt or a paparazzi chase, to take place during the cinematic magic hours of dawn or dusk. It seemed, though he was no data scientist, that it was a hit with the viewers, who were maintaining steady tune-in rates to Eutopia. However, he felt he could do one better. What if he could commandeer the iodide cannons before the next experience and make it rain, covering the streets with a photogenic, glossy sheen? Lights from the screen facades, cars, and explosions—if he could pull that off safely—would be augmented by the reflections.

The girl with the Snap spectacles started walking toward the front of the line where her boyfriend had been waiting, wheeling her carry-on luggage. First-person footage like she had been shooting, like the top-performing clips from his smash-and-grab experience, got the most attention. It immersed you like nothing else, whereas first-person films, like *Hardcore Henry*, always felt contrived. The tricky thing about all this, compared to his other directing gigs, was that he was playing with the conceit that everything unfolded organically. He didn't get to edit his scenes, choose from multiple takes; rather he steered his crowd-sourced cinematographers in the right direction.

He received a message from Sacha saying she'd "be right there."

He switched to another screen showing the top-performing user channels in Eutopia and started randomly clicking on some of the minor influencer profiles—users without the massive reach of A'rore, but who, when summed together, became impactful. He landed on a channel that was currently off the air, but by scanning through the channel's past broadcasts, he could see the user had been a witness to the smash-and-grab that morning. Scanning further back, there were a lot of bedroom scenes, featuring the same young, thin blonde. Probably a L-Uber user from the looks of it, broadcasting her exploits for added income. The strange thing, he noticed, was that she had unusually low engagement on her posts for the amount of followers she had. Proportionally way less than average. It wasn't the first time he'd seen something that felt off to him, but since he wasn't entrusted with the data analytics, nor was he by any means qualified to do so, he had decided to let the experts do their thing.

He clicked on some of the profiles of the people sharing the L-Uber user's content, and invariably they were generic in feel, with default or common avatars. While scrolling through the thousands-long list, he paused, then scrolled back up until he saw the same avatar of the blonde L-Uber girl. Inside the profile he saw the same content; the only thing different was her user name. Perhaps it was glitch? He'd had a long few days without sleep and didn't have the sharpest cognitive skills, even with the hits of Panadrine he'd been using to stave off the decline.

"Sorry to keep you waiting," Sacha said, who had suddenly appeared before him while he was still immersed in audience profiles on his tablet. "I was in the gym when I got your message." Wearing yoga pants and a tank top with a hand towel draped over her shoulders, she had flushed cheeks, her forehead damp.

"No worries," Cedric said while getting up, extending his hand. "I'm getting some work done anyway."

Sacha looked around the lobby and said, "Why don't we go up to my room? It's a little too busy down here."

Cedric followed her lead, past the lobby and the gym facilities, toward the elevators. "Look," Cedric said, as they rode up to her floor. "I might as well come right out and say it. Since I've taken on my wife's old role, I've been doing a lot of things you'd expect me to do as an experiential director. The usual branded stunts—like the nude base-jumping Red Bull experience last week, that was me of course." The elevator doors opened, and Sacha led the way down the hall.

"Yeah, I've seen those, but I was intrigued by your messages. Those don't sound like the kind of thing you were hinting at."

As she opened the door, stepping inside her room, he continued, "Well, there's that, and then there's the part we had to sign the NDA for."

"Go ahead, take a seat wherever," she said, pointing just past her bed where a coffee table and two-seater sofa were arranged. Walking to the minibar, she pulled out two water bottles, offering one to Cedric. As they both sipped, she said, "So what's this part you're talking about, if you don't mind me asking?"

"You just got here, right?"

"Yeah, about three hours ago."

"On the way in you saw the breaking news, right?"

"The smash-and-grab at the Apple store? How could I not? It was in my taxi, it was on all the screens."

Cedric stayed silent, though his eyes betrayed a smile.

"*Really*. That's . . . interesting," she said. "That's what you've been talking about the whole time?"

"You see why we have this NDA? It extends way beyond working in Eutopia. It could affect the rest of our personal lives. This whole city, on Native American land, is extrajudicial. It's built on loopholes."

"Even that, what you're doing, it's . . ."

"Gray area. Part of our covert ops, our undercover experiences. The paparazzi chases . . ."

"I figured a lot of those were staged anyway."

"At this point they're so regular I can see why. Hotel room break-ins, carjackings, bag snatchings, even that attempted rape that was filmed two weeks ago."

"That is beyond gray area, Cedric."

"No one's hurt, ever, we use stuntmen, and the victims are well taken care of."

Sacha took another sip of her bottle and sat down on a chair facing the sofa. "You're right about this being a scoop for me. But what, may I ask, is the point?"

"Nothing drives traffic like real, organic violence. We first saw it when spontaneous street fights were filmed, when some of A'rore's first, non-staged paparazzi chases were broadcast. People are wild for it."

"Was the Louvre . . . Was Mila also in a covert op?"

"I'm positive she was. But I don't think she knew it was going to turn out the way it did, and that's why she ran," he said, remembering how Sacha had implied some of the early leaks she received might have come from Mila. "I don't have anything else. You could say I'm investigating from the inside."

"Your smash-and-grab looked pretty spectacular, if I may say so."

"It went well. I'm happy with my crew. Ultimately, what counts is if the shareholders are happy. We're facing stiff competition from competing networks."

"Yeah, I'm aware of that. Even copycat cities following the same model in China and Korea."

"And A'rore is starting to lose her audience share to other influencers."

"In Internet years, she's an old maid."

"There's always someone newer, younger, and hotter. To top it off, word is Sokolov is putting a lot of pressure on upper management. She says there's not enough positive growth and that we need big ideas. She wants us to come up with something new."

LEAVING HER ROOM, HE walked past a man with short-cropped hair sitting in a chair near the elevators, fiddling with his phone. As the elevator door closed, he kept his eye on the man— mid-thirties, wearing a hoodie and jeans, nonremarkable—who didn't shift his attention from his phone. Maybe it was Cedric's sleep deprivation again, but something about the man didn't look right. And what was he doing on Sacha's floor? Memories shuffled to the forefront of his mind, of the Louvre footage he'd seen and the assailants in the garage. Those nondescript, generic tough guys—but he could also be one of dozens, if not hundreds, of guys walking around the city right now with similar dress and hairstyle. As the elevators opened on the ground floor, he hesitated, about to go back up to confront the man, then thought better of it and walked out to the lobby.

He needed sleep, that much was clear. Since moving into his wife's apartment and taking on her former role, he'd been sucked into a lifestyle of all peaks and no valleys. Even though Panadrine touted almost unlimited potential to work like the world's top CEOs—at least that was advertisements said—he didn't feel 100 percent. Hyperalert, yes, due to the intensity of the experience he had directed earlier that morning, but on a downward spiral, brought on by the cathartic conversation he'd just had with Sacha. Talking freely about the secret ops had also made him reflect inwardly. In the lobby, just past the gym and spa area, was a gift shop selling gadgets, souvenirs, and drugs. He walked in and approached the drug section, and while he was reading the label of a sleep aid, supposedly the antidote to Panadrine, he saw the hoodie guy walk out of the elevators, toward the street.

After making a quick purchase, he ran after the man, past the rotating doors, into the late-morning sun. Cedric followed him for half a block, his mind making wild, seemingly disparate connections. It couldn't be a mere coincidence that he was on Sacha's floor while he was with her, and now he was on the street just moments after Cedric had left. He hadn't had any issues with Monteiro since he started working for the city—in fact, he hadn't even talked to him except indirectly, when he was planning his covert operations—so he couldn't understand why anyone would be following him. He might be working with Sacha—to what ends he could only imagine.

Sensing someone behind him, the man looked back in Cedric's direction, briefly locked eyes with him, and quickened his gait, walking past a group of tourists taking selfies with a Kanye West impersonator. Cedric cut through the group, and the man looked back again, eyes widening in surprise. He turned around and almost ran to the end of the block, where a patrol car was parked, and approached the policemen. Gesticulating, he spoke breathlessly to one of the officers, pointing back at Cedric, who had slowed down his pace.

As he tried to anticipate his conversation with the officer—a confrontation seemed inevitable now—he suddenly became self-conscious of his outfit. Still dressed in casual clothes—a dark-gray track suit and sneakers he'd worn for the morning's smash-and-grab—with his unkempt appearance he'd likely be considered suspicious.

"Travers!"

The voice came from his right side. Looking in that direction, he saw an unmarked Charger. Inside it, he saw a man waving him over. It was Monteiro.

"Go ahead, get in. You look like you need a lift."

Cedric got in and buckled up while Monteiro placed an energy drink can in the cup holder. As they began driving off, Monteiro said, "What are you doing?"

"What do you mean?"

"You know what I mean, back there at the Gaudi."

"Just meeting a friend, that's all."

Monteiro cast a side glance at Cedric while he gripped the Charger's steering wheel and took a turn.

"You know, I know all about you, bro."

"I can imagine."

"You're in a privileged position now thanks to A'rore. You must have really impressed her."

"I can't complain. I'm doing good work," Cedric said. After a pause, he continued, "You weren't having me tailed, were you?"

"Look Travers, since coming here you've quickly become involved in the city. You dove right in, and I get that, with your wife's disappearance and all. Of course you're interested in finding out more. But you have to understand. I maintain an equilibrium here, and when something upsets that, I have to look into it. You know how that works, right? You know, Travers, we tolerate your team because it helps maintain the equilibrium." There was that undertone of menace in his voice again, as if he were modulating it to keep it from converting into a growl.

"Yeah, I do get that. Plausible deniability."

4.
On a Plain

RAMING HER POV SHOT took three attempts to get just right. First her legs, from her upper thighs to her toes, which clearly showed bright red marks left by the vibro-vacuum therapy she'd just subjected herself to. Then another, revealing a bit more skin, from just below her belly button, showing her bikini bottom, thighs and legs tapering down to her toes. This time she pulled her left foot back, knee pointing upward, her body slightly twisted, in order to highlight some of the work she'd been doing on her glutes. Her last shot revealed her cleavage, accentuated by a skimpy triangle-and-string bikini top. The sensorial lighting—warm gradations of red—and moire curtains surrounding her alpha cradle added intriguing elements to her shot, which the cleavage angle was able to highlight better. Opting for the third shot, she started populating the hashtags: #alphaspa #lux #lovemylife #vibrocup, and a copy-pasted paragraph of trending hashtags related to beauty, wellness, and fashion. The last shot, in her experience, would probably engage the best, since it showed more skin, teased her cleavage, and showed marks from her vibro-vacuum session, which were sure to generate conversation.

"I'm saving this for later," A'rore said to Sacha, who was in an adjacent cradle. "If I post it now, within twenty minutes I'll probably have some creepers up here looking for me."

A'rore had already been at the AlphaSpa, on the top floor of Bauhaus Hotel in Berlin, for a few hours by the time Sacha arrived. She'd sent a message earlier that morning while Sacha was with Cedric, saying she needed to see her urgently, without further explanation. By the time Sacha had finished talking to Cedric and managed her emails, she'd already missed the opportunity to spend the whole day with A'rore at the spa.

"It's all comped," she said, "in exchange for a post on my social channels."

A'rore had just finished AlphaSpa's signature "Vibro-Vacuum Experience," which was an updated version of ancient Chinese cupping techniques, using an AI-optimized, autonomous machine with eighty vibrating vacuum cups to "lift toxins out of subdermal regions" in order to kick-start the body's cleansing and detoxification process. "This is what all the stars in Hong Kong are doing. Three thousand a pop. Too bad you didn't come here earlier. I'd have hooked you up with the full pampering treatment. The massage boy is excellent . . . and has the most *vivifying* clitoral stimulation technique ever."

Now in the Alpha Room—a "sensorial experience chamber" as described by the spa technician who showed them in—A'rore and Sacha were in adjacent cradles, constructed with ergonomically designed acrylics and nanofabrics. Each cradle, levitating above the ground via opposing electromagnets, was held in place over the magnetic field by built-in stabilization units. The floating sensation, coupled with a soft white glow emitted by the cradle—pulsing in sync with the occupants' heart rates—allowed them to "detach" and enter an alpha state, a Zen-like place between sleep and consciousness. The LED dome overhead, synced via a kinetic tracker, showed fractal imagery that mirrored their slightest moves and the steady, droning acoustic accompaniment of binaural beats.

"It's a multisensory experience. Spatial, chromatic, aural, tactile, and olfactory," he said while A'rore and Sacha got comfortable in their cradles and engaged the levitators. A'rore, busy on her phone, already knew what she wanted but allowed him to walk through his spiel for Sacha, before telling him to put it put on the AlphaRed state. With overhead fractals in warm, red gradients—chromotherapy meant to energize and revitalize and mimic the womb—the chamber also had infrared ambient lighting, which penetrated their skin, warming their core body temperatures. The last touch was an ultrasonic diffuser that filled the room with a bespoke cocktail of essential oils.

"Nigella sativa, for its thermogenic and anti-inflammatory properties, champaca for its stress-relieving and aphrodisiac properties—it's also a holy fragrance—and essence of opium for its analgesic benefits," the technician said. "It's a twist on a formula derived by Indian scent expert Raj Kumar." As he launched the program on the machine, he said, "Enjoy," and softly padded out of the chamber.

"I can see what you'll write now, in some obscure article with a few thousand shares. 'After her meteoric rise, she hit a plateau and never recovered . . .'" A'rore said as a subtle citrus floral scent wafted over them.

Sacha, who had come to meet her on short notice mainly because she believed A'rore might have a scoop for her, quickly decided to avoid ingratiating. It would be easy to tell her she still had millions of followers, that she had nothing to worry about, but she knew in the rapidly pivoting world of social media that A'rore was already old news. "What," she said, "do you think it is?"

A'rore, after absentmindedly thumbing through her feeds, turned off her phone and rested it on her tummy. Inhaling the diffused scents, her nostrils flaring, she meditated on the answer and chuckled to herself. "You know, there's girls with the same haircut now, wearing fake prosthetics. Talk about ironic. I've become normal, average. I don't stand out."

"You're still the trendsetter. Do something else."

"They're younger," she said, running her hand along her abdomen, along her thighs, then tapping on her prosthesis, which was in sleep mode, a black mirror sculpture of her lower leg. "They're firmer, even hotter."

The rhythmic fractal lighting patterns above were still perceptible to Sacha as she lay with her eyes closed, breathing in the scents rolling over them. Her skin, exposed as she lay in only her panties in the levitating cradle, was warmed by the infrared lighting and the climate-controlled air in the chamber. Her mouth opened partially as she was about to speak, but she stopped herself. There was something therapeutic about this for A'rore, using her as a sounding board, confessing her deepest, most embarrassing fears. She could be recording this right now for a quick piece of gossip news, enough for millions of page hits and thousands in ad revenue. Instead she lay still, commiserating with A'rore, entranced by the chromatics, while strangely both enervated and relaxed by the olfactory concoction being emitted from the ultrasonic machine.

"What am I going to do? I'm as augmented as you could possibly be without becoming a plastic surgery sideshow on TMZ. This is prime grade-A beef, still," she said, cupping her glutes. "Does my age show?"

"Honestly? You don't look like a teen or college freshman anymore, but your age is indeterminate. Maybe late twenties, early thirties."

"Too old. On the tail end of the prime eighteen-to-thirty-four demographic. You're right, I have to do something else. I have to pivot."

The synchronized fractals and binaural beats coming out of

hidden speakers began to have an effect on Sacha, although she wasn't sure if it was the hypnotizing combination of light and sound or the ingredients in the aroma clouds. A'rore, for her part, sighed before continuing her confessional. As she was already perked up by Panadrine, the sense chamber did little to alter her state.

"My makeup line was a thing for a while, but that was only some rebranded white-label stuff. Just putting my face and name on it sold it. I can't fall back on that."

"Is there anything, in retrospect, you would have done differently?"

"No, I can't say so. I've had—I still have—more power and influence than most girls from obscure lower-middle-class backgrounds ever get. Right now I need a plan B."

Sacha, recalling the conversation she'd just had with Cedric about how Eutopian traffic was steady but losing market share to newer multichannel networks, said, "People are still highly engaged in everything you do, from your appearances to your run-ins with paparazzi."

"Yeah, maybe I need to step it up. There's a couple bitches in Dubai and Japan who are totally biting my style. Even down to the live paparazzi chases." A'rore paused, inhaling deeply, as if she were trying to slow her mind and her pulse. "You know," she said, "there's a guy I'm working with. Actually, kind of a scoop for you here. The new experiential director here is this Hollywood guy, Cedric Travers. Maybe you've heard about him. He used to be hot shit until about four years ago."

"He rings a bell."

"He's really good."

"Wait, isn't he, wasn't he, married to Mila Webb, the old experiential director?" Sacha said, feigning ignorance, trying pump A'rore for more information.

"I think you're right," A'rore said before taking a long pause. "I need to find a way to do things differently."

As A'rore's stream-of-consciousness talk went on, Sacha listened, chiming in every minute or so, like a gust of wind billowing the sails of a boat, propelling it further into the uncharted waters of her mind. Her obsession with youth and social media presence were brought out in stark relief; her fears and insecurities rolling off her tongue as easily as the vapor clouds misting over them.

"I'm so sorry," the technician said, who had just reentered the chamber, "but we have some fans of yours who have arrived at the reception desk. We don't know how this happened."

A'rore let out an exasperated gasp and said, "I didn't even get to do my bee venom mask."

"This is just unacceptable, I'm sorry," he said as he shut off the levitators, bringing their cradles back to their grounded positions. "We can turn them away, but more might be arriving."

"Please do. Clear the way for us to take the VIP elevator."

After the technician turned off the sense program and the diffuser, and as he exited the chamber, A'rore said to Sacha, "Some lackey must have posted somewhere about my being here. So much for rest and relaxation." They each put on their robes and slippers and made their way to the antechamber, where they had their clothes waiting for them.

While they dressed, A'rore said, "We didn't get to talk much, did we? Look, why don't you come by my place next time?"

"I'd love that," Sacha said, again feeling the pull of her charisma, drawing her into her machinations. As a writer who immersed herself in whatever she was working on, she'd already decided to let herself go.

In the elevator on their way down from the spa, they were accompanied by A'rore's driver, who had come up to fetch them. As he stood near the door, A'rore and Sacha stood on either side of the elevator, each checking the latest updates on their phones.

"You know," A'rore said, without looking up from her screen, "it's a good thing you have a semi-high profile."

"Why is that?"

"You're persona non grata here. They don't like snooping. Which company or entity does?"

"I watch my back."

"Oh, you're definitely being followed," A'rore said, laughing under her breath. "They're tolerating you, for now, because, you know. Publicity, me . . ."

"A good reason, I suppose, to finish this piece as soon as possible."

"There, just posted it," A'rore said, after uploading the picture she had taken earlier in the AlphaRoom.

5.
Tradecraft

"**S**HE'S JUST LEFT THE Louvre, again," his operative said. "She's getting a taxi."

"Tail her and send me details when she gets to her next destination."

Monteiro's operatives had been following Sacha Villanova ever since she arrived in town, logging a few meetings with A'rore and Travers, and regular daily routines like going to the gym and working from cafés. She hadn't gone back to the burned-out remains of the Louvre since her first visit, and he wondered what the interest was now. In disrepair since the failed heist, the Louvre had remained conspicuously ruined since then—a boarded-up husk in the middle of the city, like a blemish on an otherwise healthy body. He'd asked about it, curious as to why nothing was being done to resurrect the museum in the half year since it was attacked, but his inquiries fell on deaf ears. It seemed to him they were postponing the reconstruction, and he wondered if it was a sign they were having trouble with funding. Now, Sacha was snooping in it again. He made a mental note to go back the Louvre and attempt to retrace her steps.

When the text came from his operative—an address in Rome, next to the Maserati Lifestyle Lounge—he got in his cruiser and headed for the city. As the oncoming lights of the monuments and billboards loomed larger, he voice-activated the car's autopilot and began swiping through files on his tablet. Something about the particular address his operative was sending him seemed familiar.

"Destination is one hundred meters ahead," his autopilot said.

Monteiro grabbed the wheel, retaking control of the car. Driving past the Maserati Lounge—a luxury grooming and apparel outlet—he found his operative parked just a few dozen feet beyond it. He parked behind his operative's car and approached the passenger's side window. Hearing the click of the lock disengaging, he opened it and sat in the passenger's seat.

"She slipped into the service entrance, just next to the showroom," said his op, a man about half Monteiro's age, dressed in nondescript civilian clothes.

Monteiro looked through the rearview mirror and saw the entrance, painted to blend in with the Maserati mural that covered the side of the building.

"How long has she been in there?"

"Just a few minutes."

"This place, it reminds me of something," Monteiro said, pulling out his phone. "Wasn't it one of those places that Strand was visiting?"

"The spy that was with Travers?"

"Yeah, he went by Fred Green."

Pulling up his dossier, he cross-referenced his notes with the address. Sure enough, the building in Rome next to the Maserati Lounge was one of the places Strand had visited. The Louvre was there too, as well as half a dozen others. While he was in town,

Strand made it a point to visit gaming rooms, keeping up a public profile as a veteran gambler. When he wasn't in gaming rooms, he was talking to seemingly random people—off-duty croupiers in bars, influencers, hotel employees, strippers—but following up with them didn't reveal any clues as to what he was up to.

"Yep," Monteiro said. "He was here."

"I could never figure that out," the operative said. "I remember whoever we talked to said he seemed harmless and just made small talk. What was he planning?"

Monteiro's nostrils flared, and he resisted speaking. It was strange indeed. The order had come from above to follow him, that he was a threat. What he did know was the brief they'd gotten on him described him as a contracted spy and saboteur, and very possibly he was doing field work for a larger operation.

"Don't know, but it's unfortunate he died," Monteiro said. They'd gone too far in their intimidation ruse, which had been designed to look like a common mugging during the crime wave that night.

"He had a heart problem. We couldn't have known."

"Yeah," Monteiro said, eyes still fixed on the rearview mirror for the first sign of Sacha. He'd been working so many evening shifts in the last few months, he felt his mind was losing its edge. Why couldn't he piece the puzzle together? This case was nagging him. The New York reporter, the Hollywood director, the corporate spy, and the biggest influencer in the city. While his operative next to him took a drag on a cigarette and exhaled out the window, he stayed silent, momentarily lost in thought until he saw the service door open.

"There," he said. "That's her."

Sacha walked out of the service entrance. She was on her phone. Looking around, checking up and down the street, she exhibited the behavior of someone who suspected she was being followed. After a brief conversation, she started tapping and swiping on her phone screen, then walked over to the Maserati

Lounge vitrine and started window shopping, periodically looking at her phone.

"She's waiting for a cab, I'll bet," Monteiro said. "When it comes, tail them. I'm going to stay behind."

Minutes later, she turned around and approached the street, where she was met by a cab, and as she stepped in, Monteiro got out of his operative's car and walked toward the service entrance, thumbing his phone. When both cars were out of sight, he opened the door and entered.

Leading to a back entrance into the lounge next door, the hallway lit up automatically when motion sensors detected him. Bare concrete masonry, slick cement floors, and exposed pipes ran the length of the wall. This was where garbage was wheeled out and bulk items from vendors were wheeled in. Nothing remarkable as far as he could see, and he walked down the hall toward the end. Low-end oscillations from the music in the lounge bled through the walls—dull, thudding beats waiting for him to open a door and release their full sound spectrum.

When he got to the end of the hall, about to open the door, he paused and walked back a few steps. A crack in the middle of the wall running in a rough horizontal line had caught his eye, and as he followed it back, he saw it stair-step up, following breaks in masonry for a few feet, underneath some exposed copper tubing, until it closed back up again near the ceiling. On closer inspection it looked like the tubing, housing electrical cables, had been replaced recently. It was newer than other sections; even the screws fixing it in place looked like they'd recently been drilled. He followed the stair-step crack back down toward the entrance to the lounge, where it closed again after running a few feet horizontally, just inches from the ground. The steady, rhythmic bass hits resonating through the foundation suddenly made him feel vulnerable, trapped, like a rat in the hull of a sinking ship. Pulling out his phone, he took a picture of the crack, as he was sure Sacha had done, and knew before entering the hedonistic swelter of the lounge that he'd already gathered what he needed.

6.
Extreme Mainstream

AN EMERGENCY SHAREHOLDER MEETING had just been convened when the news came. Four arrests had been made in connection with a gang rape that had taken place a few days earlier. After the smash-and-grab news cycle, there had been a period of relative calm that was making everyone nervous—himself, the crew, and the rest of the city, as if their ration of violence, delivered in easily digestible snippets of video, had not been met, a palliative to cure their boredom.

They still conducted their regular car chases, bag snatches, and burglaries, which served to bump up traffic in short bursts, but nothing sensational was happening. Even a groping event, which Cedric had staged with A'rore, had failed to dominate the trending topics for more than four hours. Wearing a LaQuan Smith nude mesh two-piece—part of a retro line the brand was trying to push—A'rore was in public, going to get pizza, when a minor influencer snuck past her bodyguards and successfully kissed her rear end before getting tackled and detained. The biggest controversy around the event was the rumor that the groping was suspiciously similar to something that had happened a decade earlier to Kim Kardashian West. Although LaQuan Smith's dress and brand received millions of impressions across social media, the experience was considered a failure. The online sentiment was that the groping was fake—hashtag #gropegate— and that A'rore was desperate for attention.

Then the gang rape happened, in the underground parking of the Rembrandt Hotel. Filmed by one of the perpetrators as well as eyewitnesses, who stayed locked in their cars, the assault had been viewed hundreds of millions of times, surpassing even his smash-and-grab experience. Four Saudi nationals had lured a L-Uber user into a tryst in the underground car park, then when she resisted one of the men's rough behavior, she was brutally assaulted. Live videos from the event went viral in a matter of minutes, with a global audience expressing dismay in the comment feeds. Streams of anti-Muslim rhetoric and negative sentiment about Eutopia flooded shares of the posts, and Eutopia's traffic peaked for a solid twelve hours before plateauing again when a rival network started broadcasting an NFL playoff game with player POVs in VR.

While riding his motorcycle to the meeting, Cedric called his lead data scientist for a quick analysis. He'd need something in his back pocket in case the shareholders asked. "What do you think happened? I mean, how did it gain more traction than the smash-and-grab operation?"

"It's one of those intangibles, I think. Maybe it just felt *more* authentic."

Joining them in a conference room at the top of the Brandenburg, with a view overlooking Unter den Linden and the Fernsehturm, were a handful of visiting shareholders, Cedric's assistant, and some marketing executives. Calling in virtually was Sokolov herself, more shareholders, and Alexandra Kim, the chief creative technologist of Lab Networks. As the window tinting activated and the wall screen at the end of the horseshoe table grew brighter, showing the live video feeds of each of the participants, Cedric swiped to Alexandra's work profile on his phone. Before Lab Networks she had been in half a dozen other companies, one of them the agency his wife worked for when she helped pitch the idea of Eutopia. She was his wife's former boss, in essence his boss now. In a way, things had come full circle.

"We hit our stride three years ago," Sokolov said, her avatar now dominating the top two-thirds of the screen. Unlike the rest of the rest of the attendees, she had a gray default icon instead of a live video feed. Her voice clear, forceful, and unmeditative, it sounded like she knew what she was going to say two or three sentences before her actual delivery. "Bringing A'rore in was a game changer, and we showed the world how to monetize a geographic hub in a decentralized virtual reality. Alexandra Kim, who is joining us, was instrumental in stewarding this project. But in no time the rest of the world caught up, and now there are dozens of copycats in Macau, Mumbai, Sydney—even Vegas, in our own backyard, has retrofitted and developed its own proprietary geofencing technology. Attracting quality influencers with revenue streams is increasingly difficult, and our numbers have been flatlining, despite the work of our data scientists, developers, and experiential teams."

The screen switched to a graphic with multicolored lines, and Sokolov continued. "Normally, I'd paint a rosy picture, and I could, because Eutopia is still, overall, the leading multichannel, but if we don't act now, things are going to change."

Eutopia's line, represented by teal blue, converged with the rest of the lines at about three-quarters of the screen to the right, with a vertical line drawn over the crossing point, indicating it was a projected time in the near future. The teal line stayed flat after that, while the rest of the cities trended upward. "The question is," she said, "what do we do about it?"

One of the shareholders sitting opposite to Cedric—a young, hoodie-wearing man probably no older than twenty-five—began speaking, their conference room video feed simultaneously appearing in the chat room for the rest of the participants. "What is the plateau due to?"

"It could be the novelty or uniqueness of Eutopia has been nullified by the copycats," Alexandra said over the conference feed. "But all our brand studies show Eutopian social coin is still considered premium. Maybe we're looking at the psychographic data incorrectly. Maybe the organic excitement is dwindling on social media because what's happening in Eutopia is becoming passé. If you look at the Chinese, their new geofenced cities are showing upticks in broadcasts from their users. Their content is a little different—as you know, things like prostitution are still illegal there—but they have their share of spectacles. Car chases, honor beatings. We're just not cutting through the clutter anymore."

Another shareholder said remotely, "What do our data scientists say? Can someone chime in?"

"The data shows," Cedric's data scientist said, sitting next to him in the Brandenburg conference room, "that our audience, in line with the mission briefing, comprises eighteen-to-thirty-four-year-olds, about an even male-female skew, full range of income levels, skewing slightly higher than average. They show strong affinities toward entertainment channels involving gossip and gadgets, as well as personality-driven channels like A'rore's."

"So," Sokolov said, her sound waves visualized, rippling across the screen, "it's pretty clear we need something to differentiate and drive up viewership. Something personal, like our analyst said, that will grip the audience."

"That's a great point," Alexandra said. "Personal, but also hitting each of our targets. Entertainment-minded youth, preferably a hundred-k-plus income levels to drive higher ad premiums and purchase value."

"Who's taking minutes here?" one of the marketing directors on the conference feed said. "This is our big-ideas session."

Cedric spoke up, offering his assistant, as ideas bubbled up from the group.

"How about a brand tie-in with Tesla and A'rore on her next chase?"

"How will that move the needle? Aren't her numbers stagnant?"

"We could eventize the next UFC fight here by allowing global audience voting."

"They did that in China already."

"We could create a custom branded motion emoji pack that can only be unlocked in Eutopia."

"Don't we have something like that already?"

"We have custom filters people can add to their selfies and video feeds."

"That's totally different."

"I got something. Meme-generating lure modules. They interact with localized VR lures, incentivized by autogenerated memes unique to them."

While ideas bounced around, Cedric's assistant scribbled notes out, but neither Alexandra nor Sokolov spoke up until a few minutes had passed.

"Excuse me for being blunt," Alexandra said. "A lot of these are rehashed ideas. Some of them frankly wouldn't even have been that innovative five years ago. What can we do to *differentiate*? That's the key word."

After several more minutes of floating ideas that didn't seem to inspire any of the executives, Cedric spoke up.

"The most successful events and experiences we've run," he said, "have all had an element of user-generated content, whether real or seeded paid content that looked organic. It's normally not the execution itself, but the *surrounding* events that get traction."

Of course, there were certain elements of his job that weren't explicitly discussed. As part of the NDA he signed, there were the above-the-board experiences he was directing, mostly brand-sponsored stunts around town, the paparazzi encounters, which were at the limits of legality, and then there were the covert operations that they all implicitly understood were necessary for steady traffic—but no one ever talked about them on the record.

"That's true," the data scientist said. "We've often seen upticks in criminal activity surrounding events with A'rore, and that's when we get the highest traffic."

"We obviously can't condone that," one of the shareholders said, eliciting laughter from the group.

"But that's what people want, right? We can't help if people tune in to that," another shareholder said.

Cedric, waiting for his moment to interject again, had an idea that had been gestating for a while, and hadn't planned on presenting it yet, but now seemed like the perfect opportunity, even if some of it was half-baked.

"What about," he said, "something that engages all our strong points and is uniquely Eutopian? Eutopia is a city defined by celebrity. This is where people come to become someone, to bask in the glow of A'rore. It's like the golden age of Hollywood. People come here because they want to be power influencers— they want to be *famous*. What's more emblematic of that than a film festival?"

No one interrupted him, a good sign, and he continued.

"Like Cannes or Venice or the Berlinale. *That's* what people miss about Europe. Some of that old-world glamor that doesn't exist anymore. So we can tap in to that, except with a twist. Instead of a feature-length competition, a film festival of scenes. Short-form content for short attention spans. My idea is to get users to submit remakes of scenes from movies shot in Europe. The catch? They have to shoot the scenes here in the city, on their phones."

"We can eventize the ceremony and prize-giving," a shareholder said.

"There's definite promotional opportunities. Sponsored parties, step and repeats," said another.

"The red carpet," Cedric said. "Invite legacy celebrities to legitimize the event. The social amplification has huge potential."

"Not bad," a shareholder said. "But we're leaving a lot to chance. How do we ensure the content is any good?"

"Set constraints from the beginning," Cedric said. "Sanctioned scenes from movies that competed in those festivals. Naturally, the more sensational, the better. The most provocative ones we can find."

The conference line and room were quiet, although the shareholders in the room with him were nodding. "We involve," he continued, "people across multiple touchpoints, across the city. They shoot scenes, upload them for consideration. We can also seed the entries with our own scenes so we're guaranteed a few pieces of high-impact content."

"It's not the long-term fix, but it has potential to steer us out of the traffic slump," a shareholder said on the conference line to nods and some audible affirmations.

"A'rore as master of ceremonies," Cedric said. "It will be Cannes resurrected. Morphed into something the Snap generation can immediately recognize as relevant."

While brainstorming ideas for prizing—including allowing the finalists to take over the city's billboards for a day—Cedric received a text from Sacha, asking him if he could meet that evening—*something . . . interesting.* After wrapping the meeting and rejuvenating in an oxygen bar, he took a cab to Leicester Square.

—◊—

"REMEMBER THE GUY YOU were with the night you were attacked?" she said, just after the clack of a billiard ball break. From their dimly lit vantage point in the corner—warm lighting, faux distressed wood, and two pints of ale added to the cozy feel—they could see all the comings and goings in the pub. Brazilians, European expats, and weekenders from either coast mingled, while outside a slight drizzle had temporarily caused people to huddle under the entrance.

"Fred Green? Of course. How could I forget that?"

"It wasn't some random thing, as I'm sure you suspected."

Cedric nodded and sipped on his drink before she continued.

"You know the data dump I got a few months ago? There's an exchange between foreign investors who are worried about keeping their money in Eutopia. They see it as too volatile, and they were investigating the city on the down low. They sent in their own private detectives and data scientists to audit their own company."

"You're saying he was sent in to spy?"

"His name is—was—Caspar Stand. I know the name of the contractor the investors hired and was able to, through some contacts, find out his real name. They were trying to sweep it under the rug. Everybody—the investors, the city who found out he was spying. He's just a statistic among many that night. They assumed after the news cycle that no one would investigate it further. Lots of people come to these gaming cities with checkered pasts. Lots of people have aliases. It just turns out Fred Green was an alias of Caspar's, the undercover name he was using while here in the city."

"The way we met, or seemed to meet, was so random. Why would he look into me?"

"It's possible he had a dossier on your wife and had been watching her apartment. The Louvre thing hadn't happened long before your meeting, and you know that incident had to worry some investors."

"So he was trying to get me to open up, as someone close to her."

"Your guess is as good as mine."

"At least you can say his instincts were correct."

—⟶Ⱳ—

"I'VE BEEN REALLY BUSY the last few days," she said, as they walked on a breezeway from London to Barcelona. Low-end casinos, vape bars, and sex clubs with arabesque ornamentation lined the streets, barkers and scantily clad women cajoling inebriated tourists, like wildflowers attracting insects. "Yesterday I followed some leads I got on Caspar Strand's movements while he was here in the city. A list of addresses he had been checking out."

After hitting street level again, they continued walking for another block. "There were these recurring addresses in the data dump that I cross-referenced them with, and after some public database searches I found a lot of anonymous companies listed at the same addresses around the city. I figured it was going to be part of a minor side story in my bigger piece—shell corporations aren't exactly illegal."

She stopped next to a Zara clothing outlet. Part of a larger building with an undulating roof and slender columns, beside screens cycling between shots of a faux exterior and ads for clubs and luxury tech, it appeared to be in disuse. "This building is part of a hotel, but I've been asking around and it hasn't been functioning for the last year. There are a dozen LLCs listed here, of course, but that seems to be the case at a bunch of hotels around the city."

"Follow me," she said, as she walked to a service door next to the Zara outlet, pulling out a card, slapping it on the door's reader. After the door's locking mechanism made a click, it opened. Preempting Cedric's question, she said, "I bought this badge from a garbage man. It's universal for most of the city's service entrances."

"Resourceful."

After pushing open the door, they walked inside, the lights

automatically switching on. He followed her down a corridor leading toward the back, doors lining both sides. "These on the left lead to the hotel, now abandoned. That's where the mail drop was as well, where the shell corporations are listed. Zara is on the right, but down here, this is what caught my eye." Stopping, she knelt and pointed to a horizontal crack about three inches from the bottom of the wall, on the hotel's side. She got up and followed the crack as it widened, making a diagonal run for a few feet before tapering off. "These," she said, pointing to cracks around a doorframe, "are in a bunch of places your acquaintance went to."

"That's huge news," Cedric said. "Do you think this whole city is on unstable ground?"

"We know a lot of the region has seen seismic activity as a result of the fracking sites. But, as for the city being ready for it, I just don't know. It's one of the things Caspar Strand was looking into, that's for sure. The investors suspected something."

As they stepped back outside, the high-pitched whir of a drone startled them as it flew by overhead. Down the street, a drunken altercation seemed to be the focus of the drone's attention as it paused and hovered over it. While they were planning on how to meet up in the next couple days a nearby billboard flashed with a GIF advertisement for Club Rossebuurt in Amsterdam, lights streaking across the wet pavement. Another drone whisked by overhead, toward the fight, and then the colors changed, all over the city. The billboard turned vermillion, and buildings all around them changed to a similar hue.

"A'rore's health meter," Cedric said, pulling out his phone to check for updates. "Whenever we're doing her chases it activates, syncing with her pulse; the more it races, the redder it gets."

"What's happening tonight?"

"I have no idea," he said, looking up from his phone. He hadn't received any updates, so, whatever it was, it must be unscripted. "She could be aroused, in danger, or both."

7.
Pixel Perfect

BUFFETED BY A SUDDEN gust of wind, she quickly adjusted her stance to regain her balance. Her heel planted inches from the ledge, the exposed toes of her prosthetic foot peeking over the abyss, amethyst scan lines rippling up and down it. As her arms braced out and her calf muscles tensed, she held her breath until the wind stopped before crouching, planting one hand and sitting down with her feet dangling over the building's projecting cornice.

A'rore had been in a contemplative state, standing on the ledge of her building, forty-seven stories above the streets of Eutopia. It was one of the rare moments—with her phone placed on the ledge a few feet away from her—when her mind was free of the incessant thoughts it was normally plagued with. In the split second it took for her survival instinct to kick in and prevent her from plunging to her death, she had opened her eyes, and the present came rushing back to her, just as adrenaline flooded her body. As she sat now, a cool breeze tousling her hair, she peered over the edge at the vertigo-inducing drop, then back up at the blackness above, the stars blotted out by the intense light pollution of the city. It was as if she straddled two worlds, one hyperconnected, unrelenting, bold, and bright, the other shrouded in mystery. She took a deep breath and closed her eyes again. Out there, way out there, there was silence, and there were no networks.

How did she get up here? Lately she had been forgetting things. Whole sequences—like her morning ritual, a ride to a meet and greet fans, even the events themselves—were a blur sometimes, even completely wiped from her memory, as if someone were editing the narrative of her life, selectively showing bits and pieces to her. She'd never suffered from somnambulism before, but perhaps the sleep deprivation and nootropic enhancers were having some unintended effects. How long had she been up here? The signage around the city, synced with her heightened state of alertness, cast a red glow over everything, and, not for the first time, she wished she could deactivate the health monitor that tethered her to the city. As part of her contract she had to be wired 24/7; she had minimum number of social posts she had to make, and a minimum number of appearances. That, in essence, was the logistical price she had to pay to maintain her status as a tier-one influencer. She hadn't had a break in over a year, and looking back up at the immense impact of night above, she realized she couldn't remember what the city looked like from afar anymore. She was losing her perspective.

Another sharp gust of wind whipped her hair across her forehead, partially occluding her vision, before she brushed it back. Her phone on the ledge next to her vibrated nonstop. Thank god she didn't have to wear a geo-tracker. If she did, they'd see the altitude she was at, and the social networks would alight with speculation and trolls, and it would only be a matter of minutes until the drones came to capture her live on the edge of a building, contemplating a swan dive to her death.

She'd been in the zone, on the verge of jumping, but something had stopped her, again. She still cared, too much, about the stories. That's what it was. What people would be saying about her. Her mind, like a motor surging at max amperage, imagined everything being written about her after her death, and, most terrifyingly, not written, in the days and years to follow, when she would be relegated to the forgotten archives of the Internet.

There was the beautiful suicide of Evelyn McHale, who leapt from the eighty-sixth floor of the Empire State building in 1947, landing on top of a limousine. When they found her she was supine, face up, remarkably intact by all appearances. There was no evidence of trauma as she lay there, elegantly composed with her pearl necklace, white gloves, and serene expression, in the middle of crumpled metal and shattered glass. An amateur photographer captured the moment they found her, an unknown beauty surrounded by the violent evidence of her suicide. A perfect confluence of events, which would be impossible to recreate. She'd never be able to jump from that height and control the photogenic outcome of her death. Besides, the black-and-white memories felt as if they came from another era, and she was different—a twenty-first-century celebrity.

In her morbid research, during the twilight hours when she came home from an event, she came across the story of another immortalized jumper—Daniele Alves Lopes, a Brazilian teen who was filmed on broadcast television jumping from a building, causing a spike in ratings. If she really wanted to, she could announce her intentions, and within minutes cameras would be trained on her. But would it seem too desperate? And there was the fear she harbored that she wouldn't be able to go through with it, and her pathetic ploy for attention would be exposed. She did appreciate the way Capital Steez did it. The rapper tweeted "the end" just before jumping from a rooftop in Manhattan's Flatiron district. Concise, decisive, efficient. It had a certain flair. It was very masculine, in a way. Maybe not the right way for her. Peg Entwistle was another one. A despondent starlet, disillusioned by life in la-la land, she'd jumped from the iconic Hollywood sign. But who remembered her or, for that matter, even thought of the incident when looking at the sign today? There was a certain affinity for Leslie Cheung, the cinema icon and singer who jumped from the twenty-fourth floor of the Mandarin Oriental Hotel in Hong Kong. He was a legend who starred in some of Hong Kong cinema's most beloved movies, so his public funeral was attended by tens of thousands of people, including fans and celebrities from all around the world.

There were other methods she considered, but she wasn't too keen on them. Kurt Cobain, Hunter S. Thompson, Ernest Hemingway—all blew their brains out. Hemingway and Thompson, by their own admission, were starting to lose their minds in their old age, and perhaps the bullet was their own way of confronting dementia and the reaper head-on. Cobain was desperate, hated what he'd become, yet by killing himself at the peak of his career, he had become a rock martyr, crystallized in time. It wasn't exactly her style to end up on the list of celebrity suicides by gunshot. It was too dark, darker than jumping. Too brutal and too masculine, lacking poetry. The horrible ideation and voices, and there's the magic weapon, right there, waiting for you to feel its heft, its power, its ability to end it all in a split second.

She was still fixated on style. That's what would be remembered. Mishima, the Japanese playwright and director, committed ritual suicide by seppuku after leading a failed coup d'état. Cleopatra allegedly died of a self-induced snake bite. Marilyn Monroe was a big one. Maybe she did it right. Hers was ambiguous, spinning so many narratives and counternarratives that it was still a common topic on conspiracy forums. Was it an accidental barbiturate overdose, a suicide, a mob hit, a murder conspiracy by the Kennedy brothers? She was also thirty-six, like A'rore, when she died. She'd already peaked and went out on her own terms.

Maybe what resonated with her the most—and who knew these days, with the fickleness of social media; even she, with her in-the-weeds experience couldn't predict it—was what was truly unexpected. That's what really grabbed the public: not some downward-trending influencer, despondent over dwindling impression and engagement rates, swan-diving into the pavement. *Pull yourself together. Pull yourself together.* A mantra she found herself using lately. "Elizabeth," she'd hear in her mom's voice. "Pull yourself together."

Pinging every few seconds, the phone next to her kept vibrating on the ledge. She curled her fingers around it and held it facing her, the screen auto-activating, showing a stream of notifications stacking on top of each other. She got to her feet again, courage welling up inside her as the drop below her became more pronounced, and held her finger over the livestream button. All she had to do was press that button, and for a few moments she'd be the most talked about thing in the world.

"We should go," a gruff voice said from behind.

Norton, her faithful shadow, who'd accompanied her to the roof many times already. Even he knew it wasn't her time just yet. He'd been living on borrowed time himself, having died dozens of times in Hollywood blockbusters in violent, bone-crushing scenes of mayhem. He knew her. His brain, concussed repeatedly over the years, wasn't wired the same as normal people anymore. She could commiserate with him.

"Ms. Bowe," he said. The use of her surname brought her back to the present, back down to earth. "I'm getting calls. They're very concerned about you."

Of course they are. The AI traders don't favor volatility. In a matter of minutes, the shares of the city could plummet if she didn't make an appearance to normalize things. Hopping off the ledge to the rooftop, she strode toward Norton, who was waiting, holding the roof access door open for her.

8.
War Room

"**T**HAT ONE, RIGHT THERE," Cedric said. "Scrub it back three seconds and let it play for two."

As part of his plan to kick-start the festival entries, Cedric worked with his team to recreate a scene from *The Bourne Identity*. Working with a stuntman and a paid influencer, he directed a chase scene in a rented Fiat as it was pursued by half a dozen motorcycle cops. A mixture of handheld selfies and shots of their pursuers tailing them as they swerved through cars near recognizable Parisian landmarks, the chase climaxed with a run down a set of stairs, which the stunt driver executed flawlessly, followed by their entrance into an underground parking garage. By design, it wasn't a perfect recreation of the scene, rather an interpretation.

Exceeding their expectations, bystander footage of their stunt had been immediately uploaded to the networks. He'd already anticipated using some of it, and surveillance footage, in order to complement his influencer's footage with B-roll. Up on the large screen in the war room, dozens of tagged clips showed multiple perspectives of the chase, with audio capturing the excitement of bystanders as they witnessed the wild pursuit. Even though it was staged, it inspired hysterical responses from bystanders who didn't realize they were part of a cinema verité remake of a twenty-five-year-old action movie classic.

"That scream and that guy going 'Oh my god,' that's what I want," he said as the curation technician dropped the clip on the timeline. In its entirety, the entire scene, called "Bourne Identity Paris Police Chase," would be no longer than two minutes, the time constraint laid out in the contest guidelines. Chosen because the data scientists had seen significant video viewing drop-off rates after the two-minute mark, it was also a way they could attract more entries. Anybody with a phone and some inspiration could shoot a two-minute scene.

"Play it back from the beginning, using the Hudson filter," Cedric said. The filter, an old Instagram classic, gave the sequence a washed-out, blue-tinged look, reminiscent of the movie's original cinematography and setting.

The technician played the edited sequence from the beginning: using a healthy mix of bystander footage and their staged POV footage, and a quick moment of dialogue leading into the chase, the scene came in at one minute and forty-seven seconds, right within their sweet spot.

"Some of those shots linger a bit too long in the chase scene. See if you can trim those or add some more bystander footage. We have over forty decent clips we can pull from," Cedric said before turning to his assistant. "Check all the profiles of the bystanders who shot footage and box them into tier one, two, and three influencers. Let's maximize reach by sticking with the ones and twos. Only if the footage is exceptionally good should we go with a three."

Cedric left the curation bay and headed for the energy drink machine. While walking, he took a hit of Panadrine and checked his phone for more updates. The festival arrangements were made with an extremely short turnaround since it had been such a high priority for the shareholders to boost the traffic numbers. His regular experiential operations were like a life vest, thrown out to the city to keep it afloat amid the sea of competitors. The city was so hot a mere three years ago, and now it had fallen into the "trough of sorrow" as his chief data scientist put it, that doomed valley of non-upward-sloping trending lines. The festival, however, was working as planned.

Within three days of its announcement, they'd achieved twenty thousand comments and three million shares. They had hired an ex-data scientist from Netflix who had analyzed viewing trends across thousands of movies, marking the peak visceral moments in each, when arousal and excitement were at their highest. Using his research—which measured physio-logical indicators like pulse, breath rate, and blood pressure—and restricting the list to movies that aligned with the Eutopian brand, they announced the festival with an officially sanctioned list of scenes. Among them, moments from movies like *The French Connection, La Haine, The Talented Mr. Ripley, Taken, Shaun of the Dead, Trainspotting, Breathless, Blow-Up, Day of the Jackal, Irreversible, La Femme Nikita, Run Lola Run, Untergang,* and *La Dolce Vita.*

Submissions began to come in on the second day. Those not geo-stamped as being shot in Eutopia were automatically disqualified, as were those that went over the two-minute limit. An entry had just come in earlier that day called "Last Tango in Paris Butter Scene." This hadn't been one of the official scenes, but the work had all the right elements otherwise. Geo-stamped as being shot in Paris, with some glimpses of Eutopian landmarks— even though it was almost entirely shot indoors—the scene was superbly acted, to the point where Cedric and his assistant were getting uncomfortable watching it together. Verging on the appearance of nonconsensual sex, it starred an aging influencer in Brando's part, a past-his-prime American expat, heavyset and sweaty; and a young influencer in Schneider's part—a young mid-twenties woman, in the ideal marketing demographic. The young woman in the scene, just like the original, appeared to cry real tears as their graphic sexual encounter reached its climax. Had she not submitted it herself for competition, signing a consent form, they would have had to vet it thoroughly to ensure no actual rape had occurred. Unfortunately, since it wasn't one of the sanctioned scenes, they couldn't include it in the official selection, but his colleagues agreed with him: the scene was so obscene that a mini controversy was sure to erupt around it given the recent gang rape case. Taking a cue from Cannes, they decided to create an "out of competition" section of the festival to accommodate the influx of entries that didn't adhere to the rules and regulations.

"Last Tango in Paris Butter Scene" wasn't the only entry of this sort. Other influencers submitted a recreation of the leaked sex tape with Max Mosley, the disgraced former Formula 1 boss who'd participated in a Nazi-themed sadomasochistic orgy. The strangest, in line with the leaked-sex-tape theme, was an entry called "Berlusconi Bunga Bunga party," which was shot in a suite in the Hotel Augustus. Young women who appeared to be barely legal—dressed in top-end designer clothes—were parading in front of a very convincing Berlusconi lookalike. Shot as if a cell phone were secretly recording them, it ended with Berlusconi choosing one called "Ruby," taking her to his bedroom and having his way with her. "With all these entries," Cedric said to his assistant, "we could be creating a new genre of pornography."

With only four weeks to go until the festival, and given the pace at which submissions were coming in, the momentum was relentless, as if they were planets circling closer to a collapsing star. At least for Cedric, there was an air of finality in everything he did. Any way he looked at it, things seemed to be coming to an end. In the tech world, four years was already a longer than average run, and, especially after Sacha's discovery, he couldn't imagine staying in the city much longer. He'd been sucked into its vices in his search for clarity on his wife's disappearance—and he'd even sipped on the Kool-Aid for a while. A'rore saw what she had needed in him—someone malleable, in need of purpose; someone like her, in many respects.

She had been distant for the last few weeks, since the night she disappeared for a few hours, alarming the city when her health monitor kept pinging in the red. That night he'd gone to her penthouse to work out the details of the gala with her and was greeted at the door by an unusually modest version of her— dressed in a sweatshirt and yoga pants, not made up, as if she'd flipped a switch on her seduction mode. "My numbers," she said, drinking what must have been her third or fourth vodka cocktail, "are flat. My followers are dropping off." But then, a few days later—after sleep and rejuvenation therapy—she was back to her normal, audacious self. She had warmed to the idea of the gala and even brainstormed ideas with him for unique experiences involving her during the festivities. She liked the idea of leaking a story to the tabloids involving an international celebrity or wealthy entrepreneur with whom she'd be "caught" during the days of the festival. "I need some inroads into the Asian market. See if there's an angle there, some handsome businessman or cinema idol I can seduce or home-wreck."

After putting the finishing touches on the *Bourne* edit, he was leaving the offices to pick up some more Panadrine when his assistant stopped him in the hallway.

"Do you have a moment? You have to check out this submission that just came in. They recreated the naked gun battle from *Eastern Promises.*" He followed her back to the curation station while checking the time on his phone. It had been over forty hours since he'd slept, and while he was getting a lot of work done, his mind was losing its sharpness. He needed that refill of Panadrine within the next hour, or he'd crash hard.

"They were actually arrested after shooting it," she said, as she pulled up a submission aptly called "Eastern Promises Naked Fight." "I think they freaked out a few people in the sauna who weren't in on it."

9.
Sex is Violence

HER GRIP ON THE edge of the mattress, nails clawing into the fitted sheet, loosened as he rolled off of her. Releasing a pillow corner from her mouth, which she'd been biting into as he plowed into her, she turned her head away from him—his tumescence and body heat—and took a deep breath. The perspiration that had formed on her forehead and exposed back evaporated, cooling her as she lay, eyes closed, mindful again of the sounds in the room. Her Spotify list—one she'd created for her sessions with clients, consisting of a few hundred slow jam tracks of soul, R&B, hip-hop, and sensuous dream-pop remixes—was still playing, while her phone vibrated on the hotel room's desk every ten or so seconds.

"*Me matas papi. Me matas,*" she said.

Monteiro laughed under his breath but didn't say anything as he lay next to her, face up, watching the changing light patterns on the ceiling from the television. Her phone buzzed again, vibrating on the glass-covered table across the room from them.

It reminded him that his service pistol was also on that desk, as was his own phone.

"You're more popular than ever," he said.

"I started sharing my listening habits a few days ago, so they all know when I'm fucking. They're not clients, just a bunch of horny dudes blowing up my social," she said, turning to face Monteiro again. She reached down and grabbed a corner of the sheet and pulled it up to cover her breasts.

"Couldn't you turn it off, just once, when you're with me?"

"You know I love you," she said, kissing him on his forehead, "but this is my business, baby. It's marketing. That's what I went to school for before I got into L-Ubering."

"I get it," he said. "I get it."

"You're so grumpy," she said, running her hand down his chest and abdomen, squeezing his deflating erection playfully. "But so full of energy. What's going on lately?"

He laughed and said, "It's probably just the Virilix pill I popped before coming over here."

"Is that the new one they're pushing? Those things, I tell you, are a blessing and a curse. I get more customers, but damn do I get ragdolled. After you, baby, I can't take anymore."

He had taken a pill before coming over to visit her—*nom de guerre* Desiree, and he didn't care to find out her real name—but he'd always taken a pill to give him a little more staying power now that he was a fifty-year-old man trying to keep up with a twenty-something L-Uber star. It wasn't the pill that had changed him; it wasn't her, either.

It was this influx of wannabe influencers and tourists coming because of the festival. All the advertising promised incredible exposure and ad revenue, and people from all over were coming in to strike it rich. He had to source more security contractors to handle the influx, and he himself was pulling double shifts sometimes. A few days ago, a flash mob of influencers reenacting a zombie scene from a movie took over a shopping mall in

London, disrupting commerce and terrorizing tourists. Before his visit to Desiree, he had just finished booking some Russian influencers who were fighting naked in a spa, trying to recreate a scene from another movie. In a way, it was like the days leading up to the insurgency, when the atmosphere felt combustible, like a small spark could set the whole place off.

"Oh god, as if we don't see her enough," Desiree said, eyeing the television. A'rore, in her latest public appearance, was at the opening of an Alain Ducasse restaurant, wearing a lamé bikini top and sarong, snapping selfies with the crowd outside. "I feel like she's been around forever."

Hashtagged photos and videos from the crowd began to cycle across the screen, showing A'rore getting into her black sedan and driving off, before a new segment started on the upcoming film festival. While they were highlighting and interviewing influencers whose entries had been accepted, Monteiro said, "I don't think she'll be around much longer."

"Oh really. Do tell me, *Mr. Policeman*," she said, inching closer to him.

"There's a case from a few months ago. A guy working with her, for the city, was found dead, and we've been able to link the main murder suspect to her. They caught him in Chicago, but he is claiming he was paid by her. It's just he said, she said right now, but I think it will bring her down. She's not popular enough anymore to deflect controversy."

"She's just, *old*. This place needs some new blood, a new thing."

"Are you volunteering?" he said, reaching his arm around her, pulling her in closer, while his other hand fondled the sides of her abdomen and hips. She acquiesced to him, grinding her rear into his crotch, slowly arousing him again. As the blue light of the television danced on the ceiling and walls, off the translucent drapes screening them from a view of the neon strip down below, he was momentarily distracted by another flurry of message alerts on her phone. Even though she ignored it, he was annoyed by it. Having been her regular for a few months now, he deserved better treatment. He'd booked her for a couple hours this time, even brought her a gift of Yves Saint Laurent perfume—something she had put on her public wish list—and he wanted to take full advantage of each minute. He stroked her hair—bleach blond—and formed a fist, gripping the strands like a handful of hay. He'd take her belly-down again, from a dominant position.

There was a strange connection between sex and violence, something he was noticing now—with his increased sexual appetite correlating to the increased delinquent activity in the city—but also something he'd experienced while deployed in Iraq. His first kill was amid extremely chaotic circumstances, bullets flying at him, and he was almost numb. He didn't feel anything until he got back to base and things wound down. The next firefights he was involved in seemed less chaotic, as he was more mindful of his surroundings, but he did feel, despite himself, excitement and arousal, similar to what he was feeling now.

He had one soldier in his platoon, a devout Christian, who got a full-blown erection during his first kill, and it deeply disturbed him. His hands shaking, his voice low as he confided to Montiero, he was actually more disturbed by getting aroused than by the act of killing. *You can have the most intense training possible, but nothing will ever prepare you for the raw violence—and that's what separates the men from the boys.* Nothing ever really lived up to the camaraderie and intensity of battle in the civilian world, not to mention the cathartic effect of killing the enemy with your own hands.

There was a different alert sound, this time coming from Monteiro's phone. What could it be now? More goddamn delinquent influencers? Desiree reached to the nightstand and grabbed a remote, turning up the volume on her playlist, drowning out the incessant alerts. They were both wanted, but for another hour they were going to try to block out the rest of the world.

10.
Millions of
Monthly Uniques

H E COULDN'T RESIST THE opportunity. Despite the intense
activity of the days and hours leading up to the gala—
which was becoming more popular than any of his data
scientists had predicted—he had to stage a home invasion. A
talent agent for Dunya Novak, a former top-ranked selfie star
who had been on the short list for A'rore's spot, was attending the
film festival with her billionaire husband. Off the record, they
were looking for a boost to her social media channels and were
looking for out-of-the-box ideas.

She still had a social following worth tapping into, and her
audience of aspirational eighteen-to-thirty-year-old females
aligned perfectly with the city. Her husband, Azy Murthy, had
created the social app Covet, known as the "Instagram of luxury
goods." The copyrighted hashtag #Want accompanied pictures
of Coveters posting images of their latest acquisitions, from
designer handbags to high-powered, eight-figure sports cars.

Dunya, whose rise to selfie fame had peaked two years ago, still had eighteen million followers, and her latest posts brazenly featured a three-million-dollar Cartier necklace she said she was going to wear on the red carpet. The most popular post featuring the necklace, dangling in front of her cleavage, had been shared close to nine hundred thousand times in less than twenty-four hours. The hashtags #want #cartier #eutopiafest had spread globally, but as her agent had pointed out, there was an opportunity to augment those numbers even further—to create a "win-win scenario" for the city and her brand.

After a brainstorming session, Cedric hit upon an idea that was both media-friendly and, for those who remembered the good old days of the Cannes Film Festival, nostalgic. There had always been side stories involving disputes between actors, but the most memorable moments were the daring jewel heists carried out by local gangs in the Riviera. The combination of glamour, extreme wealth, and danger captured the public's attention in a way no other story could.

Sunday afternoon, in Paris, and the atmosphere was relaxed. The lighting was perfect, and the security cameras plus the bystander footage pretty much guaranteed a hit story. Wearing orange rebel alliance jumpsuits and helmets from the Star Wars franchise, Cedric and his assistant parked their getaway motorcycles in front of the Hotel Croisette, front wheels facing the street. Despite having their visors pulled down and wearing dust masks over their mouths, weapons clearly holstered on their sides, they walked straight through the hotel lobby without being stopped. As planned, they looked like influencers returning to their rooms after a day on the town. Marching straight to the elevators, they rode to the twenty-third floor, one floor below the twenty-fourth where Dunya and Azy were staying in their presidential suite.

"Their security guard left the stairwell door open for us," Cedric said, "so all we have to do is walk one flight up, and we'll be just down the hall from them. It will be a plausible explanation for how we were able to circumvent the restricted access to the twenty-fourth floor."

After entering the twenty-fourth floor, they marched toward Dunya's suite, guns drawn and aimed at a security guard standing in front of her door. With nowhere to run except down the hall, he held his hands up and followed their orders. Since no audio was being recorded, Cedric didn't bother to script dialogue for this part of the robbery, only giving the security guard commands from under his mouth mask, as if he were blocking a theater production.

Once inside it was relatively easy, since there were no cameras present. Inspired by Kim Kardashian West's infamous 2016 hotel heist in Paris, with the couple's full cooperation, his assistant tied them up and locked them in the bathroom. Cedric went through the apartment and staged a brisk robbery, opening drawers, overturning valises—and, as planned, ransacking an already open safe, grabbing the Cartier necklace and two luxury watches, a diamond-encrusted Chopard, and a Patek Philippe, giving them a total haul worth over $7 million. When his assistant was done with the couple, they loosely tied the security guard and timed his escape to allow them a minute of lead time.

On the ground floor of the hotel, they walked calmly through the lobby, Cedric wearing a backpack with the couples' stolen items. When they were about three-quarters of the way through the lobby, faces still covered by their rebel alliance disguises and masks—the people around them still assuming they were a couple of influencers dressed in full regalia—the guard burst out of the elevators behind them and began shouting.

"Robbery!" he said while sprinting after Cedric and his assistant, who were already out of the hotel and starting up their motorcycles. Just as the guard exited the hotel, followed by hotel security who were ignorant to the stunt, they took off, gunning their motorcycles through stalled traffic and jumping a red light.

By that time, organic video from bystanders had already been shot from inside the hotel's lobby and outside, where Cedric and his assistant made their escape in dramatic fashion.

"Great stories write themselves," Cedric said to his assistant as they reviewed the footage back in the war room. Where had he heard that? It was true, at least in the line of work he was in now. He'd worked his entire adult life, unsuccessfully trying to make a name for himself in the entertainment industry, trying to leave a legacy, only to find out that the stories that resonated the most weren't carefully crafted by committees of Hollywood movie executives. They were stories that felt real, that were told by real people, shot with no filters or CGI effects.

In the next hour, after they curated the story using security footage and bystander footage from the hotel lobby, Dunya's popularity index peaked at the highest it had been for over a year. It stayed steady as she released a series of posts showing marks on her wrists where the home invaders had bound her, as well as the aftermath of their robbery. The hashtags #Chopard #Patek #Cartier #eutopiafest #want #dunyazy #robbery were trending worldwide. As they sipped coffees and watched the comments stream in, half of them commiserating with Dunya and Azy, the other half claiming it was an inside job—which he could care less about, since all they cared about was the notoriety—he even noticed copycats. Influencers around the city were posting pictures of their own luxury wearables, trying to draft off Dunya's breakout success. Despite his misgivings, and the distance he tried to create for himself while doing this job, Cedric had to admit to himself that he enjoyed manufacturing these experiences—like an undercover cop in a gang, getting hooked on the violence and drugs.

The public relations officer was in the middle of telling him who they'd finally landed for A'rore's festival scandal—a married Russo-Chinese action movie icon named Constantine Wei—when he received a text from Sacha.

"At A's with news. Need to see u asap."

She'd flown back in town a few days earlier to cover the festival—which she called the city's "swan song"—and had been trying to meet up with him. He'd been too caught up directing to find time, although he'd been communicating with her regularly via text and email. Using encrypted channels, he had been passing her the documents she needed to complete her story—logs from the war room, raw footage showing collaboration with the police to manufacture violent experiences for the sake of online traffic. Whatever he did, and however much he received guilty pleasure from it, he knew it was coming to an end. In a way, despite the very real consequences of espionage, which he had witnessed firsthand, he went ahead with it. Was it his conscience finally nagging him, or the foreknowledge that this whole thing was about to be blown up and exposed? He was conflicted—the Venn diagram of fame and notoriety overlapping, finding him in the sweet spot, where legacies are born.

After parting ways with the public relations officer, promising to go over the details of the tabloid scandal with her as soon as he got back, he headed out of the Haussmann offices toward his motorcycle. While mounting it, he noticed another person, face obscured by a downturned visor, mounting a motorcycle. As he pulled out in the opposite direction, the other motorcycle rolled out of its space, following, visible in his rearview mirror. In the last couple of weeks there seemed to be more instances where he perceived himself being watched or followed, and shaking these tails was starting to become second nature to him. A'rore had expressed her fear earlier, but he had chalked it up to a cognitive distortion brought about by her waning stardom. However, he also felt like he was under increasing scrutiny—after all, Monteiro had dirt on him now if he wanted to get him out, and it was A'rore's clout that had landed him the job in the first place, and she was losing her influence.

Rolling between cars with his hand loosely gripping the

throttle, he reached the edge of a crosswalk just as the lights were turning from yellow to red. Gunning the engine, he shot through the intersection just as the cross traffic started rolling, horns blaring as he accelerated toward the cars ahead of him. Checking his rearview mirror, he felt relieved not to see the other rider anymore and rode at a steady pace the rest of the way toward A'rore's building. Was it a charade put on by Monteiro to keep him paranoid and under his thumb? At times he wondered if his pursuers were figments of his sleep-deprived imagination.

"We don't have much time," Sacha said, closing the door behind him. Setting his helmet down on the kitchen counter, next to an open bottle of vodka, he walked to A'rore and greeted her with a perfunctory kiss on the cheek. Despite their half dozen intimate encounters, she always kept it strictly business when she wasn't interested in using him sexually. This was the first time he'd seen A'rore and Sacha together, despite all their connections. Had A'rore also seduced Sacha, using her like she so masterfully did with him and everyone else in her circle? He wouldn't put it beyond her, but Sacha, despite exuding an innate charm, had always been braced around him. Even if A'rore's star was dimming, she still eclipsed him in terms of charisma.

"So, what's going on?" he said, taking his jacket off, draping it over A'rore's sofa, and taking a seat facing both of them. Clearly observing the casual way in which he moved about A'rore's penthouse, a look of realization came over Sacha—her eyes and an almost imperceptible nod betrayed it. Glancing from A'rore to Cedric, she said: "I've told A'rore everything we talked about. It's only fair, since she's going to be the nexus of my story."

"The spell," A'rore said, "is beginning to wear off." She laughed, not unpleasantly, and took a sip on her cocktail.

"I've got a piece of news that is going to change everything," Sacha said. "I owe it to the both of you since you're both such big parts of my story—and it's going to come out regardless, in very short order."

"I think I might need a cocktail too," Cedric said. "Go on. Nothing surprises me anymore." In the early evening, the city's powerful digital screens shone brightly in the panoramic vista from A'rore's apartment. Vibrant colors, representing a million different brands attempting to break through the clutter, danced along the curves and hard edges of the city's architecture.

"Another reporter on my staff back east has been working on a story about a massive black market for hackers in the dark web, used by corporations and nation states. She has sources deep in the organization who are heavily involved in traffic fraud and who operate the biggest bot network she's ever seen. She's basically going to blow the lid off this thing, exposing nearly all the top web properties as fraudsters, buying viewership from shady traffic brokers. Eutopia is one of them. One of the worst, in fact."

"But the people here, coming here, that's all real," he said.

"The audience numbers are inflated, Cedric," A'rore said. "Meaningless. Even my audience numbers, she says, might be off by factors of two or three."

"You mean all of this?" Cedric said, getting up and walking toward the window with its view on the sea of screens and neon. What would happen, he thought, if no one was watching, if there were no metrics to incentivize the masses? *That's the twenty-first-century version of a tree falling in a forest.*

"This is going to be a nuclear detonation in the media and advertising landscape," Sacha said. Cedric, still lost in thought as he looked over the city, was remembering old pictures from the Tunguska meteor impact, which flattened two thousand square meters of Siberian forest.

Cedric turned around, facing both women. A'rore, unusually serene, sat cross-legged looking at him with her mouth and silver eyes formed into a relaxed smile, one he'd never seen on her before. Sacha, standing behind her, was stroking her hair. "This is going to be huge when it comes out," he said. "That means all the influencers here, the key thing motivating them, is a complete farce."

"Exactly," Sacha said. "It's not going to be pretty when they find out their ad revenue is bogus, that they won't be getting paid."

"When is the story coming out?" he said.

"That's the thing. That's why I called you over. They're on an accelerated timeline because they're worried about moles leaking the story." She smiled before saying, "Ironically, they're also worried about ad revenue and page views. It's set to come out in the next forty-eight hours."

"Just in time for the gala," A'rore said.

"Maximum impact," Cedric said. "Goddamn. And this will be actual genuine news. We'll go out with a bang."

"Yep," Sacha said. "Who knows what's going to happen, but one thing is for sure: the value of the city is going to drop the second this news comes out."

That smile on A'rore's face was so disconcerting, Cedric realized, because it was real, genuine, and vulnerable. Her poise and confidence were what initially drew him to her, but somehow this new facet of her stirred feelings inside of him, as if he recognized a part of himself he'd been trying to suppress while playing the game in Eutopia. Sacha bent down and whispered into A'rore's ear, and A'rore set her drink down and stood up. For a split second they were both looking at Cedric, and he knew they'd carry on, whatever the outcome. He nodded, affirming their complicity.

As Sacha and A'rore walked to her bedroom, Cedric recalled something A'rore had said to him the night her health stats plummeted, when she was on the verge of a breakdown. "We women, you have to understand, have an expiration date in the entertainment world. The data doesn't lie." The data didn't lie, just like her health sync to the city, translated to colors, changed the signage outside to Coca-Cola red.

"Dim the lights to ten percent," A'rore said, and as the ambient light grew darker he saw her lips move, mouthing something inaudible to Sacha as they entered her bedroom, leaving the door open as they began to undress. His phone vibrated in his pocket and he took it out. The anonymous texter again—always appearing in moments like these—with another random number, *55.551898.*

He set his phone face down on the counter and began unbuttoning his shirt, aware in his animal brain of the subtle shift in power dynamics, of something finite, vulnerable and human, as the signage outside dissolved to a selfie of A'rore, poised and immaculate.

11.
Parallax View

ONSUMED BY LAST-MINUTE CANCELLATIONS and logistical adjustments, Cedric had barely kept up with the news and had achieved a mere seven hours of sleep in the last seventy-two hours according to his sleep tracker. "Adpocalypse" or not, he was intent on staging the online event of the year, if not decade, and for Sacha, with her insider's view, to record every last detail for posterity. It wasn't as if they could do anything about it until the news was dropped. It was business as usual, as if they were all on the same freight train hurtling down the tracks to parts unknown.

That's it, a Scorsese-esque freeze-frame. Cedric exhaled a cloud of Panadrine, the nanoparticles curling toward the ceiling, an amorphous shape shrouding everybody in a Gaussian blur. He felt like an impartial observer, like they were animals moving about, unaware of the scrutiny they were under. In the biopic of his life, this would be the sequence leading up to one of the major set pieces, his minions typing and swiping furiously at their workstations, powerwalking in and out of breakout rooms, on calls with vendors and talent, sealing deals at the eleventh hour. It was the freeze-frame moment, with a short voice-over saying, in the end, "How did it come to this?"

His team, composed mostly of transactionals born in the early 2000s, were able to tap into the audience mix for maximum effective reach. While they had some marquee names attending, including A$AP Rocky, Daisy Ridley, Zoë Kravitz, and Michael B. Jordan, they'd successfully managed to attract a combination of lesser known names that their data scientists determined would bring greater market penetration and possibly even more scale. Constantine Wei—the It boy of global cinema at the moment—was due to arrive in an hour or so, and Cedric's PR team had already leaked details of an alleged secret rendezvous between him and A'rore. Gossip site columnists and social media managers were already posting rumors to their sites. As expected, this provoked indignation and new hashtags, created to denounce A'rore's latest scandalous affair. Constantine, married to Shiloh Nouvel Jolie-Pitt, five months pregnant, was painted as a hapless victim to A'rore's outrageous and sexually predatory behavior.

Besides the Eurasian action star, they had Jayson Spiegel, whose virtual gaming company had just been valued at several billion dollars, adding a level of hip tech entrepreneur pedigree. Former UFC title holder Conor McGregor was set to attend, as well as *League of Legends* champ Lee Sang-hyeok. Most of the world's top influencers—like A'rore—were contractually tied to other networks, but through partnerships, they were able to secure a strong list of up-and-coming indies, including beauty vlogger Becca Zaldana, the teen heartthrob and Instagram icon Billy Brouex, and lifestyle blogger Enrique Castillo. Incentivized by the promise of massive viewing numbers, they had been comped penthouse suites atop hotels around the city and ensured red-carpet treatment. No one in the city was the wiser, except for Cedric, A'rore, and Sacha, to the truth about those viewing numbers. But in the end, would it matter?

As Cedric stood up, he remembered what Monteiro had said: "A lie can travel halfway around the world while the truth is putting on its shoes." Really, who cared about the deception as long as it attracted attention? The social proof of millions of viewers would attract more viewers, providing more viral potential for his experience. He walked past the breakout rooms to the editing bay to check on the progress of the last bits of content. After the semifinalists were chosen—all having passed through a rigorous analysis and logistical regression model measuring audience scale, gender split, and potential revenue—Cedric had then produced over a dozen mini docs spotlighting the competitors, which were seeded out to the media in the run-up to the festival. Inspired by the pre-fight docs used to build up boxing and WrestleMania matches, they pitted the competitors against each other to create tension and mythologized their struggles to become famous in order to endear them to the public. With his eye for aesthetics encompassing all the official content being released, all in all it was a work of art he was proud of, larger in scope and more tangible than anything he'd ever done.

After inserting a clip of A'rore in front of a monitor watching competition entries, the editor slid his fingers over the ends of an adjacent clip, adjusting the timing. His producer, a freelancer he'd flown in from Hollywood who had just wrapped work on *Star Wars Episode XIII*, looked at the storyboard on her tablet and directed the editor to a new piece of footage.

"What's the ETA on this?" Cedric said.

"Just tweaking a few things," she said. "With the final render I'm guessing an hour and a half?"

"What's the running time?"

She ordered the editor to pull it up, and, half-turning so he was facing both the producer and Cedric, he said, "Six minutes, thirty-eight seconds."

"Good," Cedric said. "Keep it under six minutes thirty, and we're ready to rock and roll. Ping me as soon as you have your final cut." His analysts had shown him the long-format viewing trends for the last month, which showed a significant view-through drop-off between six and a half minutes and ten minutes. After ten minutes, forget about it. Less than one percent of the audience could stand anything longer than that, and, if they could, they were almost all in the undesirable forty-plus demographic.

Leaving the editing bay, he had one other stop before he had to go to the Coliseum to scope out the venue, where crews were prepping for the gala. The public relations officer wanted to update him on the planned scandal involving A'rore and Constantine.

"We've already tipped off select independent paparazzi who work closely with TMZ and OMG," she said. "And we have reservations at the Rossellini."

"So, they have all the key message points, hashtags, and the rest?"

"Yep. It's basically the same thing I did to reboot Blanket Jackson's career, so there's precedent. For Blanket we leaked surveillance footage of him and Selena Braxton groping each other in an elevator. In this case, the paparazzi will be hiding outside the restaurant and catch them leaving. Once those pics start circulating, we can bump up traffic by leaking surveillance footage of them in a private booth in the restaurant."

"Can't we step this up? What about live footage?"

"Hmm. We can do that. I have an idea for that. But we'll have to work with some of the stuntmen and motorcycles."

He left headquarters and headed for the main venue. As he steered through traffic, a strange sense of nostalgia overcame him. The intense lightshow around him, the bold and bizarre architecture, the trompe l'oeil facades, the thousands of influencers, each with their own perspective, their own channels, their own egos, what was going to happen to them after his experience? It was as if he'd had a recollection from the future of the moment the lights went out.

Just as he was in the middle of this musing, to his right, a sign wrapping the facade of a gaming room stuttered and distorted. A nuclear-green ad for Spotify froze, then went black, and a message in stark white on black appeared: *THX 4 DA ADREV. URS. ROFLEX.* After glitching and reverting to black for a split second, a selfie of A'rore appeared on the screen. In light of the news Sacha had revealed, the hijacked billboard message, and those that had preceded it over the last few months, finally made sense. Was this the final rehearsal? Had ROFLEX been warning them the whole time of an imminent network implosion? As he gunned his engine on the green light, leaving the rest of the traffic behind him, his reverie suddenly gave him a drone's-eye view from high above. He saw himself, and the denizens of Eutopia, as mere data points in a closed ecosystem—a cold, dispassionate view, as if he were a scientist observing a curious computer simulation.

IT WAS 3:00 A.M., the day of the festival, and he'd just taken a deep hit of the newest Panadrine analog, CEO 2.0, the nootropic opening the taps in his brain, letting information flood through. The task at hand—going though his wife's apartment, gathering his and her personal belongings—suddenly became easier to manage, all his preoccupations shelved in a corner of his mind. The idea wasn't to grab everything—only portable things, and things that spoke to him, like her notebook, a bracelet he had given her, a hand mirror. The only things he had accumulated were clothes, new phones, and watches. As he was stuffing a data drive into a backpack, the wall monitor activated with an incoming call from Sacha.

"I'm just getting ready for tomorrow," he said, zipping up the backpack.

"Good thing you are," she said. "I just got confirmation they're ready to publish the ad fraud story. I was able to delay them by a few hours, but they won't wait any longer. There are rumblings already among some tech reporters, and it's just a matter of time."

"So, what do we do? Should we leave now?"

"They're waiting for the film festival in order to maximize impact, so we're safe for now. But as soon as it's over, when the news starts going viral, we're going to have to get out. Besides, I know you're just as eager as I am to witness this thing unfold. Just admit it."

Cedric smiled and nodded. "I guess you're right," he said. "What about A'rore?"

"I told her. She said she'd take care of herself. She's ruthless enough, anyway."

"What do you mean?"

"Look, I didn't tell you the other night, because of the way things went. But I meant to. She's behind Eddie Costello's death—she confessed to me she had Norton take care of him and make it look like a common L-Uber user had done it. I think it was a power play, that's all, because he wanted her out."

"That's why I ended up getting the job."

"And trust me, she's expecting you to finish it."

AFTER THE LAST OF his hype clips aired—about the influencers behind the remake of the head-slamming scene from *Lock, Stock and Two Smoking Barrels*, freely interpreted using gory DIY blood-spatter effects to enhance and embellish the original clip—his chief curator cut to live footage of the celebrity arrivals. Constantine Wei's arrival by helicopter, landing on top of the Hotel Augustus, was also captured by paparazzi on adjacent hotels, who had been tipped off by his team. Real-time traffic stats, which he knew were grossly inflated, nevertheless showed the strongest performance he'd ever seen. They were also the number one trending topic across every network, worldwide, and that couldn't be faked.

As the celebrities, influencers, socialites, and businessmen walked down the red carpet, all shot from a dizzying array of angles as curators pulled in live feeds from the surrounding crowds, he felt a sudden thrill, a rush of excitement, knowing this entire experience with its subplots and metalanguage could very well be his masterpiece. The gala itself was secondary to everything else that was happening in the city—everything he had orchestrated. The realness, the organic spontaneity, was more visceral than any Pollock or Basquiat, quaint twentieth-century expressions constrained to rectangles of canvas. A'rore taking the stage to announce the winners was going to be a prelude to the bacchanal to follow.

Two hours later, after the last award had been announced for the most audacious adaptation—a virtual tie between "Last Tango in Paris Butter Scene" and "Gomorra Solarium Execution," after Cedric's own "Bourne Car Chase" clip was disqualified for public endangerment—he was waiting for A'rore backstage as she gave her farewell speech and ushered in the closing musical act. He'd been following the public sentiment online, and he had never seen ratings so high. Each of the twenty-five semifinalist clips were available online—including some bonuses, which had been disqualified for risqué or unsanctioned content—and they had already received over thirty-five thousand interactions since going live with the official gallery an hour ago. Part of him wondered if the massive spike had enough legitimate traffic to save the city.

As applause rippled in from the Coliseum's main stage, he met A'rore while she walked back to her dressing room.

"Great job, you killed it," he said, following her down the hall. Busy stagehands were rushing past them in the opposite direction, and some B-roll cameramen, live-broadcasting behind-the-scenes footage, were following both of them. Cedric turned to them, right before they tried to enter her dressing room, and held out his hand.

"Cut it here, move on," he said.

As they entered her room, closing the door behind them, she said, "Thanks. The energy out there is crazy. You can't tell me it's not real." Pointing to a monitor mounted next to her makeup counter, showing the streams of comments pouring in, she continued, "I wanted to go out with a bang."

"You did tonight, but it's not over."

They paused, their eyes locking for a split second of clarity. No matter what the actual numbers looked like, the raw enthusiasm across the city was real.

"I'll enjoy the feeling while it lasts," she said, turning her back toward him. "I need your help with this."

As he helped her step out of her red satin evening gown, with its ultra low-plunging neckline, inspired by Bella Hadid's racy 2016 Cannes ensemble, she said, "How are we going to get out of here?" Still wearing her stiletto heels, she revealed a completely nude body as the gown crumpled to the floor around her feet.

"Trinidad's set is going to last another ten minutes so you have time to leave through the back entrance. Norton is waiting for you there—he'll take you to the next stage at the Rossellini, where Constantine is waiting."

As she pulled on a new, less flashy outfit consisting of skintight trousers, a swimsuit-style top, and a pair of black satin stilettos, she turned her back to him again as he helped her into a black Armani jacket. Her skin, when he brushed against it, was damp with perspiration. She hadn't paused once during the entire ceremony.

"How long will this take? I'm wiped out." After removing some of the heavy foundation on her face with a wet washcloth—no longer needed since she wasn't going to be under ultra-bright lighting and ultra HD optics—she patted her face dry, picked up a vape stick from the counter, and took a long drag.

"We'll alert you when we're ready. It's a quick paparazzi chase, with the twist this time that you'll be with Constantine."

She was silent, hands resting on the counter, watching him through the reflection in the makeup-flecked mirror.

"C'mon, A'rore. It's great exposure for you in Asia. It's what you're going to need once this place is done."

As they exited her room, a photographer who had been lingering outside her door started snapping pictures. The exhausted woman who seemed to be shrinking in front of him just a few moments earlier suddenly transformed into a poised, confident queen—like an exotic bird, proudly displaying her plumage—as they strode toward the back exit. When they got there, Cedric shut the door behind them, keeping the photographer inside. Norton was waiting next to the open door of her black Mercedes, and Cedric acknowledged him with a silent nod.

Her eyes, even though they were slightly creased into a smile, were like liquid, deeper than he had ever seen them, belying a certain sadness. After she sat in the back seat, Norton closed the door behind her, the tinted window separating then now like a black mirror, reflecting starbursts from the overhead sodium lights of the underground garage.

—◊—

While A'rore was still at the restaurant with Constantine, Cedric got a call from Sacha.

"I couldn't delay them any longer. They're going to publish

the story at six a.m. Eastern Time, in order to make the Eurasian nightly news cycle."

That left them with about four hours. After the chase was over, they'd have a few hours of calm before the news hit. As he sat in the war room—points of light relaying ephemera across the networks on the giant screen in front of him—he wondered again how much of it was authentic, and if it really mattered. Over the course of his brief career as an experiential director, machinating fake authenticity but generating real-life reactions, activity on the networks had come to have a Pavlovian effect on him. He was then struck with a premonition of the lights in the city shifting from blue to red, then the black impact of nothingness as tourists and influencers and their global audiences came face-to-face with the truth. For now, in this moment of irrational exuberance before the bubble burst, perhaps the illusion of fame was enough. There were always Rasputin-like figures manipulating public perception, even in the golden age of Hollywood, only these days celebrities and their agents were able to jumpstart their careers by buying followers on social media. Was it a storm in a teacup? Would the outrage fizzle, subsumed by the next trending topic in the next news cycle?

His assistant in the restaurant pinged him that A'rore and Constantine were about to leave. With the paparazzi alerted and livestreaming, semi-grainy footage of the couple stepping out of the restaurant appeared on OMG's gossip channels. Zoomed in, under low-light conditions, the shot, as he had requested, was partially obscured behind a parked vehicle to give it a spontaneous, voyeuristic quality. Live commentary on the channel announced the couple had just been caught secretly having a dinner together, while the viewer count rose so quickly the number counter was a blur.

IIRC Constantine & Shiloh were having a baby?
A'rore home wrecking again
Get help A'rore

Leave him alone
#aroreconstantine #eutopia #cheater #followme

The comments flooded the feeds, and the sentiment tracker showed a slightly more hostile attitude toward A'rore. As the paparazzi got up from their hiding spots and approached the couple, asking them for their own comments, they shielded their faces from the lights of the cameras. Just then, Norton pulled up with her car, cutting off the photographers. After parking the car, lights still on, he got out and stalked toward the them, gloved hand outstretched, palm facing forward. As the paparazzi backed off, their field of vision widening, Norton held the door open for A'rore and Constantine. Comments started coming in, clamoring for A'rore and Constantine to start livestreaming themselves, but starting their streams now would tip their hand, contradicting the narrative that they didn't want to get caught in their surreptitious rendezvous. They'd opted, in this case, for the less-is-more approach.

After closing the door behind them, Norton got in the driver's seat and, without missing a beat, floored the acceleration pedal, launching them into the two-lane boulevard, before making an aggressive U-turn. The paparazzi, following close behind on their motorcycles, barely missed the rapidly approaching oncoming traffic.

People were already starting to bet on the outcome of the chase. Live stats showed the odds heavily in A'rore's favor, the skill of her driver, her track record, and their head start factoring into the real-time probability analysis. Norton, according to the script, drove toward the Champs-Élysées, where they planned on evading the paparazzi in a spectacular, all-out, pedal-to-the-metal drag race. With the paparazzi POV, aerial drone footage, and bystander footage, the chase sequence would be one of the most photogenic they'd ever produced. Inspired by the many car chases on the real Champs in Paris—from the De Niro film *Ronin* to the drug-fueled pursuits involving Saudi princes in their McLaren F1s—Cedric had chosen to end the chase here, with paparazzi bailing from their motorcycles just before they launched into a large Eutopia-branded billboard.

At the intersection where her car was supposed to turn toward the boulevard, however, it kept going straight. Unbeknownst to the audience, clamoring for more action, Norton had taken them off script. Cedric's chief curator turned away from the monitor.

"What's going on?" he said, removing one of the earmuffs on his headset.

"I have no idea," Cedric said. He typed out a quick message to his PR person, asking if anything had changed. The few seconds that followed, with the ellipsis in the speech bubble showing she was typing back a response, seemed like an eternity. "WTF" was her reply. "I thought you knew."

With no way of contacting Norton, except indirectly through A'rore, he pulled out his phone and called her. No answer, but her health tracker on the war room screen, and projected on buildings across the city, showed a quickening pulse and hues of red. Constantine's feeds were still silent, and Cedric wrote to PR to see if she had been able to contact him. She answered back in seconds with a negative.

A'rore's vehicle started accelerating, widening the gap between it and the paparazzi. Then, at the next intersection, it braked and took a sharp turn. The POV cameras mounted to the paparazzi's helmets showed onrushing asphalt, then the speeding taillights of A'rore's car coming into view again.

Suddenly Cedric realized the trajectory Norton was on. There was only one way for him to go forward—the Continental Tunnel, which would take them to the other side of the city. For what purpose, he had no idea. A'rore's health tracker was entirely in the red zone.

As the POV from the paparazzi sped toward the tunnel, the red lights of A'rore's car racing ahead of them, Cedric felt his abdominal muscles tighten as a sense of impending doom seized him. Norton's brutal aura had always made him uncomfortable. He envisioned his face, teeth gritted, driver's gloves bulging as his muscular hands gripped the steering wheel, the powerful sedan an extension of his explosive mien. As they entered the tunnel, the overhead lights reflecting off the car's sleek black body, he gasped. They couldn't. She couldn't. But he knew the truth, and part of him wished she would broadcast one last time.

As the car raced ahead, A'rore's health tracker was solid vermilion. Commentary on her feeds had trickled to almost nothing as her global audience watched, fraught with anxiety, hanging on the suspense of the moment. At a bend in the tunnel, the sedan kept going straight, embracing a concrete pillar in a horrific flurry of twisted machine metal, splintering carbon fiber, shattered circuit boards, sparks, and blood.

Everyone in the war room remained silent—even the comments across social media had paused—as they collectively tried to understand what had just happened. At the same time, A'rore's health tracker downgraded from a steady, saturated red glow to cooler hues of blue. Within another twenty seconds, her pulse had flatlined.

WITHIN ANOTHER MINUTE, THE chatter ramped up as replays started to cycle across the networks. The curator turned toward him again, eyes wide. Cedric shook his head, ripped off his headset, and got up, pushing his way past scrambling media coordinators trying to get back to their stations. The jig was up. With the volatile atmosphere outside—these thousands of influencers about to be rudderless, without a focal point for their angst and dreams—he knew something unprecedented was going to be unleashed on the city.

His phone, jammed in his pants pocket, began vibrating with incoming messages and phone calls. Ignoring it, he stepped outside, onto the streets, where he felt he belonged now after his final experience. People were gathered in front of screens, watching replays of the accident and live footage of rescue workers pulling two bodies from the back of the mangled wreck. They pulled a third body from the driver's seat but laid it on a stretcher. Norton had somehow pulled through. People started yelling and booing at the screens, furiously typing on their phones. Others were taking selfie videos, broadcasting their live reactions to their audiences.

Then, a programmatic ad for Nike took over almost all the signage around him. The crowds erupted in jeers, demanding their story come back uninterrupted. Then the screen cut to drone footage at Piccadilly Circus, where people were overturning a car. People began cheering as new drone footage showed a group of people hurling objects at a Nike store.

He took his vibrating phone out of his pocket.

"I, I'm in shock," Sacha said. "I can't believe what just happened."

"They went off script. You have to believe me."

"I know, I know. Do you think she . . ."

Her voice trailed off and he paused, unsure any comment was necessary. "Shit is getting out of hand. You probably saw what just happened at Piccadilly."

Overhead a helicopter flew past, probably carrying a fleeing celebrity or businessman who had seen the writing on the wall. All over the city, he imagined, other helicopters were also preparing for takeoff, like large scavenger birds about to carry away their precious carrion.

12.
Proof of Concept

FTER TAKING THE STAIRS two to three at a time, Cedric
made it to the ground floor of his apartment. With his own
data dump contained entirely on a thumb drive, thrown
into a backpack with some other personal effects, including the
heirloom ring he had originally come for, he headed for the
edge of Paris. A police drone flew by, hovering briefly overhead
before swaying with forward momentum as it zoomed toward
the nearest conflagration or roaming band of wild influencers.

Sacha's site had just published the story about widespread
bot fraud, and news of it propagated virally across the globe and
throughout the city in mere minutes. The double blow of A'rore's
death, leaving the city without a figurehead—one they never knew
they needed—and the revelation that their traffic numbers were
inflated, essentially eliminating their ad revenue and their sense
of self-worth—had turned the denizens of Eutopia into nihilistic
rioters. Hashtag #adpocalypse was trending worldwide, and the
city's networks, overloaded with real traffic, were beginning to
collapse. The city was taking a knee to the canvas, blood-spat-

tered, dazed, clinging to a vague sense of purpose. The signage everywhere was glitching, intermittently blacking out, and the illusion of light gave way to a city of dark screens. All the hopes and dreams of influencer fame had been dashed in a few hours after the euphoria of a festival celebrating their works of art.

Cell phone coverage had been jammed for a couple hours already as the security forces tried to regain control of the city. Having anticipated something like this, Cedric had a beacon that Sacha had given him. Connected to a secure mesh network, even without satellite coverage for their phones, they would still be able to find each other. It looked like their contingency planning had paid off. After several blocks—passing by looters and roving gangs of disgruntled superheroes and pop culture icons—Cedric came upon a bistro near the Concorde obelisk. The sidewalk in front of it was strewn with overturned chairs and tables, and it appeared abandoned, an ideal place to alert Sacha, who was going to meet him with a getaway car she had procured: a stolen Tesla with flashed firmware and no autopilot function. He kicked aside a chair and stepped into the darkened bistro. From a refrigerator near the bar, he pulled out a bottle of water. After dropping his face mask, he took a few swigs of water and set it down. Then, after placing the portable beacon on the counter, he activated it, sending the signal to Sacha.

He stood facing the door as a group of teens dressed as the Suicide Squad ran past, one of them, dressed as the Joker, picking up one of the woven rattan chairs outside and hurling it at the window display of an adjacent store. Something about the detail of that chair, which would not have been out of place in a Paris café, and the faux patina of the bar he was standing next to, the chalkboard menu knocked over near the door, reminded him of a curious story he'd read, which for some reason had not surfaced until just now. Over a century ago, during WWI, the first fake Paris was built, complete with its own Champs-Élysées and Gare du Nord. Intended to fool German bombers, it was situated on the outskirts of the capital, and even had functioning streetlights, replica buildings, and copies of iconic monuments. Famous *arrondisements*, including those around the Arc de Triomphe and Opéra, were built as if from top-level blueprints, wooden replicas of the city's most visibly striking architecture.

Was Eutopia also a sham city, meant to distract the world? Maybe it had an expiration date by design. Quickly and cheaply built, it was never meant to last, as if it were the logical extension of the technology and gadgets they were all using. After churning a profit, what use was this city of the future? In a matter of minutes it had become a thing of the past, planned obsolescence in the name of market efficiency.

Impatient, he stepped outside and tapped his pockets, searching for his Panadrine stick. His heart sank a little when he realized he had left it back in the apartment. Just then a group of stragglers walked by, wide-eyed, going at a leisurely pace. From the look of them, they were economy tourists from somewhere in Asia, stranded in the city, unable to communicate with the outside world. They walked through streets littered with discarded cell phones and tablets, some freshly looted from stores and dropped, others jettisoned by frustrated influencers who could no longer connect to their audience, who didn't, for that matter, have any faith that they even existed in the first place. Their mad dashes for fame were futile now that their idol and revenue sources had disappeared.

Tires screeched, and from around the corner came a car, coming to a swift stop in front of him. Sacha, gripping the wheel, shouted at him as he opened the passenger's side door.

"Get in! The police are right behind me."

As Cedric was about to get in, a black Humvee with Eutopia livery blocked the road behind them. Monteiro got out, followed by another officer, both dressed in black tactical gear, each armed with a Glock. While his partner spoke into his watch, eyes scanning the periphery, Monteiro advanced, gun pointed at Cedric and Sacha.

"You!" he said, gun trained on Sacha. "Get out of the car and hold your hands where I can see them." Next, aiming at Cedric, he said, "Travers, you know what to do. Back up and get on your knees and slowly put your hands behind your head."

Cedric and Sacha looked at each other, silently calculating the risk of disobedience. Cedric, his hands behind his head, stepped back to the curb. Sacha was getting out of the car when suddenly a large object came tumbling out of the sky. A spinning television screen hit the pavement right in front of Monteiro, glass shrapnel and circuitry scattering everywhere. Monteiro, momentarily stunned by the impact, pointed his gun toward an open window about seven floors up in the hotel above the bistro. Two masked rioters, one with an arm outstretched, filming the attack with a phone, ducked back inside as soon as the gun was aimed at them.

Behind Monteiro's car, a group of five youths carrying Molotov cocktails ran past, followed by a police drone and another Humvee. Monteiro was unperturbed, and he couldn't suppress the beginnings of a smile. He'd been waiting for this moment for over a decade, ever since his last tour of duty. Cedric and this reporter, they weren't the problem here, only symptoms of it.

Calling over his partner, he pointed to the open window above, and they both made their way toward the entrance just as a chair and a coffee table were hurled out the window. He stayed focused on the window and dodging the furniture, but when he was three car lengths away from Cedric, he looked at him and nodded, as if saying, "I never saw you," then went straight into the hotel followed by his partner.

A Humvee with four more men in tactical gear tore around the corner, pulling up next to Monteiro's vehicle. As the men were disembarking, Cedric got in Sacha's car, placing his backpack between his legs. She punched the accelerator, and the torque produced by the speeding car as it drove through the detritus in the streets to the outskirts of Eutopia pinned him against the seat, his stomach feeling as if he were on a roller coaster drop.

The last of the buildings rushed by, and they were out of the city for good. Behind them, it was already a dark shell, with plumes of smoke rising from different points around the city. A group of three military Humvees drove past them, toward the city, and to the left, the billboard of A'rore welcoming visitors to the city whipped past. Still working, the looping images of the erstwhile icon against the remains of the city were like a siren luring sailors to perilous waters. Sacha and Cedric remained silent as they drove on, dawn breaking, shades of purple, then gray, then mauve painting the horizon over the open road.

13.
Unblockable

A SUDDEN DECREASE IN SPEED forced Cedric against his seatbelt, and he opened his eyes. A white wall of water was coming down, graying out everything in sight, the vehicle in front of them just two red brake lights and a wake of mist kicking up from its tires.

"This rain is insane," Sacha said, glancing at Cedric.

"How long has it been?"

"Since leaving, or the rain?"

"I don't know, Jesus, I'm tired."

The wipers, on full speed, barely kept up with the heavy downpour, and they continued at a steady pace through the plume of road spray. Behind them, another car had slowed down; behind that, another. Cedric patted down his pockets and was about to reach for his backpack when he sat up again.

"Did you forget something?" she said.

"Yeah, my Panadrine. I was so rushed I forgot to grab some. I've been going on three days now with barely any sleep. It's the only thing that was keeping me going."

"I told you that stuff makes people lose their minds."

"Yeah, I know, but it's the only way to keep up."

"Was," she said, taking advantage of a pause in the downpour to speed up and pass what turned out to be a truck in front of them. "That's three hours behind us."

"How much charge do we have left?"

"Probably a couple hours. I'll wake you up when we get to a station."

Cedric felt his phone vibrate in his pocket and pulled it out. Network coverage was available again, and his phone had accumulated dozens of alerts with headlines about Eutopia. Too tired to read them, he pushed his phone back in his pocket and shifted to his side, his eyelids falling shut, heavy, like velour theater curtains. The thrum of the rain and the hypnotic, metronomic sound of the wipers soon lulled him back to sleep.

BRIGHT LIGHT BEAMING THROUGH the windshield woke him up, and he squinted while shielding his eyes. They were driving down an open stretch of the interstate under a brilliant blue sky speckled with puffy white cotton ball clouds. The plains on either side and the ridges of the rock formations in the distance shimmered with a golden transparency, and the large cumulus overhead cast wide swaths of shadow every few thousand feet.

"Have we stopped yet?" he said.

"There's a charging station and diner up ahead in a couple miles."

While reaching for the console screen, swiping through the radio stations, he said, "Any news?"

"It's useless out here. The satellite radio is spotty, and I tried terrestrial. Just preachers and conservative talk radio."

He swiped out of the radio interface and leaned back into his seat. Still groggy from sleeping uncomfortably in the passenger's seat for the last few hours, he kept his half-lidded eyes on the road in front of them. A UFO-shaped billboard for a diner called Crash '47 flew past them on the right, with the words "Gas, Food, Lodging" written in a space-age font, like something you'd see in a mid-twentieth-century advertisement for X-ray glasses, or a pulp science-fiction novel. After another half minute, another standard interstate sign, weather-beaten and covered with stickers, indicated they needed to take the next exit, two miles ahead.

The off-ramp was dark and dust-free from the recent rainfall and led them over a gently sloping hill to a valley where the Crash '47 was. Plated in aluminum, with neon trim, the service station and diner were something straight out of the atomic age, retro-futuristic with an upswept roof and sharp angles. As they pulled up to a set of old gas pumps, some now retrofitted with electric charging options, the diner's metal facade shimmered in the early afternoon light. A gray alien, no bigger than a five-year-old child, greeted patrons at the door of the diner. Cedric got out of the car and stretched while Sacha hooked the vehicle up to the charging line. Everything about the place was old, yet new, as if they had driven into a strange fold in space-time where the past and present were mashed into one.

The waiter, a young man wearing a white apron, black bowtie, and red-and-white paper hat, led them to their table, past a handful of other patrons, each waiting for their cars to charge outside. They sat near the window, with a view of the covered charging station and the interstate in the distance, just past the hill, with only the tops of passing cars visible. Cedric, facing Sacha, had his hands and elbows resting on a tablecloth with a motif of whirling electrons and atoms.

"I'm almost afraid of looking at the news," he said, glancing at a sphere-shaped television on the counter playing silent loops of vintage advertising—Betty Crocker, Alka-Seltzer, Coca-Cola, and other commercials from the atomic age. The clear, reassuring tones of Chet Atkins's fingerpicked guitar wafted out of a radio somewhere, like echoes of a bygone time.

After ordering coffee and apple pie, Sacha pulled out her phone and began thumbing through alerts and messages that had been accumulating for the last few hours.

"Wow," she said, "look at this." She pressed on a video in her social feed, expanding it to show a helicopter lifting off of a high-rise, hovering as it stabilized in the wind, then tilting as it began its flight over a canyon of black screens, cutting through puffs of smoke that looked like an ominous shape-shifting alphabet. "They're saying that the helicopter was carrying Barron Trump and his girlfriend."

While the waiter placed their slices of pie in front of them and poured their coffees into alien-themed mugs, Cedric pulled out his phone, which, since sitting down, had been vibrating with incoming alerts. He took a sip of the steamy, watered-down diner coffee, ignoring the dish of half-and-half the waiter had left on the table.

"They're estimating about thirty to forty thousand people are trapped in the city," Sacha said, reading through another story on her phone. Cedric, swiping past videos of street violence—a strangely anodyne act after having actually been in the thick of it—was looking for mentions of A'rore. Had she already been relegated to the dustbin of Internet history? Images of stranded tourists in the Eutopia airport; more helicopters, like giant insects, taking off from helipads across the city; police in military vehicles racing to the next fire or looting. "It looks like two other networks were affected by the ad fraud, although they're not taking a hit like Eutopia."

"To be fair, we had a pretty major spectacle."

"And here," she said, pointing to an article on a conspiracy site. "They're already saying A'rore's accident was staged and that it was copying Princess Diana's in the nineties."

"Of all the things, that was the only one that wasn't staged,"

Cedric said, although deep down he knew he was responsible for it. That kind of mystery was exactly what A'rore had always cultivated for herself, and he'd been drawn right into the middle of it.

"This is concerning," Sacha said. "Your name is surfacing in connection with the accident."

"Someone on my staff must be leaking information to the media."

Despite being hundreds of miles outside of Eutopia, a few hours removed, and definitely retired as the city's experiential director, the old, anxious feeling he'd perpetually had while there was seizing him again. He placed his phone on the tablecloth, face up, on top of an atomic burst of bright colors.

"I need some pie," he said and dug his fork into the slice in front him. "I need to relax."

They were both silent, sipping their coffees and watching the tops of cars zoom by in the distance, while country-western music and the hushed conversations of fellow travelers droned on in the background. A dozen cars had passed, each spaced a few seconds apart, when their phones started vibrating with alerts again.

"God damn," Cedric said. "I can't get rid of these things."

"What's that?" Sacha said as Cedric thumbed his phone on the table, stabbing at the apple pie again with the fork in his other hand.

"This," he said, pointing to a message he just received, containing a string of numbers and decimal points. "It's weird spam I keep getting from blocked numbers."

Using her index finger she spun his phone on the tabletop so that it faced her.

"Those look like geo coordinates. Do you have any more?"

He tapped the phone lightly, spinning it back around.

"No, I just delete them as they come in. Do you really think they're geo coordinates?"

"Maybe someone is signaling you."

Cedric pursed his lips and glanced at the atom-shaped ceiling fixtures. Then, coffee mug raised with his elbow on the table, he turned it so the oblong alien head, with its large, bug-like eyes, seemed to observe him. There was no iris or pupil in those opaque, liquid eyes, but for a second, he saw a reflection of his own.

ACKNOWLEDGMENTS

The idea for a near-future theme park based on Europe was sparked by my move back to the United States after living in Barcelona and Paris for fourteen years. Entering the media and advertising world in Los Angeles gave me deep insight into ad tech and influencer marketing, so I'd be remiss if I didn't acknowledge the many boardroom sessions and meetings with account executives which helped shape the details of this book. I always had a notebook on hand, but those notes were for my story.

I'd like to thank my editor, Lindsey Alexander, for her diligent work. What you've read is the perfected version of the shaggy dog I initially delivered to her in 2015. Thank you for getting it, and for letting my voice shine through.

Bob at California Coldblood Books has championed this book ever since I sent him the first query in 2016. Thank you for believing in it, and for adding me to your roster. Lauren and the rest of the team at CCB: my eternal gratitude for the work you put into marketing it.

Last, but not least, Olga and Alice, my wife and daughter, for putting up with my early morning and late-night writing sessions, and for giving me the space to do it. You are my inspiration and motivation. This book is for you.

ABOUT THE AUTHOR

DREW MINH is a digital strategist currently residing in Los Angeles, with firsthand knowledge of our current social media revolution. He's lived in Barcelona and Paris, where he worked as a freelance writer, ghostwriter, and digital consultant. His fiction has appeared in 3AM Magazine, Word Riot, Litro Magazine, and other publications. He also wrote a fictional crime column for weekly newspapers in Spain.

CPSIA information can be obtained
at www.ICGtesting.com
Printed in the USA
JSHW021512081019
1853JS00001B/1